I M

Death March on Mount Hakkōda

"*The higher they climbed, the stronger the gale blew. Once they reached the ridge, the men found that the wind had swept it comparatively free of snow, but they were buffeted by gusts so strong they found it almost impossible to keep their eyes open. This was no gale, or even a storm—this was a blizzard. The wind boiled and swirled in complicated patterns caused by the rugged terrain over which it blew. Each soldier blindly followed the footsteps of the man before him. What else could he do? Not one of them had any idea where he was or where he was going.*"

—along the route of the Death March

THE ROCK SPRING COLLECTION

DEATH MARCH ON MOUNT HAKKŌDA

A DOCUMENTARY NOVEL BY

JIRŌ NITTA

Translated by James Westerhoven

STONE BRIDGE PRESS / *Berkeley, California*

Published by STONE BRIDGE PRESS
P.O. Box 8208 • Berkeley, CA 94707

Originally published in Japan as *Hakkōda-san shi no hōkō*
by Jirō Nitta. Copyright © 1971 by Nihon Bungei
Chosakuken Hogo Dōmei. English translation rights
arranged with Nihon Bungei Chosakuken Hogo Dōmei
through Japan Foreign-Rights Centre.

English translation and afterword copyright © 1992
by James N. Westerhoven.

Book design by Polly Christensen.

Printed in the United States of America.

Library of Congress Cataloging-in-Publication Data

Nitta, Jirō, pseud.
[Hakkōdasan shi no hōkō. English]
Death march on Mount Hakkōda : a documentary novel /
by Jirō Nitta; translated by James Westerhoven.
p. cm.
Translation of: Hakkōdasan shi no hōkō.
ISBN 0-9628137-2-9 (pbk).
1. Japan. Rikugun. Hohei Rentai, Dai 5—Fiction. 2. Japan.
Rikugun. Hohei Rentai, Dai 31—fiction. I. Title.
PL857.I8H313   1991
895.6'35–dc20   91-24157
                                                        CIP

CONTENTS

BACKGROUND NOTE

Japan in 1901 considered itself a threatened nation. It had won its war against China in 1895, but victory did not bring a sense of security. While Japan had been allowed to keep the island of Formosa, intervention by Russia, France, and Germany forced it to return the Liaotung Peninsula with Port Arthur to China. Three years later Japan watched from the sidelines as the European powers themselves did what they had not allowed Japan to do: carve off pieces from the dying Chinese empire. Russia, which had already gained the right to build a railroad across Manchuria to Vladivostok, now claimed Port Arthur for itself—leased it, to be more precise—and began to turn it into a naval port, connected to Moscow by yet another Russian-built railroad. Worse was to come. When the Boxer Rebellion broke out in 1900, Russia sent its army into Manchuria but did not bother to withdraw it when the rebellion was quashed. Russia also showed signs of extending its influence into Korea, a peninsula which points like a dagger to the heart of Japan and which Japan, for that reason, had earmarked for its own sphere of interest.

Though by and by the intransigence of both countries would lead to the Russo-Japanese War of 1904–5, this was by no means a foregone conclusion in 1901. But Japan was not taking any chances. In order to prepare for a war that might be fought in the icy Siberian climate, the Japanese Army ordered a series of winter exercises to be held in the snowy northeast of Japan's main island of Honshu. This book is about one of them.

—*the translator*

Route of the Death March, January 1902

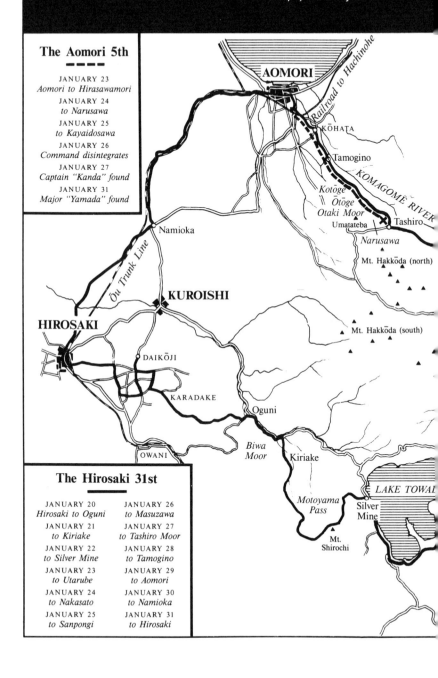

The Aomori 5th

JANUARY 23
Aomori to Hirasawamori

JANUARY 24
to Narusawa

JANUARY 25
to Kayaidosawa

JANUARY 26
Command disintegrates

JANUARY 27
Captain "Kanda" found

JANUARY 31
Major "Yamada" found

AOMORI

Railroad to Hachinohe

KŌHATA

Tamogino

KOMAGOMÉ RIVER

Kotōge
Ōtōge
Otaki Moor
Umatateba
Tashiro
Narusawa

Namioka

Ōu Trunk Line

Mt. Hakkōda (north)

KUROISHI

HIROSAKI

DAIKŌJI

Mt. Hakkōda (south)

KARADAKE

Oguni

Biwa
Moor
Kiriake

OWANI

LAKE TOWAI

Motoyama
Pass

Silver
Mine

Mt.
Shirochi

The Hirosaki 31st

JANUARY 20
Hirosaki to Oguni

JANUARY 21
to Kiriake

JANUARY 22
to Silver Mine

JANUARY 23
to Utarube

JANUARY 24
to Nakasato

JANUARY 25
to Sanpongi

JANUARY 26
to Masuzawa

JANUARY 27
to Tashiro Moor

JANUARY 28
to Tamogino

JANUARY 29
to Aomori

JANUARY 30
to Namioka

JANUARY 31
to Hirosaki

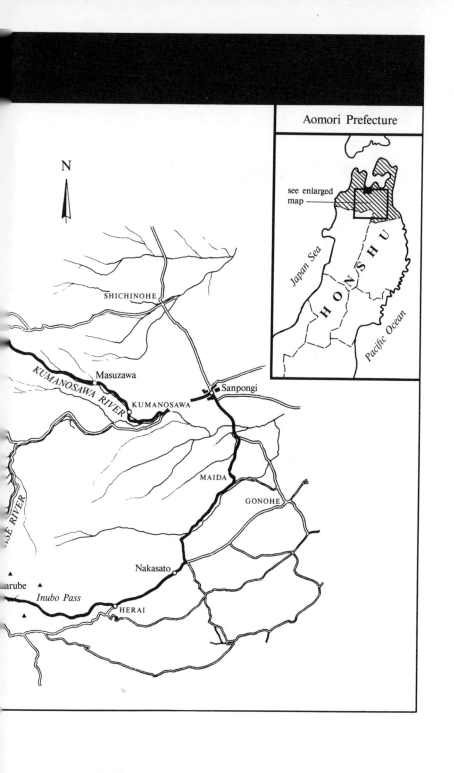

LIST OF CHARACTERS

Commander of the 8th Division
LIEUTENANT GENERAL TACHIKAWA

Tachikawa's Chief of Staff
COLONEL NAKABAYASHI

Commander of the 4th Brigade
MAJOR GENERAL TOMODA

THE 5TH REGIMENT OF AOMORI	THE 31ST REGIMENT OF HIROSAKI
Commander Lieutenant Colonel Tsumura	*Commander* Colonel Kojima
2nd Battalion Major Yamada	*1st Battalion* Major Monma
E Company Captain Kanda	*B Company* Captain Tokushima

PART ONE

PREPARATIONS

All temperatures throughout this text are given in Fahrenheit.

I

$\mathbb{P}$EOPLE WERE SHOUTING, running up and down the street. At the point where they converged, the crowd spilled over the side of the road, until a wall of people reached to the two adjoining buildings that housed Division Headquarters and Brigade Headquarters.

When the continued cries of "Fire!" showed no signs of abating, Major General Harunobu Tomoda, commander of the 4th Brigade, got up from his chair and turned to the window. The other persons in the room rose as one and positioned themselves behind him, all taking care that their differences in rank were expressed in the distances that separated them in space.

The fire was directly across the street from the headquarters of the 8th Division next door. From a square red-brick chimney, an unusual feature in the house of a commoner, arose bright-red flames. The crowd in the street had grown, but very few people made any attempt to help extinguish the fire. Most seemed to be hoping that the flames the chimney belched forth would rise even higher. The people who lived in the immediate vicinity of the burning house were running around with tubs and buckets, the tense expression on their faces in sharp contrast with that on the faces of the onlookers. A woman with her hair in disorder came dashing out of the burning house in her bare feet and screamed something, but it was impossible to make out her words. As the flames from the chimney flared up higher, smoke began to curl up from the roof of the house as well.

General Tomoda looked over his shoulder and seemed about to say something to the person standing closest to him, but without speaking he reverted his gaze to the fire. The flames coming from the chimney now changed into a black smoke that erupted explosively and subsided at once, its color fading as suddenly as it had appeared. Soon a report was brought up to the room: The incident was no more than a small fire in a confectionary. A policeman shouted angrily at the crowd. The smoke from the chimney dwindled even more.

Tomoda turned around and went back to his seat. For about ten minutes he had stood at the window, through which the sunlight now fell brightly on the well-polished conference table. When the general sat down, the others returned to their seats too. Tomoda did not say a word concerning the fire, and as long as their commanding officer ignored the subject, none of the others so much as even whispered about it.

"Well, shall we begin?"

As if he had been waiting for Tomoda to speak these words, the Chief of Staff of the 8th Division, Colonel Nakabayashi, who was sitting next to the general, rose to his feet and spread out a large map on the table.

"In the event war should break out between Japan and Russia, the first thing to be considered is the possibility that the enemy fleet will seal off the Tsugaru Strait and Mutsu Bay. If that should happen, we must anticipate naval bombardments destroying our highways and railroads so that traffic between Aomori and Hirosaki or between Aomori and Hachinohe will have no option but to use roads across Mount Hakkōda. Now, in summer this ought not to cause too many problems, but it is at present totally unclear whether these roads are passable in winter. To this day there has not been a single study to investigate the feasibility of the army moving troops over these roads in the deep snow and extreme cold of winter, nor of the steps that should be taken to make this possible if it is not."

Although Nakabayashi had his map before him while he delivered this speech, it was obvious that he was not using it to demonstrate some detail of strategy; he was introducing the problem in general terms. Consequently his finger had touched the map only once, at the beginning of his presentation.

But his eyes were active. They roamed across the room, relentlessly searching other eyes, intent on finding unanimous approval and unwilling to allow the slightest room for doubt. If he caught but a gleam of skepticism somewhere, the colonel would talk on until it had disappeared.

Sitting at the conference table were—besides General Tomoda and Colonel Nakabayashi—the commander of the 31st Regiment, Colonel Kojima, with Major Monma of its 1st Battalion and Captain Tokushima, who was in charge of that battalion's B

Company. Also at the table were their counterparts of the 5th Regiment: Lieutenant Colonel Tsumura, Major Yamada of the 2nd Battalion, and Captain Kanda of 2nd Battalion's E Company.

The 31st and 5th Regiments belonged to the 4th Brigade, which in turn was part of the 8th Division. Though the division commander was not present at this meeting, Colonel Nakabayashi, his chief of staff, could be considered his representative. This was therefore a meeting of division, brigade, and regiment commanders, but what gave it a special character was the fact that battalion and company commanders were also attending.

"So far I have discussed the possibility of hostilities between Japan and Russia in hypothetical terms," Nakabayashi continued. "However, if I should be asked what the probability is of such a war breaking out, my answer must be that it is no longer a question of whether, but of when. Our armed forces are concentrating all their powers on the preparations for the battle against Russia. Our guns are primed, our soldiers ready. But at this moment there is one thing the army clearly lacks: winter equipment, winter training. To be able to fight the Russian army, which is equipped to cope with Siberian cold and which can fight even at arctic temperatures of 0°, our army must acquire equipment that beats theirs. However, I am sorry to say that in this respect there have been precious few studies or experiments. If you take winter exercises as an example, you will find that we have not much more to go by than the Hirosaki 31st's ascent of Mount Iwaki in January of this year. Now, the army has benefited tremendously from that exercise, but it was too brief, the distance too short, and the weather too good for it to be of much value as an experiment.

"If, as chief of staff of the 8th Division, I may be allowed to express a desire, it is that someone investigate if a company or platoon of soldiers can actually cross the deep snows of Mount Hakkōda in the coldest part of winter. Mind you, gentlemen, this is not an official order. I am merely expressing a personal wish in my capacity as chief of staff of this division. Until it officially becomes an order, you may consider it the chief of staff's private plan if you like. And I am not telling you that you must march your men through the frozen wastes of that mountain at any cost or sacrifice. All I want is a clear and true picture of what it really means when people talk about cold and snow."

Here Colonel Nakabayashi paused and looked at General Tomoda to give him an opportunity to add some comments of his

15

own. Tomoda turned to the two regimental commanders and said, rather sternly:

"Mount Hakkōda lies right in the middle between Aomori and Hirosaki—eminently convenient for both the Aomori 5th Infantry and the Hirosaki 31st Infantry if they should decide to stage such an exercise."

But when he turned toward Captains Tokushima and Kanda, who were sitting at the bottom of the table, his tone was gentler.

"I understand that both Captain Tokushima and Captain Kanda are authorities on the subject of winter exercises."

Addressed directly by their brigade commander, before their immediate superiors had been heard, both captains jumped up so briskly that their chairs flew backwards. Tokushima spoke first.

"If the General please, I know very little about snow or cold, and certainly not enough to set myself up as an authority!"

And Kanda said, "I have participated in winter exercises on level terrain, Sir, never in the mountains."

"But don't you think it might be interesting to see if you can't cross Mount Hakkōda in winter?"

This was extraordinary: Tomoda had gone over the heads of the commanders of regiments and battalions and addressed the question directly to the two captains. Tokushima and Kanda knew that such a question, coming from their division commander in person, was as good as a direct order. They also realized it was an honor.

"Yes, Sir!" they answered in unison, stiffening that very moment under the burden of the responsibility.

"Splendid!" Colonel Nakabayashi said. "Really, I'm very pleased that you are willing to undertake this. But willingness alone is not enough. Preparation is everything! If the exercise is to be brought to a successful conclusion, it will be as the result of careful anticipation of every contingency. The best thing would be if each regiment—the Hirosaki 31st and the Aomori 5th—tried it its own way."

"Tried it its own way." These were words fraught with meaning. The colonel was not telling them in so many words to make a contest out of it, but a contest is what it amounted to: Each regiment should work out and implement its plans in secret.

16   This concluded the meeting.

General Tomoda and Colonel Nakabayashi stayed behind while the other six officers left Brigade Headquarters. The crowd that had blocked the street was gone. It was hard to believe that this had been the scene of such an uproar.

The six walked down the street in double file, in order of rank. With two regimental commanders, two battalion commanders, and two company commanders walking in the same direction, it was impossible not to form a double file.

Colonel Kojima of the 31st said to Lieutenant Colonel Tsumura, who was walking beside him, "If we go through with this, the exercise will be held at the end of January or the beginning of February of next year."

"Yes. If we start preparations today, everything ought to be just ready by that time, and the worst cold and deepest snow will be about then too," Tsumura agreed.

"How about this? Since the object of the exercise is essentially to gather information, we could leave from Hirosaki and Aomori and meet each other on Mount Hakkōda," suggested Kojima. For a few seconds he halted in his stride. The four men walking behind him also stopped and listened closely, aware that an important decision was being made.

"Good idea!" Tsumura said, "Then we'll decide the date of departure after mutual consultation, so weather and terrain conditions will be identical for both sides."

"Right. Conditions will be the same, but for the rest each side will make its own arrangements, as it sees fit."

Here Kojima coughed lightly: a civilian passerby was approaching.

Major Monma, who was walking right behind Kojima, felt slightly troubled by the regimental commanders' conversation. He really wanted a word with Major Yamada, who was walking to his left. As battalion commanders, Yamada and he were in the same position, and Monma wanted to find out what Yamada thought of their superiors' idea. Monma slowed down a bit and spoke softly so the two colonels in front could not hear him.

"If this exercise really does take place, we'll both have a rough time of it."

"A rough time? I don't see why. Nothing rough about it, is there?" Yamada looked at Monma, his eyes glittering.

Monma found it difficult to say anything after such a reply. He walked on behind his colonel, looking as if he had lost interest.

"We're the ones who'll have a rough time of it," Tokushima said to Kanda.

"Yes," Kanda agreed. "This could turn out a lot worse than we can tell now. At least the 31st has had some experience, with your ascent of Mount Iwaki, but for the 5th this is all new. . . ."

17

"Not much experience, really. We did it only once, and the weather was fine then. There's not much to be learned that way." Unconsciously, Tokushima had fallen into step with Kanda. "It's getting cold."

"It's the end of November already."

Together they looked up at the sky.

2

On the first Sunday of December, Captain Kanda put on civilian clothes and went to visit Tokushima at his home in Hirosaki. He had written that he was coming, so Tokushima welcomed him at the door. Kanda presented the two big bottles of fine saké he had brought with him as a souvenir from Aomori.

"I'm sorry to make such demands on your time, but there's no one I can ask for advice but you," he apologized.

Throughout his visit Kanda behaved deferentially. First he inquired about Tokushima's preparations for his ascent of Mount Iwaki the previous January.

"I have very little specific advice to give you," explained Tokushima, "except that after heavy snowfall you can't distinguish the road any longer. So I put some local people up front, planted poles as landmarks at every important point, and tied strips of red cloth to the branches of the trees. That was very useful. Even in fine weather it's difficult enough to find your way through the snow, but when it comes down really hard you'll find the red strips absolutely indispensable."

Tokushima was a broad-minded person. As he saw it, there should be no secrets in the army: Both the 31st and the 5th Regiments belonged to the same 4th Brigade, and if both were going to try to cross Mount Hakkōda, they ought to succeed together.

"You should also be fully aware that maps will become useless because the landmarks that appear on them become hard to recognize. So I really wonder if it ought not be army policy to employ guides on winter exercises."

"Policy? You feel that strongly about it?" Kanda asked.

"Yes. Maps are not infallible; people are better. It's obvious that you're better off using local guides." And Tokushima explained in further detail why guides were indispensable.

Then Kanda asked the question he had really come to ask: "Is it possible to bivouac in the snow?"

"That depends on the depth of the snow and the state of the weather, but with the sort of equipment the army has now, I can only say it's dangerous. You'd be courting death if you camped out, especially on Mount Hakkōda. No matter what precautions you take, that cold will get the better of you."

When Tokushima said "that cold," he seemed to be recalling the January weather on Mount Iwaki.

"Then, footwear. The kind of straw boots the local people wear seem to be best. You'd better prepare an issue of those boots so you can have your men put them on when it becomes necessary. Also, rice will freeze until it is as hard as stone. So, to prepare food, you simply must have fire."

Tokushima filled Kanda's cup with saké. Because Kanda's visit was a social one, they did not limit their conversation to the coming exercise; they digressed. Once they began about the past war against China, they both talked until they were red in the face. But Kanda had come to ask advice about the basic preparations for the Hakkōda Exercise. They could not just sit there entertaining each other. Soon they stuck their heads together again and reverted to the discussion of snow, ice, and equipment.

"Is there any information about the equipment foreign armies use during winter maneuvers?" asked Kanda.

"I was wondering about that myself, so I inquired at Brigade Headquarters, but Brigade doesn't seem to have anything really helpful—at best some pointers about the kinds of fur or cloth they use against the cold. Then there are things called skis, which you wear when walking over snow, but our army apparently has no plans yet to try them out. But if you're looking for literature on protective clothing in foreign armies, I know that there is some at Division Headquarters. Why not check it out?" Tokushima suggested.

But Kanda answered, "No, I went only to the Training Corps. I don't know any foreign languages."

At the time there were two ways to become an officer: by going to the Military Academy and by being promoted from the ranks of the noncommissioned officers. Captain Bunkichi Kanda had taken the latter route. He had been born in 1867, in a fishing village in Akita Prefecture. At the age of nineteen, he had joined the NCO Training Corps. At twenty-one, he had been promoted to sergeant, and after successive elevations in rank he had been made a second lieutenant at age twenty-eight. In May 1901 he had gained his captaincy. Of course it had been to his advantage that the war with

19

China had forced the army to expand, but the fact that he had been so promoted after leaving the Training Corps was entirely due to Kanda's exceptional ability. Most officers were descendants of samurai or of the aristocracy; it was extremely rare for a commoner to get a commission. The old feudal way of thinking was still very much alive. Because it was difficult to enter the Military Academy unless one belonged to the old samurai class, persons who really wanted to make their career in the army tried to do so by way of the Training Corps, like Kanda. The commoners who traveled this road had all turned out to be excellent officers, and Kanda was no exception. There had been no need for him to explain his background, for Tokushima was already aware of it.

But the fact that Kanda had done so meant that he had lowered himself before Tokushima. Or, to look at it in a different way, it meant that he was talking to Tokushima as if the latter were slightly higher in rank. Kanda was a little older, but Tokushima had been a captain longer.

When he heard Kanda's reason for not knowing any foreign languages, Tokushima, recognizing Kanda's deference, was momentarily at a loss for words.

"Oh, but I myself don't know any either," he admitted. "Everything I just mentioned about foreign armies was based only on hearsay." He changed the topic. "With enthusiastic people like you slaving away, the 5th must be making steady progress with its preparations. Over here they seem to feel that next year is early enough to start thinking about next year's business, so our planning hasn't got anywhere yet." He burst into laughter.

"No, at the 5th it's just the same. I, as the company commander in charge, may be breaking my head over things, but it hasn't even been decided yet whether we'll send out a company or a platoon. The only thing that's more or less certain is the road we'll take."

"I suppose you'll go from Aomori to Sanpongi via Tamogino, Tashiro, and Masuzawa."

"Exactly. There is no other way from Aomori to Sanpongi across Mount Hakkōda, so the route at least was clear from the start."

"If the 31st crosses Hakkōda, it'll have to be in exactly the opposite direction: Sanpongi, Masuzawa, Tashiro, Tamogino, Aomori. But if we go at all, it will be as a platoon—that much I can tell you now. I think it's impossible to try it with a company. I learned my lesson when we climbed Mount Iwaki. No, I intend to go with a small, select group. We'll travel as light as possible, and we'll spend every single night in civilian housing," Tokushima said resolutely.

These plans were part of the 31st's secret preparations. Why should Tokushima divulge them to—of all people—the officer in charge of the rival 5th's planning? For a moment, Kanda's eyes opened wide in amazement. He wondered if there might not be some ulterior motive behind Tokushima's words.

"You said, 'If we go at all.'"

Kanda was under the impression that, the previous month, their superior officers had decided to go ahead with the exercise.

"If we go at all," Tokushima repeated. "Neither Nakabayashi nor Tomoda gave a direct order; they merely expressed a desire. For the rest they left it to the discretion of the 31st and the 5th. So it's not as if we have to go. And I feel very much like advising our colonel that missions like crossing Mount Hakkōda in the coldest part of winter are irresponsible. Shall I tell you where all this started? With just a handful of people in pretty red-brick official housing—with the administrative staff, whether of Division or Brigade makes no difference. You won't catch *them* taking part in any winter exercises. They're only onlookers. Yet they're the ones who cooked up this plan and decided it might be nice to have a little contest between the 31st and the 5th. But if the big brass issued official orders, they'd have to listen to a lot of moaning about how there's not enough equipment and how there's not enough money. So they're leaving the regiments holding the bag. Mark my words, if anything should go wrong, both Brigade and Division will take the line that the regimental commanders acted on their own initiative. I'm telling you, in this army the people who make the plans look at things very differently from the people who carry them out!"

"So you don't think Tomoda will issue a formal order?"

"No, what I think will happen is this. As brigade commander, Tomoda can't very well involve himself actively in every little regimental exercise. So if the whole thing could be over and done with in three days, his permission won't be needed."

"You think they'll tell us to do it in three days?"

"No. I'm just speaking hypothetically. I myself intend to get Tomoda's permission to stay away for about ten days, but the colonel might tell me to choose a route that would get us back in three. Anyway, when people move, it costs money—which they haven't got. So they'll tell us to make up for the money with morale. But I ask you, can morale alone keep you from the cold? Can morale dig you out when you're buried up to your chest in snow? The brass has a tendency to close their eyes to reality and think that the spirit always triumphs over the body. And that's dangerous. Very dangerous."

The saké must have begun to take effect, for Tokushima's face was beet red.

Kanda looked as if he had been hit by a huge, invisible object. Tokushima's vision had given Kanda a new understanding of Mount Hakkōda—of the cold, the deep snow, and the equipment and the food needed to conquer them.

Kanda took out his pocket watch. It was time to go home.

"Once we're into next month, I'll be so busy with preparations that I probably won't have a chance to see you again. I suppose our next meeting will be on Hakkōda, in the snow," Kanda said as he was about to leave.

While Kanda was putting on his shoes in the entrance, Tokushima continued counseling. "Everywhere you'll bump into people who have no idea what things are really like. There's only one way to open their eyes: show them in person what it means to suffer from cold or frostbite. If you have half a chance before the Hakkōda Exercise, organize a practice march to some nearby mountain."

Encouraged by this good advice, Kanda offered a smart salute and left.

On his way from Tokushima's house to Hirosaki Station, Kanda passed in front of Division and Brigade Headquarters. He looked across the street from the two buildings, at the brick chimney from which bluish smoke now floated up peacefully.

He walked past, his eyes glued to the chimney as if he had received the order "Eyes left!" He recalled how the scarlet flames it spewed had changed instantly into black smoke. That moment had left a much stronger impression on his mind than the spectacle of the fire, for that was when Tomoda had turned round to begin the meeting that would lead to the Hakkōda Exercise. When the worried look in the general's eyes seemed to combine with the black smoke, Kanda had been assailed by a fear he could not explain. The fear had nothing to do with the fire. Rather, it resembled the fear he had felt once when he had a premonition of an enemy attack. This had happened in Taiwan, just after the war with China. Toward evening one day he had seen a column of smoke rising up from the middle of the forest, and a cold charge had

run down his spine. And sure enough, that very night the platoon under his command had come under fire and suffered heavy casualties.

He walked on. He had to get that chimney off his mind.

3

Because he had secured his superiors' permission for his unofficial visit to Tokushima, the first thing Kanda did when he reported for duty the following morning was to visit the office of his battalion commander, Major Yamada.

After they had exchanged salutes, Kanda submitted a report that listed, item by item, everything Tokushima had told him. It filled several pages of lined paper, kept together with a string looped through a hole. On the cover of the report was the title "Ideas for Winter Exercises as Suggested by Captain Taizō Tokushima of the 31st Regiment."

Yamada glanced from the report to Kanda's face and began to read.

Kanda always worked hard at everything he undertook. The fact that he had gone all the way to Hirosaki to talk to Tokushima was a case in point, and no one but he would have put Tokushima's thoughts on paper the very night of his return to Aomori and presented them as a report to his superior officer. The promotion of the commoner Kanda to the rank of captain was an aberration from the norm, a mutation as it were, in that very special society known as the army. Kanda's promotion truly showed that he possessed no ordinary talents and motivation. He devoted all his energy to his work, gave everything he had to the tasks with which he was entrusted. He worried particularly about overstepping his authority and never failed to consult his superiors about matters that fell beyond the scope of his instruction. This was part of the secret behind his promotions. Toward officers lower in rank, let alone his equals, he never behaved in a way that could have earned him their dislike. And he always kept in mind that he was a commoner, an officer who had come up from the ranks of the Training Corps.

"Did you warn Tokushima that you were visiting him in a private capacity?" asked Yamada after reading the report.

"I visited Captain Tokushima's home in civilian clothes, and I had made it plain to him that I was meeting him as Kanda, the private individual."

Kanda's face seemed to ask if there was anything untoward in his report, so Yamada told him:

"Well, on reading this, one gets the impression that its contents are rather far removed from what one might expect from a private visit. You seem to have brought the 31st's complete preparation schedule home with you."

"I had rather the same feeling."

"You didn't think it suspicious?"

"I thought that if anyone was to be trusted, it was Captain Tokushima."

"Tokushima perhaps, yes. But can you read Major Monma's thoughts? Do you know what's going on in Colonel Kojima's mind?"

"So my report. . . "

"Is to be considered as one possible way of looking at the problem, nothing more. The 5th will draw up its own plans, without relying too much on Tokushima's ideas."

Yamada stood up.

"I have one request to make, Sir," Kanda said. "I would like to take a platoon out on a march through the snow to the mountains nearby. It wouldn't take more than a day."

"Tokushima really put his spell on you, didn't he? Well, all right. If it takes no more than a day, I suppose there's no harm done. Which mountain did you have in mind?"

Yamada turned toward the map that was fixed to the wall.

"As far as Kotōge, on the way to Mount Hakkōda. I imagine we could easily get there and back again in a day, and I expect the snow will be quite deep."

"And when do you intend to go?"

"Soon after New Year's. I will need some time to evaluate what the results of that march say about our equipment and so on."

Yamada gave his approval.

A few days later, Kanda and First Lieutenant Katō, Sergeant Major Fujimoto, and Corporal Satō, all of E Company's 1st Platoon, set off to Tamogino to ask the villagers about the route.

The barracks of the Aomori 5th Infantry were located on the southern outskirts of Aomori City, in the middle of the rice fields. The road that passed in front of the barracks traveled southeast through the village of Tamogino; up the mountain; and to Sanpongi, on the eastern slopes of the Hakkōda Range. Tamogino would be their gateway to Mount Hakkōda. The last settlement— if one could call it that—on the western side of the divide was the

24

hot-spring resort of Tashiro, 8 miles deeper in the mountains than Tamogino.

From the barracks of the 5th to Tamogino it was about 3 miles gently upward. When they reached the village, Kanda asked for someone who knew his way about Mount Hakkōda well. Tamogino, though called a village, was really not more than a hamlet of sixteen households that survived mainly on farming and charcoal burning. Most of the able men were off in the mountains. Corporal Satō walked through the village and came back accompanied by two old men—Genbei, sixty-five years old, and Sakuemon, seventy-three. Genbei had a slight speech impediment, perhaps caused by the fact that he had suffered a light stroke, but Sakuemon's back was still straight and his voice was that of a young man.

"Have any of the people here ever used this road to go to Sanpongi around the end of January, beginning of February?" Kanda asked.

"When you say 'used this road,' you don't mean, did anyone ever go down this road to Aomori, take a train to Hachinohe, and then walk to Sanpongi. You mean, did anyone ever actually go up this road, across the mountains?" asked Sakuemon, who refused to be intimidated by the fact that his questioner was a military man.

"That's exactly what I meant," said Kanda. "Has anyone ever traveled up this road, to the southeast, and gone to Sanpongi via Tashiro?"

He had spread out a map, but Sakuemon did not even look at it.

"Nobody here would be that crazy."

"Crazy?" thundered Lieutenant Katō. It seemed to him that Sakuemon was making fun of them and their plans to cross the mountains. Then it dawned on him that no one had as yet referred to the exercise with so much as a single word, so he changed his tone and asked, more quietly: "Why would it be crazy?"

"Because in January and February the snow is so deep and the wind so strong that you couldn't possibly get through. You'd die if you tried. And people who go places where they know they'll die are crazy."

"I see, I see." Kanda took over now. "I'd like to have some more exact information about the weather. Specifically, how deep is the snow, how strong the wind, and how bad the cold."

"Well now, once you cross Ōtōge, you're in a white hell. The snow reaches as high as your chest. Walking is out of the question. And between Ōtōge and Tashiro there are practically no trees—it's all flat and white, as far as you can see. But you can't see the road, because it's buried under the snow. And when that snow starts drifting in the wind, you can't see where you're going either. With snow flying into your eyes, you can't walk a step. And as for the cold . . . oh, it gets cold enough to freeze saké."

Here Lieutenant Katō groaned. That sounded unmercifully cold to him.

"But I've heard that at Tashiro there are hot springs where people live year round," said Sergeant Major Fujimoto.

"Yes, there is one family that stores up on food and fuel at the end of autumn and passes the winter there. But they stay to see to it that their house won't collapse under the snow, not to lodge guests. Oh, there have been idiots who thought it might be nice to take a bath in the springs and left for Tashiro as if it were a lark up a summer road. They were buried in the snow and died."

"Did that happen recently?"

"Not what you could call very recently. About four years ago. Some young people from around here went off into the mountains on the feast of the mountain god, and all eight of them died. And some thirteen years ago the same sort of thing happened, except twelve people died. So it makes no difference how many people you try it with. Impossible is impossible."

Sakuemon put heavy emphasis on his last words.

"Especially on the feast of the mountain god, the second half of January, it's dangerous to go up the mountain, for the god gets angry and will surely punish you," quavered Genbei, who had thus far remained silent. "My own son was one of the eight who left for Tashiro that time four years ago. His body wasn't found until the next April, at Sainokawara. He hadn't gone 2½ miles beyond Ōtōge before he froze to death. You soldiers are not like my son. Your clothes are good and your bodies are strong, but you simply can't go up this road to Tashiro in the middle of winter. And supposing you make it to Tashiro, nothing can save you if you get lost between there and Masuzawa!"

Because Genbei appeared to take it for granted that the army was preparing for a winter exercise, Kanda changed the subject and asked what sort of shoes the people of the village wore in the snow and what kind of food they could recommend for provisions. Round snowshoes were best, Sakuemon told him, but since Tamogino was not a hunting village whose men had to spend days on end in the snow searching for game, they had no special food to

26

suggest. Carry your food near your skin and heat it up over a wood fire if it froze, that was about all you could do, he supposed, and for that purpose rice cakes or parched rice seemed best.

It was a short winter's day. While they had stood talking to the two old men, Tamogino had become dark and cold.

As they were leaving, Kanda told Sakuemon that he had one more question. "Suppose someone told you he absolutely wanted to go to Tashiro. Would anyone be willing to guide him?"

Sakuemon thought for a while.

"That would depend both on the guide and on the people he'd be guiding," he answered.

Kanda felt he should no longer beat about the bush. This was, after all, no army secret. It would be best to tell the old man honestly what the rough plans for the exercise were.

"We're thinking of sending a platoon on a march through the snow to Sanpongi, via Kotōge, Ōtōge, Sainokawara, Tashiro, and Masuzawa. The exact date hasn't been fixed yet, but it'll probably be toward the end of January. I really would appreciate it if you could find us a reliable guide then."

Sakuemon appeared won over by the new, grave tone in Kanda's voice. In broad Tsugaru dialect he discussed the request with Genbei. Then he said:

"In that case I suppose this village has the duty to produce two or three guides."

But his face showed what he was thinking: It may be our duty, but I doubt whether there'll be any volunteers.

4

Although Tokushima had told Kanda that he had made no preparations at all, he had in fact considered the problem carefully and hit on a strategy that might give him a chance against the snow. The day after Kanda's visit he began to work out his ideas, and one week later he presented them in outline to Major Monma, his battalion commander.

"The plans to cross Mount Hakkōda? I suppose the colonel had better see them too," said Monma, observing that Tokushima's face was unusually tense.

27

On seeing Tokushima and Monma enter his office together, Colonel Kojima said, as if he had been waiting: "Ah, there are the plans for the Hakkōda Exercise."

"With permission, Sir. I have prepared a summary that, if it is approved, I intend to use as a a basis for more detailed planning. But before I start my explanation, there is something I would like to say to both of you. Do I have the Colonel's permission to speak?"

Tokushima had spoken fast, as he always did when he was nervous. Monma stared at him with a concerned expression in his eyes.

"Oh, yes. By all means." If Kojima was surprised, he did not show it. Not a cloud darkened the serene look on his face.

"Sir, I wonder if it isn't possible to reconsider this agreement to rendezvous with the 5th Regiment on Mount Hakkōda this winter. In my personal opinion, we should not stare ourselves blind on Hakkōda. It would be better if the two regiments held separate exercises."

"You think Mount Hakkōda too difficult?"

"I can't say that until I've tried it, but I can state positively that the risks involved are extremely high."

"Does that mean that these plans you two brought in here are not for the Hakkōda Exercise?"

"I cannot go against orders, Sir. These are the plans of the Hakkōda Exercise, and they are as good as I could make them— within the limits of the possible."

"Well, as long as they are finished. But tell me what you're worried about, Captain."

"In the first place, Sir, I am worried that Division and Brigade are merely using us to earn feathers in their own caps. In the second place, I am worried about the snow. And in the third place, I am worried about the men who have to struggle through it. For all these reasons I wonder if we could not forget about these plans and schedule another exercise—on Mount Iwaki, but on a larger scale from last winter's."

Though the way Tokushima had openly criticized Division and Brigade had cast a shadow over Kojima's face, the colonel let it pass. He said, gazing at Tokushima:

"You're worried about the men?"

"Sir, whether this exercise ends up as a death march or as a brilliant success depends entirely upon the participants. To save one straggler in that kind of snow, ten others will have to fall behind, and to save those ten, the whole platoon will have to risk disaster. They don't call Hakkōda a white hell for nothing."

This was indeed something to worry about.

28

Colonel Gunzō Kojima had grown gray in the service. He looked
not merely at home in the army after all those years—he looked as
if he had the army in his blood. He had had many officers like
Tokushima under him, and whenever one of them spoke as Tokushima had just done, it meant that the problem at hand was graver
than anyone thought. More than once, the officer in question had
hinted he would not be able to accept the responsibility for a
certain course of action. I have to be careful, the colonel thought.
At such a time it's best to let someone have his say.

"All right, Captain, you may speak frankly. Tell us exactly what
you have on your mind," he said in a quiet, persuasive tone.

"Sir, I respectfully request to be put in charge of the entire
organization of this exercise. I honestly believe we have no chance
against the snow unless I am allowed a free hand."

Kojima thought he discerned an emotional undertone in Tokushima's words.

"But wasn't it decided at the very beginning to leave everything
up to you? And you have proceeded on that understanding. What
freer hand could you want?" wondered Monma.

"I was referring to organization from now on, Sir. I am afraid
I must urge you to accept the plans for the number and composition of the participants and their equipment exactly as they
are formulated in my report. We will have great problems if
you don't."

With these words Tokushima handed the folder containing his
preparation plans to Monma, who quickly leafed through them
and placed them in front of Kojima.

The colonel put on his glasses.

Time passed, marked by the tramping of boots entering and
leaving barracks.

"This is amazing! You write here that you'll need eleven days
from the moment you leave Hirosaki to the end of this exercise.
And you estimate covering a distance of some 150 miles." Kojima
looked up from the report. "Look Captain, just a moment ago you
were complaining about the high risks involved in this exercise;
but if these plans don't look dangerous, I'll eat my hat. Can't you
organize a shorter march, in fewer days?"

"If we are to cross Mount Hakkōda to Aomori, there is no other 29
possible route, Sir. It's this plan, or none at all. If you think this is
too difficult, I suggest you change the site of the exercise from
Mount Hakkōda to Mount Iwaki," Tokushima said resolutely.

Kojima asked no further questions about the route, but read on. A few moments later he cried out, "What is this supposed to mean!" It was not a question, but an exclamation of surprise.

Tokushima's report recommended that the force sent out on this exercise consist of himself as the officer in charge, one first and one second lieutenant, seven probationary officers (a rank between noncommissioned officers and officers), two probationary medical officers, twenty NCOs, and five enlisted men.

In number this was certainly a platoon, but its composition was most unusual. It was basically a mixture of probationary officers and NCOs, with a sprinkling of ordinary soldiers. Moreover, this recommendation was followed by a number of conditions the participants would have to meet:

1. All participants are to be volunteers, recruited from the whole regiment.

2. The selection of the volunteers is to be left to the judgment of the officer in charge.

3. All volunteering NCOs and enlisted men must be able to function as guides during the entire exercise, or at least part of it, or be familiar with mountains in winter. No NCO or enlisted man can be shorter than 5 feet 2 inches.

"Shall I explain, Sir?" Tokushima offered, but neither Kojima nor Monma spoke a word. Judging from what Tokushima had said so far, they could imagine why he had come up with this extraordinary plan.

"I have considered various alternatives, but I believe this is the only viable course of action. I require so many NCOs and probationary officers because the main object of this exercise is to gather information, but also because, if something should go wrong, the nation will accept the news easier if all participants enlisted in the army voluntarily."

Kojima and Monma did not have to be told what Tokushima meant when he said "if something should go wrong." He seemed to have thought of every contingency, including the public reaction against the army authorities if there should be casualties among the enlisted men.

"All right, then," Kojima said to Monma. "Let's leave everything to Tokushima."

That very day the plans for the Hakkōda Exercise were presented in outline to the officers of the 31st, and recruitment of volunteers began. Several officers from other battalions objected to the fact that Tokushima was in total charge of the selection, but Colonel Kojima and Major Monma managed to talk them around.

"If this were an ordinary case, you'd be quite right. But for Tokushima this exercise is literally a matter of life or death," argued the major, and this made the other officers see reason.

Tokushima had stipulated 5 feet 2 inches as the minimum height for NCOs and enlisted men because he wanted only volunteers of superior physical strength.

From the recruitment posters it was obvious to everyone that the Hakkōda Exercise was not going to be a pleasure trip. Because most NCOs and enlisted men in the 31st hailed from Aomori Prefecture, they already knew that Mount Hakkōda was virtually impenetrable in midwinter. They knew also that they would be risking their lives. Nevertheless, a great many men of the required height volunteered. Tokushima studied their career histories, interviewed them individually, and consulted their immediate superiors. Only then did he make his final selection. He could still recall vividly how, during the ascent of Mount Iwaki in January, one of the soldiers had developed frostbite on his feet and had become a tremendous burden to the rest of the platoon. In the snow one could not allow a single person to fall behind.

By December 25, Tokushima had finished the selection of his platoon: one first and one second lieutenant, seven probationary officers, two probationary medical officers, one sergeant major, twenty corporals, and four enlisted men. When the local newspaper *Tōō Nippō* heard of the 31st's daring plan, it requested and received permission to send a military correspondent along. With the addition of the journalist Yūjirō Saikai, the total strength of the platoon became thirty-eight.

This task accomplished, Tokushima assigned reconnaissance problems to each member of the platoon and sent officer and probationary officers to each town, village, or hamlet on the route to investigate the state of the roads, the depth of the snow, the availability of guides, and so on. Everyone from probationary officer on up was told to cancel his New Year's leave and to work on the preparations for the exercise.

5

The Tokushima Platoon's tentative marching schedule reached the 5th Regiment on January 6, 1902.

"It seems the 31st is all set to go."

Lieutenant Colonel Tsumura, the regimental commander, had summoned Major Yamada of the 2nd Battalion and showed him the schedule.

"They're too ambitious, Sir. To hike full circle all the way around the Hakkōda Massif from Hirosaki would be difficult even in summer. No, I'm afraid Tokushima must have gone off his head." Yamada looked incredulous as he continued, "These plans are totally irresponsible! I don't care how many guides he says he's going to use, there is no guarantee that he'll be able to find enough of them to guide him all the way. And anyway, the whole idea of relying on civilians for quarters every night is impossible."

"Use guides?" asked Tsumura. The schedule he had received did not go into such details.

"Yes, Sir. When Kanda went to visit Tokushima in Hirosaki, he was told that the 31st plans to use guides throughout."

"Oh. And what did Kanda have to say about that?"

"Tokushima seems to have bowled him over completely, so now Kanda is all in favor of using guides, too. Though the whole thing will last for only three days, we'll still have to cross some snowy terrain, he says, and we'd better use guides from Tamogino onward."

"Three days?"

"Yes, Sir. According to my battalion's plans, the first day we will pass through Tamogino, cross Kotōge and Ōtōge, and strike out across Mount Hakkōda toward Tashiro in the southeast, where we'll spend the first night at the hot springs. The second night we'll spend at Masuzawa, the third at Sanpongi, and the fourth day we'll board a train and return to barracks. This is only a rough plan, of course. The final details will be thrashed out after we have finished our practice march to Kotōge."

"But if you intend to cover such a distance, shouldn't you also use guides? I mean, you're venturing into unknown territory once you enter those snowbound mountains."

"But Sir, isn't the military object of this exercise to open up unknown territories? If we're going to follow guides, we won't learn a thing. No, we'll obtain the best possible results only if we rely entirely on maps and compasses while we're in the snow."

"Still, I think you'd better leave such decisions to Kanda's judgment, seeing that he will be in charge of the platoon. You don't meet officers as outstanding as Kanda every day. He started his career in this regiment, you know."

Colonel Tsumura had advanced ideas. To his mind, restricting the Military Academy to the descendants of samurai was totally out of tune with the times. Captain Kanda illustrated the new order beautifully: he was not born in a samurai family, he had not graduated from the Academy, and yet he was the most brilliant officer of the 5th Regiment.

"Yes, Sir," Yamada agreed. "Kanda is an excellent officer, and the 5th may be proud of him. And because he is so good, he is not just popular among the lower ranks—they'd follow him through hell— he is also well liked among his fellow officers. That is why I recommended he be put in charge of the exercise. However, I'd like to see a little bit more individuality in Kanda. I'd like him to come up with final plans so good that anyone would agree only the 5th could have produced them."

"And you think it is individual not to use guides?" asked Tsumura, his eyes flashing ominously.

"No, Sir, that was not what I meant."

As Yamada fell back a step, Tsumura continued instantly.

"When will this march to Kotōge take place? I don't suppose we'll be able to think about the equipment or the number of the participants for Hakkōda until we have the results from the practice march."

"The practice march will take place after the tenth, Sir."

"The 31st has already finished all its preparations."

Tsumura did not raise his voice, but he could not quite hide the irritation that darkened his brow.

6

Preceded by a detail of twenty men on snowshoes, Captain Kanda's E Company was working its way toward Kotōge. They had had snow on the road since they left barracks, but the squad up front had not put on their snowshoes until just before Tamogino. Behind the trailbreakers marched the individual platoons, and the rear was made up by four soldiers, relieved every twenty minutes, who were pulling a sled carrying some 240 pounds of luggage.

There was not a cloud in the sky. The snow lay sparkling in the sun, and the men hauling the sled were bathing in sweat. 33

The people of Tamogino, who had hardly expected the army at this time of the year, came flying out of every door and walked along part of the way. The whole company was wearing straw boots over their army issues. The snow was fairly hard and did not offer many problems to the main body, which had the added advantage of being able to walk in the footsteps of the twenty trailbreakers.

Boys were pointing and shouting, "Look! The soldiers are wearing straw boots!" They had always associated soldiers with leather boots, and for them now to wear the same kind of straw affairs as the people of the village struck the village youth as quite unusual. The sight of soldiers was less unusual to them. When there was no snow, an occasional platoon or company, at times even a battalion, might take this road on its way to the mountains. But soldiers in midwinter—that was something they had never seen before.

Every fifty minutes, not a minute sooner or later, the company would take a ten-minute break. As the slope became steeper, the snow grew deeper and it became more difficult for the snowshoe detail to clear a path. At the rear, more and more men were needed on the ropes that pulled the sled. Nevertheless, E Company handled the problems. No one was complaining about the cold, and frostbite was the last thing on anyone's mind. And, since it was a windless day, there was no snow drifting or flying about. When it was time for the fourth break, Kanda did not give the order to stop; he had the men march on for fifteen minutes more. After sixty-five minutes they finally halted at Kotōge, the object of that day's march. As the name Kotōge—"Low Crest"—indicated, the place looked like a hilltop but, in fact, was not: the road went much higher.

On receiving the order to fall out for midday rations, the men sought sunny spots for themselves and sat down on the snow. In the always moving pools of sunlight among the scrawny bushes, it was so warm that it was hard to believe it was winter.

"The snow lies 4 feet 10 inches deep, Sir," First Lieutenant Katō reported to Kanda.

"I imagine it will get deeper very quickly as you get nearer Ōtōge," said Kanda, looking in that direction.

Ōtōge—"High Crest"—did its name credit. Kanda's map showed 765 yards between Kotōge and Ōtōge, but on that stretch the slope suddenly became very steep. Beyond Ōtōge, at an altitude of 1,640 feet, lay a snowfield.

"Captain, why don't we push on to Ōtōge after the men have eaten?" suggested Katō, between bites from his rice cake. "It would be tremendously valuable for the exercise if we could check out what the snow is like on the other side, before we return to barracks."

"Yes, that mightn't be a bad idea, provided there's time. But let's finish chow first," Kanda responded noncommittally. He concentrated on his meal.

Thirty minutes had been scheduled for the midday break, during which the men ate the rations they had carried with them in boxes made of willow bark. To a man they looked as cheerful as if they were on a winter picnic.

Some five minutes before the end of the break, Katō again broached the subject of going on to Ōtōge, adding that the other platoon leaders agreed with him.

"From barracks to here it took us four hours, so it should take, at most, two to get back. If we return now, we'll be back by two o'clock. If we decide to get back by four, we could go on for another two hours," he said, looking up into the blue sky where the sun stood shining brightly.

"You're right, Lieutenant. But today's plan was to go as far as Kotōge. That was all Major Yamada gave us permission for, so that is all we'll do. We'll return to barracks according to the original plan," Kanda said firmly. He had made his decision while he was eating lunch.

Looking visibly dissatisfied, Katō stared from Kanda's face to Ōtōge and back, but he decided there was nothing he could do about Kanda's conclusion. Katō went back to his platoon. He had grave doubts about the wisdom of Kanda's refusal to march one step farther than he had planned. It was quite unlike the captain, he thought. Since the object of this march was to prepare for the main exercise, the officer in charge should have been given enough leeway to deviate from his orders somewhat, even though the orders had contained no reference to any point beyond Kotōge. In fact, Katō thought, for refusing to proceed to the snowfield at Ōtōge, Kanda could be accused of temporizing.

In his mind Katō compared Major Yamada's face with the captain's: the one frowning nervously when lost in thought, the other at times looking as if he were gazing very far away. Among the officers of the battalion there had been rumors that Captain Kanda, who had done all the planning, and Major Yamada, to whom he was responsible, did not see eye to eye in this business of the Hakkōda Exercise. Katō had even heard that the major had

35

chewed out the captain about his preparations. The real point of contention, Katō knew, was whether they should follow the captain's recommendation to send only a platoon or the major's wish to send a company. Today's practice march to Kotōge would settle that question. Katō assumed that the captain had refused to exceed his instructions because he did not want to offend the major over some minor matter. He was playing it safe, that was it.

The wind had risen and blown up clouds of snow over Ōtōge. It was time to leave. The company marched down the hill, back to barracks, according to plan. It was 2:00 PM when they arrived in Aomori.

After dismissing his men, Kanda wrote up the notes he had taken on the march and went to Yamada's office. By then it was just past 4:00 PM.

Yamada was pleased with the report.

"Well, judging from today's result, I think we should send a company after all. And that's not going to be your company, Kanda, but one that will be formed from the whole regiment. Also, I'd like your plans to provide for the fact that the staff of the 2nd Battalion will go along as well." The cold look on Yamada's face showed plainly that he was not going to argue about this.

At this piece of information, Kanda started. Even if the battalion staff would not actually be part of the company, it still meant that he, as officer in command of the company, would be outranked. Kanda's position had become truly difficult. Why did he not tell Yamada that, if he chose to participate in the exercise, then he— rather than Kanda—ought to take full responsibility as commanding officer?

Kanda kept silent. Anything he said would be a waste of words. Ten days before, when he had submitted his recommendation to stage the exercise at platoon strength, Yamada had looked far from happy. Yamada's objection had been that the 31st was already sending a platoon and for the 5th to do the same would show lack of individuality. Recommendation rejected. At that time Yamada must already have been toying with the idea of sending the battalion staff along.

The presence of the battalion staff meant trouble, Kanda thought. An army formation with even the slightest doubt about the line of command would flounder in an emergency.

"Any questions?" asked Yamada.

"No, Sir. I will select the men as soon as possible."

36

"Try to get it done by the morning of the twentieth, the day after tomorrow. That's when the 31st will leave. So get things moving, will you?"

Yamada seemed very concerned about the movements of the Tokushima Platoon.

With a heavy heart Kanda passed through the barracks gate. The snow that had melted in the warmth of the day had hardened after dark. More than once Kanda's feet slipped on the frozen surface. He was exhausted by the day's march, and Yamada's orders weighed heavy on his mind. From the barracks gate all the way to his house, the road was covered with snow.

When Kanda got home, Private Zenjirō Hasebe—his orderly, who had come to prepare his bath—stood stiffly at attention as he handed Kanda an envelope. He muttered something too fast for Kanda to understand.

The envelope contained a letter addressed to Hasebe, from Kichinosuke Saitō, a career corporal in the 31st Regiment. The letter said that, on January 20, Corporal Saitō would be leaving on the Hakkōda Exercise. He had received permission to visit his aunt in Aomori on the eighteenth and, because there was a danger that he might not come back alive from that white hell if they bungled things, he would very much like to meet Hasebe to say good-bye to him.

"What relation is this Corporal Saitō to you?"

"He's my elder brother, Sir. When I was a child, I was adopted by relatives, and my name was changed to Hasebe."

Kanda gave Hasebe permission to go and see his brother.

But when Hasebe reached his aunt's house, his brother had already left. He had taken an afternoon train back to Hirosaki.

"And he had so wanted to see you. . . . " sobbed his aunt. But Saitō had asked her to pass on a message to his brother:

If the 5th should start recruiting volunteers for the Hakkōda Exercise, you must under no circumstances step forward. I suppose there's little you can do about it if they tell you that, as your captain's orderly, you have to join. But try to avoid going if you can help it.

"It's all very well for Kichinosuke to say I shouldn't go, but how can a captain's orderly refuse to join his captain?" Hasebe asked his aunt. He explained that his participation in the exercise was a foregone conclusion.

"If you really have to go to that awful place, you ought to at least drop your brother a line to tell him."

"But Kichinosuke is leaving the day after tomorrow. If I wrote a letter right away, do you think it would reach him?" His aunt continued to look worried. "Oh well, these winter exercises are nothing to get worked up about, let them say what they will. Anyhow, I've heard we'll run into the 31st, so I'll see Kichinosuke then, I guess."

When he was still very young, Hasebe had been adopted by relatives who lived in the town of Tsukidate in Miyagi Prefecture. Unlike his brother from Aomori, therefore, he had no idea how terrible snow can be. The same could be said of all the lower ranks of the 5th, who mostly came from prefectures like Miyagi or Iwate with a much milder climate.

When Kanda came home the following evening, the nineteenth, he asked Hasebe if he had been able to meet his brother.

"No Sir, I wasn't. But my aunt gave me a message from him."

"And what was the message?"

That was a difficult question for Hasebe to answer. He could not very well tell the captain to his face that his brother had advised him not to take part in the exercise.

"Oh, you know how it is, Sir. My brother's always worrying about things, so he gave me all sorts of advice about the exercise."

"All sorts of? Let's hear some of it."

Again Hasebe was at a loss for words. Because he was not the sort of person who dodges such questions easily, he turned red and hung his head. From his silence, Kanda could well imagine what his brother's advice had been.

"He told you to stay out of it. Is that it?"

Hasebe turned pale now and began to tremble, but Kanda did not press any further. Instead he said:

"Well, if you think it's too dangerous, you don't have to go. There is absolutely no reason why I should take you along."

That night Kanda put the last touch to the plans, which he had brought home with him. The next day, the twentieth, he presented them to Yamada, who took them to Lieutenant Colonel Tsumura.

"So you're not sending a platoon?"

38

Tsumura looked surprised. Still, he had never explicitly told Yamada to drop his plans to send a whole company. He skimmed through the plans. He had no objection to recruiting volunteers from the entire regiment and giving the command to Kanda, but as regimental commander he disapproved of sending the battalion staff along, even as observers.

"Remember that Kanda will be in command," he warned Yamada. If they were going as a company, the officer in charge would be the company commander; there was no need for a battalion commander to go along. But the colonel told himself that Yamada wished to participate not so he could command Kanda's company but because he wanted to use the biggest winter exercise in the history of the regiment to broaden his own professional experience.

"Yes, Sir. I will leave the company command to Kanda in every detail," Yamada assured the colonel. "The main mission of the battalion staff will be to give guidance in matters pertaining to the gathering and processing of information."

For all that, Tsumura did not affix his seal to the document immediately. He sat momentarily lost in thought, gazing at the paper.

"The 31st left its barracks in Hirosaki this morning before dawn, Sir," said Yamada.

Tsumura knew this, of course, but Yamada was suggesting that at this stage there was no more time to revise the plans.

Tsumura grunted under his breath. "The 31st has left, eh?"

With these words he put his seal on the plans for the Hakkōda Exercise.

As soon as this was done, he ordered Yamada to get on the phone and tell the commander of the 1st and 3rd Battalions to come to his office with all their company commanders.

Within one hour, posters announcing the Hakkōda Exercise had been put up in every nook of the barracks. Participating officers and lower ranks would be selected by their platoons.

The whole 5th was in a fever. Not a single person thought of the exercise as possibly dangerous. When he read that the company would spend one night at the Tashiro hot springs, one corporal sighed:

"Ahhh! Mountains, snow, a hot bath, and a drink! What a great idea."

The NCOs around him quite agreed.

The same day, Kanda received a letter from Tokushima.

39

I am so busy with preparations for our departure the twentieth, that I have been unable to find time to meet you and discuss your plans. I hope, therefore, that you will forgive this short note. I daresay you have already received our itinerary. Since you are leaving later than we and have not yet decided your schedule, it is too early to forecast where we will meet, but I suppose that by the time our platoon reaches Mount Hakkōda, you will not be far away. Because I am well aware that the most difficult part of this march is the stretch from Masuzawa via Tashiro to Tamogino, I want to take this opportunity to ask for what I know your chivalry will not refuse: to come to our assistance if our platoon should find itself in danger. Most of all, however, I am writing to assure you how sincerely I wish for your safe return.

This letter convinced Kanda that in the matter of the Hakkōda Exercise he was one step behind Tokushima, in every sense of the word.

PART TWO

SNOW

It was 5:30 am when the Tokushima Platoon passed through the barracks gate of the 31st Regiment in Hirosaki. Snow was coming down from a jet-black sky. Led by a soldier functioning as guide, the platoon marched toward Daikōji, but at Nisato they turned off the main road, which would have taken them there in less than 1 ½ miles. Instead the men made a detour of some 6 miles through the still-dark hamlets of Kawai, Samukawa, Harada, Fukiage, and Kashiwagi. Tokushima decided on the detour because he wanted to impress on all his men that the purpose of the exercise was first and foremost to gather information.

After forming his platoon, he had given each of its thirty-seven members an assignment, with topics ranging from weather, equipment, provisions, and billeting, to the most effective way to march through snow, the reading of maps in snow-covered terrain, the influence of the cold on fatigue, and the prevention and treatment of frostbite. Important problems he had assigned to several men, who would work on them as a team. One assignment, which began at the moment of departure, was to investigate the correlation between marching speed and fatigue when moving through snow over level terrain. From time to time, therefore, he made his men run or spread out in battle formation. Since the platoon was not subdivided into squads, there were no squad leaders; the formations most resembling squads were the various observation teams. Of the four enlisted men, two had joined to serve as guides, one was Tokushima's orderly, and the last was Takejirō Kaga, the bugler. An assignment for him had not been forgotten: bugling conditions at extremely low temperatures.

Before their departure, Tokushima explained once more to all the men the exact object of the exercise, so that from the moment the platoon marched through the gate each soldier was able to concentrate on the task entrusted to him.

43

At the time of departure, the temperature measured 26° on Probationary Officer Shigeo Funayama's thermometer. Funayama's responsibility was to check the temperature at every break.

At 7:30 AM they arrived at the village of Daikōji, where the people stared, full of admiration, at the way the soldiers marched smartly in formation so early in the morning. The officers and probationary officers wore uniforms and greatcoats of black wool; the NCOs and enlisted men, blue uniforms and khaki greatcoats, also of wool. From each backpack dangled two pairs of straw boots—when they arrived in Daikōji the men were still in short army boots, leggings, and spats. All wore caps of a similar design: they were almost 4 inches high at the rim, which sported two yellow bands separated by a black one, and the golden star of the army glittering over the peak. The greatcoats were equipped with hoods, but no one was using them. And, in spite of the piercing cold, no one had put on earmuffs, either. Marching in step, their white gloves swinging, delighted children skipping around them, the soldiers offered a pretty sight as they passed through the village.

Because the men of the lower ranks were all splendidly built, the rifles they carried seemed not in the least heavy. The only thing that seemed a little unusual to the villagers was the presence of so many probationary officers.

The roofs of Daikōji groaned under a heavy load of snow, and icicles hung from every eave. Because the people had been warned that the Tokushima Platoon would be coming, they had arranged for each house to take in a few soldiers and give them some hot tea or, in some cases, food or even saké.

But Tokushima had warned each household that no soldier was allowed to drink saké on the way, not even during breaks. Included in the prohibition was the saké Colonel Kojima had presented as a gift to the platoon. The colonel's saké had been rationed out that morning, so that every canteen was now filled with a standard measure, enough for one deep drink. As for equipment, the platoon was traveling as light as possible. Cooking gear, rations, and provisions had not been packed together. Instead every man carried his midday and emergency rations with him, the policy being to buy everything necessary in the villages on the route and to depend for meals and quarters on the people. Colonel Kojima's saké had been distributed so as to make every man's burden similar. Tokushima had considered that water would be easy to come by the first day and had told his men to use their canteens for the saké, giving

44

strict orders, however, that no one was to touch it until they had reached that night's billets.

The snow, which had momentarily stopped while they were resting, began to fall again when the platoon resumed its march eastward.

After about 2½ miles they rested again at the village of Karadake, whose headman, Tokunosuke Sōma, had ridden out on horseback to meet them. The platoon was billeted among the households, where—in spite of the fact that each was carrying his own rations—the men gladly accepted the warm meals they were offered. But they stubbornly declined any offer of saké. Some men ate so much that they became drowsy and stretched out beside the hearth or by a footwarmer. It was not until 2:00 PM that the platoon was to set out for the goal of that day's march, Oguni. They could rest for two and a half hours—long enough to shake off almost all their fatigue.

The 15 miles from barracks to Karadake had been marched along a level, well-marked road, but the leg from Karadake to Oguni was a mountain path some 6 miles long, through an area deeply covered with snow. It was obvious that this would be the greatest hurdle of the day. Nevertheless, Tokushima seemed to be in no hurry.

The slow pace was getting on First Lieutenant Sanjurō Tanabe's nerves. Winter days are short, and Tanabe failed to see why Tokushima, who was always going on about how winter march objectives should be reached by 3:00 PM, had broken his own rule on the very first day. He discussed the mystery with Second Lieutenant Keiji Takahata, but Takahata did not understand either. What they both agreed on, however, was that the captain had not been his usual self since they had left barracks. His features were as cold as if his face had frozen up, and his characteristic hearty laughter or the pleasant smile he always had for civilians was conspicuously absent. It was hard to find any expression in his eyes other than that of the officer in charge.

At 2:00 PM Sōma, the headman, went up to Tokushima and suggested they should be getting ready to leave. Outside, a hunter stood waiting; he was wearing a bearskin that reached to his hips. Sōma had put on a straw coat with a peaked hood that made him look quite tall when seen from behind.

"Yabei here and I will be your guides, so you need not worry, even if it should turn dark or if we get caught in a snowstorm," Sōma said with a look over his shoulder at Yabei. His face expressionless, the hunter took off his cap and bowed slightly to Tokushima.

At Karadake they left the Hirosaki Plain and headed into the mountains. From there to Oguni the path would be all uphill and downhill, in the snow. And no sooner had they set out than it began to snow. Unlike the snow that had been falling off and on since that morning, this snow consisted of thick, heavy flakes that covered their footprints immediately and made them feel as if they were making their way through a narrow corridor cut in a forest. It was a good thing that Sōma and Yabei were walking at the head of the column; if Tokushima's men had relied on a map, they would have had to stop within one hour after leaving Karadake. The farther they went, the deeper the snow became.

On orders Tokushima had given before they left Karadake, all men now wore straw boots over their army issues. He himself wore them over his fine leather officer's boots. He had also given permission to officers and lower ranks alike to put up their hoods at any time.

Probationary Medical Officer Kenji Nagao made his rounds, instructing the men that he wanted anyone who was bothered by the cold or who thought he had frostbite to speak up immediately. But there were no complaints, neither of one nor the other.

Assisted by his NCOs, Probationary Officer Shigeo Funayama of the meteorological observation team recorded the depth of the snow and measured the temperature. The velocity and direction of the wind they estimated with the eye.

Corporal Kichinosuke Saitō counted paces, for his assignment was to keep track of the distance covered. From afar the incessant murmuring of his voice sounded as if he were reciting a litany.

The storm was turning day into night. All the men were seriously worried about the road ahead. Tokushima, walking with Sōma, at the head of the line, could sense the fear of the men behind him.

"All right!" he shouted. "The observation teams may continue as they are, but the rest of you will sing!" And he burst into "Marching Through Ice and Snow," a well-known army song. All the men joined in, except for Corporal Saitō, who raised his voice and continued counting.

In deviation from army practice, Tokushima did not stop after fifty minutes for the usual ten-minute break. He left the tempo entirely up to the guides. Yabei did not walk fast. If anything, he seemed a bit on the slow side to the men. On the other hand, he showed no signs that he was ever going to stop. His motto could have been No rush, no rest.

Sōma, the headman, had said that it would take about five hours from Karadake to Oguni, and he had wondered if the platoon would be able to walk for such a time without a long break. Sometimes, when Tokushima ordered an equipment inspection or told them to measure the depth of the snow, the platoon would halt. On those occasions the men felt how cold it was. They gradually began to understand that it might be better not to rest but to go on, no matter how slowly.

At 4:00 PM it turned totally dark. But since the guides obviously knew their business, they never got around to lighting the small lanterns they had brought along.

On and on went the road, up and down in the snow. The men began to worry if Oguni would really lie waiting for them at the end of the journey, if Yabei and Sōma really knew the way there.

Then Yabei stopped. Sōma told Tokushima they would rest for a moment. They were halfway up a slope, in a hollow protected from the wind. Three and a half hours had passed since they left Karadake.

When Tokushima gave the order to halt, the NCOs and enlisted men stacked arms and sat down in the snow, unable to hide their exhaustion. Tokushima told Kaga the bugler to try out his instrument as part of his research assignment. The bugle sounded as if to pierce the curtain of drifting snow. From then on Kaga blew his bugle at every major rest stop. During the break, the probationary officers positioned themselves in a ring around their captain, to give him every possible protection against the cold. But there were others who had no time to rest, because they had to carry out their assignments.

On orders from Tokushima, the provisions team checked everybody's rations. The team found that rice balls in the backpacks were frozen almost solid, whereas those packed into duffel bags worn underneath the greatcoats were not; rice cakes that had been carried close to the skin were actually still warm. The men lost no time eating these.

They started moving again. The road became steep now, while the increasingly severe storm dumped ever more snow on them. Panting, sinking to their waists into the drifts, the men struggled upward. Some whispered among themselves.

"Are we going to be OK?"

"Is this really the right road?"

Tokushima could hardly have heard them in the storm. Yet, whenever such whispers arose behind his back, he unfailingly ordered a rotation in the ranks. In the deep snow, the men up front had to work that much harder at clearing a path—talking was a waste of strength.

When some of the men got stuck in the snow and fell down, the team investigating fatigue checked to see if they fell because they were tired while the equipment team checked if anything was the matter with their straw boots. There was only one case of frostbite: a man who complained that the tips of his toes were frozen. On instructions from the medical team, he massaged his toes and changed into dry socks. But as more men developed problems walking and got bogged down in the snow and as more complaints about frozen toes came in, it became impossible for the medical team to attend to each case individually.

"Are we going to be all right?"

"Aren't we on the wrong road?"

At last it became clear that these whispers reflected the mood of the entire platoon. The corporals passed on their uneasiness to the sergeants, the sergeants to the probationary officers, and so on up in rank, until it reached the lieutenants. When Tanabe shouted the men's fears into Tokushima's ear, the captain yelled back:

"In a few more steps we'll be at the top, and then it's downhill all the way to Oguni. Pass it on!"

Some of the men developed a violent thirst when they got tired, but their canteens contained no water—only saké, and that they weren't allowed to touch.

The medics went around warning against eating snow. "Don't ever do it. Your belly will start aching, your temperature will drop, and you'll run a high risk of frostbite. And don't drink the saké in your canteen, either. It'll pep you up for a while, but you'll soon be unable to move, because you'll get twice as tired and cold as before."

Everyone was gasping for breath. Just a few steps more! Just a few steps more! They made swimming movements with their arms as they climbed up through the drifts.

When they reached the top, they could see—in between flurries—the light of a fire, The people of Oguni had lit a beacon to guide the Tokushima Platoon in.

At this point Tokushima held roll call. After inspecting every man's clothing and apparent physical condition, he ordered Sergeant Major Itō to check if any of the lower ranks had drunk the saké in their canteens. The canteens of the officers and probationary officers were inspected by Lieutenant Tanabe.

Itō and Tanabe both reported that they had found everything in order. Actually some of the men had drunk a little, but under the circumstances it was only normal to protect one's subordinates.

"Good!" said Tokushima. "If any of you had touched that saké against orders, I'd have sent him back to barracks right away! And it's a good thing we have no such misfits with us. We'll have to go on like this for the next eleven days, and I don't want anyone to disobey orders, ever. Just because one of you does not do exactly as he is told, the whole platoon may freeze to death. Never forget that!"

After he finished this speech, Tokushima ordered Yabei and Sōma to the rear and took the lead himself. Singing an army song, the platoon descended into the hamlet of Oguni.

It was 7:00 PM when they got there. The men were immediately taken to the billets that had been prepared for them and where hot soup and rice stood waiting. They were told to see to it that their wet uniforms were dry by morning, and were then inspected for exhaustion, frostbite, and blisters.

When they turned in that evening, Tokushima told Tanabe, "The results of today's night march were very good, excellent."

Only then did Tanabe realize that they had proceeded so leisurely to Karadake because the captain had intended all along to practice a march in the dark. Nevertheless, he was a little worried because Tokushima had placed such absolute confidence in their two guides, so he muttered, mostly to himself:

"But didn't we rely too much on our guides?"

"More than anything, an officer has to be able to tell who he can trust, and who he can't," Tokushima told him. "I left everything to Yabei and Sōma because I felt they were reliable. People who can't trust others will soon find they can't trust themselves either."

He pulled the blankets over his head. Soon, thunderous snoring filled the room.

Tanabe recalled the count Corporal Saitō had given him. This first day they had covered about 21 miles. The following day they would go from Oguni to the hot springs at Kiriake, a mere 4 miles. But although the distance was only one-fifth of that covered the first day, they would have to cross the vast upland called the Biwa

49

Moor. There, even local people were known to have lost their way when it snowed. In the report of one of the investigative teams sent out to prepare for this exercise, Tanabe had read that, about three years before, five persons from Oguni had left for Kiriake, and two of them had frozen to death in a snowstorm on the Biwa Moor. The cold of the night drove home to Tanabe what was lying in store for the platoon.

The howling of the storm continued until dawn.

2

Yūjirō Saikai, the correspondent for *Tōō Nippō*, was walking almost at the end of the line. There was only one person behind him. The previous day he had actually been the very last man, but that morning, January 21, when the platoon was about to leave Oguni, the captain had ordered Lieutenant Takahata to the rear. Tokushima's concern betrayed how difficult the second day would be; it also showed that on a march through the snow it is more important to keep an eye on the people in the rear than on those up front. As for Saikai, he felt a lot better for the fact that there was someone behind him.

Before their departure, Tokushima had made a short speech— only a few words, brief and to the point, far removed from those regrettable and bombastic proclamations so characteristic of the army. There was to be no unnecessary talking, he warned; anyone suffering from exhaustion or frostbite was to mention his condition immediately to the medical officers or their assistants, and observation teams were to continue their work of the previous day. He also announced a new experiment: four NCOs would wear straw boots over three pairs of socks instead of over their army boots. The wearing of tinted glasses as protection against snow blindness was left to everyone's personal discretion.

For Saikai this was not only his first stint as a military correspondent, it was also the first time he had ever experienced military life, so everything seemed strange to him. But he felt that on one point his ideas about the army had been mistaken. He had heard that the higher-ranking officers strutted about like peacocks, but that the further down one went in rank, the harder life became. However, in this special platoon there were only four enlisted men and no squads, so he had been unable to observe even one example of NCOs persecuting privates or of officers harassing NCOs. In fact, the eagerness with which the various observation teams seemed to compete with each other to get their results in, despite the incredible number of assignments, struck him as quite unlike the army.

The main reason *Tōō Nippō* had picked Saikai for this job was that he was young and strong and might reasonably be expected to keep up with the soldiers. He wore a greatcoat equipped with a hood and around his neck, a muffler. Over his coat he carried a bag of the type mountain people use. Like the soldiers, he wore straw boots.

No sooner had they left Oguni than the men received orders to put on their hoods. As if it had been waiting for their departure, the snow, which had let up for a while, came lashing down with a fury. And the snow was not the only enemy they had to fight. When they approached Biwa Moor a violent headwind blew straight into their faces. One moment the snow would fall down from the sky, the next it would blow up from the ground. Everything around them was one white blank. It was all one man could do to follow the man in front of him. Because of the wind, the cold seemed to cut straight through their bodies.

They walked in double file. From time to time instructions were passed down the line.

"In this kind of wind your crotch may freeze, so check if your fly is buttoned up."

"Stamp your feet during breaks."

"Rub your hands while you walk, to avoid frostbite."

When Saikai passed these messages on to Takahata behind him, all he got in reply was a curt, almost angry, grunt.

The gale did not continue all that long. It was the sort of weather in which the wind dies down and the snowflakes drift gently from the sky, and just when you think the worst is over, the storm lashes out again. Whenever the drifting snow made it impossible to see what lay ahead, the platoon would halt and stamp its feet. On this road they would not have been able to proceed one step without guides.

In some places the snow seemed deep enough for them to sink in to the waist but would turn out to have a surface hard enough to allow them to scuttle across, half sliding, half running. On the whole, however, the snow lay deep, and once someone got stuck, it was no easy matter to get him out again. If he was pulled out forcibly, as often as not his straw boots slipped off his army boots and remained behind in the snow—and it was an awful chore to dig them up again. And, to make matters worse, when someone had this kind of mishap, he kept the whole platoon waiting.

That day too they hardly rested, but walked on in the teeth of the storm. Yet Saikai never worried. He had every confidence in Yabei and Sōma.

When the descent began, the two guides were sent from the front to the rear, changing places with Lieutenant Takahata, who had walked at the end of the line all day long.

"Kiriake is at the bottom of this slope," Yabei told Saikai.

"So that is why our guides were sent to the rear," laughed the journalist.

The wind diminished to a pleasant breeze, and a pale sun broke through. The whole platoon raised its eyes to the sky and murmured gratefully. They felt as if they had not seen the sun for days. But less than five minutes later, thick clouds hid the sun again and dumped more snow on the soldiers.

"It's been really foul weather today," Saikai remarked to Yabei. "If that gale had continued just a little longer, I don't know what would have become of us. You can't have many days as bad as this."

"Oh, today was nothing. You've got to think of this kind of weather as more or less normal in winter. We get much, much worse."

"Do people go outside when it gets that bad?"

"Go out? Anyone fool enough to go into the mountains on that kind of day won't come back alive. When the sky turns pitch black in the west and the western wind creeps in low over the ground and blows that fine, grainy snow—why, then it gets so cold even this bearskin won't help you. You feel yourself freeze from the waist down. Then you'd better drop whatever you're doing and turn home, or else. Days like that we have, oh, two or three times every winter," Yabei said.

Two or three times every winter—and suppose we hit one of them, thought Saikai.

The platoon was singing now. The wind tugged at the wisps of steam that curled up from the springs of Kiriake.

Before entering the hamlet, Tokushima lined up his men and held roll call.

"I thought I had mentioned clearly this morning that there was to be no unnecessary talking, but quite a few of you don't seem to have taken it very seriously. All right, everyone who remembers he opened his mouth for no good reason, one step forward!"

Nineteen men obeyed. Tokushima turned to Lieutenant Tanabe.

"Take their names," he ordered, his face expressionless. He continued, "By six o'clock this evening I want each observation team to present a report on its findings of the past two days to Lieutenant Tanabe. I hope Mr. Sōma will be good enough to see to it that the reports reach Colonel Kojima tomorrow."

The platoon was dismissed and the men went to their billets. It was a few minutes past noon.

Saikai found himself sharing quarters with Sergeant Major Itō and three corporals.

"In the army, do they always take the names of soldiers who talk out of turn?" he asked Itō. "It seems a little childish, if I may say so."

"Oh, normally you just get chewed out on the spot. Childish, eh? . . . Well, yes, I suppose you could call it childish, but then I think the captain has his reasons."

Saikai looked puzzled. "What reasons?"

"He can't get it out of his mind that this exercise will last eleven whole days, so he worries all the time. It cramps his style. But if he doesn't relax a bit, he won't last till the end. It'll get him."

"What will get him?"

"Why, the snow of course! Our enemy is the snow! We've come to battle the snow of Mount Hakkōda, haven't we? But if the snow gets the captain, that means it'll get the whole platoon. The captain thinks—and all of us agree—that when you fight the snow there's only two ways it can possibly end: either you come through together or you die together. It's one or the other. So, to give us a chance, he feels he has to come down on us a little hard and see to it we obey orders. He's afraid that giving an inch, even on some tiny thing, will have grave consequences."

With these words Itō turned to the three corporals and told them to sort out their notes of the past few days, so that they could put together their report on the guidance of lower ranks during winter exercises.

Saikai had his own work: The head office of his paper was expecting an article on the first two days of the exercise. So he sat down by the hearth, with a tray on his knees by way of desk, and

53

began to write. But although the fire was burning lustily, his pencil moved stiffly over the paper. The cold had penetrated the room.

On January 20, 1902, before dawn, a special platoon under the command of Captain Taizō Tokushima left the barracks of the 31st Regiment Infantry in Hirosaki. It was snowing hard. . . .

When he had written this much, his unwilling hands no longer bothered him. He filled up page after page.

As far as Saikai was concerned, this second night was a good night, for after a nice hot bath he fell asleep immediately and was dead to the world until Kaga the bugler sounded the reveille the following morning.

The dawn of January 22 broke with a snowstorm. Probationary officers went from billet to billet to pass on Tokushima's instructions:

1. The provisions team has found that rice balls do not freeze if they are first wrapped in cloth and again in oiled paper, and are carried in a duffel bag under the greatcoat.

2. Be prepared for extremely difficult conditions today. Because there may not be time to rest for rations, everyone will keep an issue of hardtack within easy reach so that he has something to eat when necessary.

3. Because the water in the canteens may freeze, be certain to leave each canteen one-third empty and to shake it about while walking.

4. Yesterday's experiment has proved that it is not only more convenient but warmer to wear straw boots over three pairs of socks instead of over army boots. From now on everyone will store his army boots with his luggage and keep one pair of straw boots in reserve.

5. It was found that walking through snow is less fatiguing if the tips of the toes have some room to move. This will also prevent frostbite.

6. It was found that oiled paper wrapped over socks is also effective against frostbite.

Saikai felt a profound respect for the swiftness and decisiveness which Tokushima put the findings of the first two days to everyone's advantage. This was clearly no ordinary officer. The men under his command would have no reason to worry. As instructed, Saikai wrapped his rice balls in cloth and oiled paper and then—because he had no duffel bag—in a kerchief that he tied around his waist, under his greatcoat.

The platoon lined up in the center of the hamlet to send off Sōma and Yabei, who had guided them these two days. When Tokushima gave two large fifty-sen coins to Yabei for his two days of service, the hunter took off his cap and bowed many times over. The one was receiving his wages, the other paying them, but it struck Saikai that both faces expressed the same emotion. Feeling as if he had just peeked into Tokushima's soul, Saikai turned his eyes away, to the sky. Its darkness intimated how thick the snow clouds were.

After the two old guides had left, five new ones were introduced to the platoon. The five were sturdy fellows all, with faces tanned by the snow. Three of them were hunters who wore bearskins over their clothes and carried guns. Just like Yabei, Saikai thought. Because they were joining the platoon as guides, there was no real need for the hunters to bring guns along, yet they would not go without. In this they resembled the lower ranks of the platoon, who carried rifles, though this was not a combat exercise.

Tokushima gave the order to depart.

Seen off by the people of Kiriake, the platoon set out for that day's destination: the silver mine at Lake Towada.

3

Probationary Officer Kuramochi had eyed the spectacle of Tokushima paying Yabei with scorn. What airs the captain was putting on! Two fifty-sen pieces for two days of work was a considerable reward. Fifty sen alone would buy twenty pounds of rice, or forty pounds of horsemeat, or fifty bean-jam buns (which had been introduced not long before and were still expensive), or five to seven haircuts at a city barber's. It was easy to see why Yabei couldn't help grinning from ear to ear. And it was quite all right that the guide should get his wages, except the time and place were wrong. By paying Yabei in front of the men, it seemed as if the captain had wanted to show all the world how generous he was. And if his intention had been to suggest that he was paying Yabei out of his own pocket, it was worse than putting on airs. It was shamming! He should've told Takahata to pay out that money last night.

Kuramochi had first begun to have his doubts about Tokushima's way of doing things the previous day, just before they entered Kiriake, when the captain had ordered the men who had talked in the ranks to step forward. It was natural that he should wish to reprimand them for acting against orders, and it was proper that they should get a roasting, but to tell Tanabe to take their names! Kuramochi did not agree with that. Probationary officers are officers in training, and they should be treated on exactly the same footing as officers. You shouldn't just lump them together with the lower ranks.

Kuramochi was also skeptical about the way the members of the platoon were forced to spend all their energies on those endless assignments. But what he found particularly hard to stomach was that, on the third day, they were already changing their routine on the basis of only two days of observation.

The wearing of straw boots over army boots had been adopted for the Hakkōda Exercise only after a thorough evaluation of the results of the ascent of Mount Iwaki in January last year, when it had been tried out for the first time. But here the captain went and decided that straw boots should be worn directly over three pairs of socks after only one experiment! An experiment, what was more, that had been tried out on only a few people. Well, hunters and local people wore straw boots over their socks, so maybe there was no harm to it, but this rapid switch seemed a little rash. Even if you believed in the saying that too early was better than too late, you had to admit that this decision about footwear—the most important part of a soldier's equipment on a march through the snow!—should have been made after a bit more deliberation.

The platoon was now proceeding in single file. Their five guides were leading them through a gorge that seemed wedged in between two mountains, past spots where it was impossible to imagine a path. The deep snow that was forever hampering their progress and the darkness that reigned in the gorge seemed to fill the minds of the men with gloom. Kuramochi, who had not anticipated having to cross such difficult terrain so soon after leaving Kiriake, could not shake off the feeling that this dark path through the snow symbolized what lay ahead of the Tokushima Platoon.

The previous night he had scrutinized that day's projected route with the other probationary officers in his billet and committed it to memory. After proceeding in a southeasterly direction for a little over a mile, they were to turn south and follow a path up a steep slope for some 6 miles, all the way to the top of Mount Shirochi, at an elevation of 3,392 feet. There they had to change course again and move north for about 2½ miles until they reached Motoyama Pass, from where it was only a mile or so due east to the silver mine at Lake Towada. It was a route that, for the most part, led over exposed mountain ridges, and Kuramochi anticipated that the wind might make their journey very difficult. This dark gorge would soon come to an end, he thought, and then the road would take them over a ridge, where they would have some light.

The sound of the wind became stronger. So far it had been comparatively quiet, but suddenly the mountains seemed filled with a rumbling noise that got louder as they marched on. The trees shook down the snow that had accumulated on the branches. Everywhere in the gorge the wind blew up snow in swirling eddies.

They had passed through a few of these whirlpools when such an earsplitting roar arose from ahead that they thought a whole mountainside had collapsed. They had heard an avalanche: a layer of fresh snow had slid down over the surface of an older layer and filled up the gorge in front of them. The clouds of snow thrown up by the avalanche were so dense that the men were temporarily unable to move.

It appeared as if the avalanche had blocked the platoon's progress. The guides huddled together to discuss the situation. After hearing their opinion, Tokushima ordered the men on again, without a word of explanation about the cause of the incident.

The platoon swam through the snow, but hard as they tried, they could not get through it. It lay too deep.

"Swim for your lives! And hurry up, before there's another one!" yelled Lieutenant Tanabe, who was holding on to the bough of a silver fir that had been carried down by the avalanche. He looked and sounded like a drowning man who desperately clings to a piece of driftwood.

After their guides extricated themselves, they threw out the ropes they carried about their waists and one after another pulled up the soldiers, who were still struggling below. Everyone was covered with snow; ranks and faces were indistinguishable.

When they reached safety, Tokushima held roll call and ordered an equipment inspection. Still panting, the soldiers checked each other's gear and commented on the dangers they had just faced.

"I think it's getting a little lighter," said Kuramochi, peering ahead through the shadows. It seemed as if there, at the end of the gorge, a bright open space lay waiting for them. The sound of the wind had clearly changed too. The noise that came from ahead was no longer a subterraneous rumble. It was definitely the howling of a storm.

But it was no bright open space they found—merely a small, snow-filled clearing in the forest, plus a miserable excuse for a shed.

"This is where we'll start the ascent of Mount Shirochi. The wind appears to be very strong, so everyone will check his clothes before we go," Tokushima instructed.

All sorts of orders filled the air.

"Put on earmuffs!"

"If the oiled paper around your socks is torn, change it!"

"Wear two pairs of gloves!"

"Put on your mufflers!"

Rabbit-fur earmuffs and flannel mufflers had been especially for this exercise.

While the team leaders were conferring with their men, the wind picked up ever more speed. In a gale so strong that Tokushima's order to move was virtually inaudible, the platoon set out again to face the elements.

The path had been cut through a sparse forest of beech trees interspersed with tall conifers, which the guides seemed to use as landmarks. They were climbing now, struggling up in snow so dense it was impossible to tell whether the flakes came falling out of the sky or were blown up from the ground. At places the slope was so steep that the boots of the man in front almost kicked off the hood of the man behind him.

The higher they climbed, the stronger the gale blew. Once they reached the ridge, the men found that the wind had swept it comparatively free of snow, but they were buffeted by gusts so strong they found it almost impossible to keep their eyes open. This was no gale, or even a storm—this was a blizzard. The wind boiled and swirled in complicated patterns caused by the rugged terrain over which it blew. Each soldier blindly followed the footsteps of the man before him. What else could he do? Not one of them had any idea where he was or where he was going.

Though the ridge had been swept so clean of snow that the men could occasionally see the bamboo grass that grew there, the wind made it as good as impossible to walk upright. And when the path wound around, away from the ridge and on to a slope, the platoon was out of the wind but mired in the snow. Following a very roundabout route, they worked their way up Mount Shirochi until they had almost reached the eighth station. Then they suddenly changed course and made straight for the top. So far they had had the wind behind them but now the northwester blew straight into their faces. Climbing conditions could not have been worse.

The storm cut off their breaths. For every two steps forward, they had to take one back. With backs bent, the men inched toward the summit. The tips of their fingers and toes had gradually grown numb, but there was no time to massage them. They could tell from its relative humidity that the snow whipping into their faces came from the sky and not from the ground. Faces waxen and lips purple, they slugged on. Nobody spoke a word.

At one point it seemed as if the guides would be blown clear off their feet. Kuramochi, who was walking near the front of the line, saw them confer briefly and go to the captain. But Tokushima closed his fist over the hilt of his sword, which he was using as a walking stick, and shouted angrily. In answer to the guides' advice to turn back, Tokushima seemed to be ordering them to continue.

The platoon resumed its climb toward the top. Here and there men uttered strange cries, in between shouts and screams. Some went about helping those who had fallen back to their feet; others yelled at their legs to stop trembling. All these different voices mingled in the moaning of the storm.

A succession of terrific blasts was often followed by a few seconds of calm. During such lulls Kuramochi could distinguish the voice of Corporal Saitō, who was walking right behind him, counting paces. Even in these extreme circumstances he never stopped. Each time he reached 100, he moved a soybean from his left pocket to his right.

Cursing his own weakness, Kuramochi yelled into the blizzard, "Come on, damn you! You're almost at the top!"

The summit of Mount Shirochi was free of snow; the storm had carried it all off. Tokushima wanted to hold a roll call here, but because the wind made it impossible to stand up straight, they moved to the shelter of a hollow a little bit farther down, east of the top. There he checked if everyone was present. The men were too exhausted to feel any satisfaction at having made it to the top. Tortured by the elements, all they wanted was to get down as soon as possible. They stamped their feet, shivering all the while. The wind had scoured the snow until it glittered in the sun. Tokushima ordered Kaga to blow his horn, but the bugler's lips froze to the mouthpiece; he could not produce a sound.   59

At Tokushima's command, the guides resumed their places up front and led the descent toward Lake Towada. Because the cold and the wind had made the snow near the summit as hard and smooth as ice, the way down was very slippery.

"Look! The lake!" shouted one of the guides, so suddenly that in the middle of the line someone slipped and fell. Through a gap in the clouds the sun shone down on Lake Towada, illuminating an iceless surface of a blue so dark it was almost black.

Together, the five guides and their thirty-eight wards stared at the waters of the lake that came boiling up amidst the uniform whiteness. Whitecaps stood on its surface, and the shore where the white land and the black water met glittered white in the sun. But not for long. Soon the black of the lake was hidden by the white of a snow flurry.

Although the descent was easier than the ascent, it was afternoon and their bodies felt the cold more keenly. In the unremitting blizzard the men had found neither time nor place to eat. Whenever they halted in the snow, they had just nibbled on hardtack— almost all the rice balls were frozen solid and inedible, although they had been treated according to the instructions issued that morning. But the water in their canteens had not frozen, though when Probationary Officer Funayama measured its temperature he found that it was 21°.

By the time they reached the top of Motoyama Pass, the wind had lost considerable force. From there on, footprints led them toward the silver mine, just over a mile away.

"Guides to the rear!" Tokushima ordered. At the resonant tones of Kaga's bugle, all the miners came out and put themselves at the front of the platoon to beat out a path in the snow.

Because the mine had received advance notice of the Toku-shima Platoon's arrival, that night's quarters had already been allocated. Everybody from probationary officer up was to stay with Yūki Kudō, the superintendent of the mine; the lower ranks were to be put up in the workers' dorms.

When they arrived in front of the mine buildings, Tokushima lined up his men.

"Today's conditions were the worst we've had since leaving Hiroshi, but you've all done extremely well. I'm very pleased with your performance. Now tonight I want everyone to get all the rest he can, for you'll need your strength tomorrow. One more thing: the ancestors of Mr. Kudō, the superintendent of this mine, used to serve as samurai to the lords of Nanbu, so I expect everyone to watch his manners."

Kuramochi found that last remark, about watching their manners, hard to swallow. He was a commoner—a very rare example of a commoner who had been admitted to the Military Academy. The six other probationary officers in the platoon were all of samurai descent. Kuramochi resented this tendency to distinguish between samurai and commoners. He worried that it might lead the army up the wrong road, sometime.

Just as Tokushima was about to dismiss the platoon, Kuramochi raised his hand.

"Question, Sir."

"Yes, what is it?"

"On today's march I have spoken out of turn, Sir. Should I take one step forward?"

This was such an outrageous question that Tokushima was momentarily baffled. He fixed a cold eye on the speaker.

"I will have you remember, Kuramochi, that you have spoken out of turn merely by asking such a question."

He told the men to fall out.

That night, superintendent Kudō gave his ten guests a lavish reception in the biggest room of his house. In front of each man stood a low table with a tray filled with food and saké. Since leaving barracks the men had been offered saké whenever they stopped, both in the afternoon and at night. The orders were not to drink in the afternoon, but for the evenings there was no such prohibition. Everybody drank, from the captain on down.

When someone offered to fill his cup for him, Kuramochi would sip a little saké, but he never returned the courtesy. Kuramochi had his reservations about the excessively generous welcomes the civilians gave their soldiers. True, civilians had very little contact with the army. That was part of the explanation. And he supposed they also wanted to show their trust and respect. But when civilians were requested to quarter soldiers, they were actually forced to go to great expense. They might bid those soldiers welcome with smiles on their faces, but in their hearts they wept, no doubt about that. I suppose it can't be helped, he thought. We've got to sleep somewhere. But we should refuse all entertainment, and the army should defray the people's expenses. All right, so that day's march had been dangerous. But was it really part of a military exercise to eat and drink your fill and snore the night away in a civilian's home? He had yet to hear a good answer to such questions.

"Hey, Kuramochi, what's eating you?" shouted Tokushima from the other end of the room, where he sat drinking with their host.

"Nothing, Sir. I'm enjoying my saké."

"Then look as if you do, man, for heaven's saké!"

"Yes, Sir! I'll enjoy it, Sir!"

And Kuramochi drained the cup in front of him in one gulp. The saké had become cold. The breaking of the waves on the shore of Lake Towada sounded like the booming of huge cannon. During the evening, Tokushima's eyes occasionally strayed from his cup to Kuramochi, but he did not raise his voice again.

4

At 7:00 AM, January 23, the Tokushima Platoon left the silver mine for its next destination, Utarube, on the eastern shore of Lake Towada. Because the mine lay on the western shore, the day's march would describe a semicircle of about 10 miles along the southern half of the lake, which would therefore be on the platoon's left. Their guide was Private Satō, a former worker at the mine who had joined the platoon specifically to lead them this part of the way.

The shores of Lake Towada were virtually uninhabited. Virgin beech forest stretched between the mine and Utarube, a community so small it did not deserve to be called a village. It consisted of not more than about ten households, the families of farmers who had settled here recently to open up the land. Tokushima had taken these facts fully into account in his planning, and he had not neglected to explain them to his men before leaving.

From the mine to Utarube there was only one road. It hugged the shore of a lake in turmoil. Crashing waves sent spray flying through the air and covered the trees with ice, so that it seemed as if the platoon were walking through a forest of fossils. The din of the breakers almost completely drowned out Tokushima's orders. Close to the shore, the flying spray had transformed the road into an ice floe. Because they had difficulty negotiating its slippery surface and because they might get drenched, the platoon was forced to leave the road and walk through the forest, where the snow lay up to 10 feet deep.

That day too there blew a fierce northwester. It had hit them straight in the face the previous day, and the men had steeled themselves against this happening again. About the time they stopped for midday rations at Wainai, the storm began to grow worse. As they bit into their rice balls, they could see the grains of rice freeze before their eyes.

Saikai remembered what Yabei the hunter had told him: when black clouds fill the sky from the west and the wind comes in low, scouring the ground, and you feel the lower part of your body grow numb with cold, you'd better run home as fast as your legs can carry you. He looked up. In the west and in the east, the sky was ink black; the wind, which blew in low over the surface of the lake, carried granules of snow with it and was so cold that he felt it would freeze not only his lower parts, but his whole body. This was no longer the alternation of flurries, drifts, and occasional lulls they had experienced so far. The weather appeared to have taken an ominous turn for the worse.

Saikai was not the only one to have noticed this. Most men wolfed down their rations, their faces plainly showing that this sudden change in the sky had frightened them and that they wanted to move on not a minute later than necessary.

Tokushima called over Probationary Officer Funayama of the meteorology team and asked his opinion. Funayama reported that the thermometer had suddenly dropped 4° and now stood at 14°.

"I believe it's a sign of a giant blizzard coming our way," he said.

"I see. A giant blizzard, eh?" said Tokushima. He looked up at the northern sky. Mount Hakkōda was invisible, and he thought of Captain Kanda, who by now must be somewhere on its slopes. When Tokushima left Hirosaki, the 5th had not yet finished its preparations. Apparently the regimental officers hadn't even decided whether they'd send out a platoon or a company. But he could hardly imagine that now, when he and his platoon were on their way, the 5th would break the agreement to meet on Mount Hakkōda by staying home. No, the 5th must have left. And it wouldn't surprise him a bit if Kanda, just like himself, had found that the burden of command was a heavy one indeed.

The march past the frozen, fossilized forest was cold and depressing. The first three days of the exercise had not exactly been filled with brightness and joy, but the platoon had never felt as gloomy as today. The men marched on as gravely as if death lay in wait for them at the end of the road. Could it be the bleak gusts of wind that blew in over the lakeshore with their grainy load of snow? Or was it the unceasing roaring of the waves, which so deafened the ears that it was impossible even to sing a marching song? There were no hills to climb, no snow to wade through—all

63

they had to do was simply march along, yet not one of them understood why he felt so despondent. Everyone had his hood pulled over his face and his eyes turned to the ground.

About one hour after they left Wainai, part of the platoon was held up: Corporal Matsuo could no longer keep up with the rest. Matsuo was the soldier who had slipped and fallen near the top of Mount Shirochi when the guide had suddenly shouted that he could see Lake Towada. At that time he had slightly sprained his ankle. During the descent to the mine, he had looked quite unconcerned, and in the evening he had gone to the medical team for treatment. When they left the mine his injury had not been all that painful, but after Wainai it had gradually become worse. Now he was limping. The corporal walking by his side was carrying his rifle for him, but even so Matsuo had trouble keeping pace with the others. After hearing the medic's report, Tokushima immediately assigned two corporals to look after Matsuo. The three men's rifles were given to some probationary officers to carry; their backpacks and other equipment were distributed among the corporals.

If only one man becomes disabled on a march through the snow, his injury affects the movements of the whole group. Tokushima knew this very well, so when he had to face the reality of Matsuo's sprained ankle. he could not help feeling depressed.

By 4:00 PM, when they arrived in Utarube, the storm had developed into a full-scale blizzard. It was dark as night.

The dwellings in Utarube were hovels that only barely managed to protect their inhabitants against the wind and the snow. Most of the people were pioneers who had moved here from the village of Herai, across Inubō Pass. The existence of these settlers, in an area that until their arrival had been uninhabited, was hard beyond description, for no one came to their assistance. They were glad if they managed to keep body and soul together. In winter, most of the younger people went elsewhere to earn some money; none but old people, women, and children remained.

They knew that the Tokushima Platoon was coming, but the settlers could offer nothing except shelter. After the men had found their billets, each man produced the two pounds of rice and one can of beef he carried with him and requested that these be cooked and divided into three portions—two for the evening meal and one for the following day's midday rations. None of the families had any bedding to spare, or indeed any space for the men to lie down in, so after finishing their meals they spread dried kindling on the dirt floor, covered this with straw mats, and built a wood fire in the center of the floor. Firewood was the only thing the people of Utarube had plenty of. But, though the soldiers were so exhausted after the day's march that they could hardly keep their eyes open, they could not sleep for the cold. They put straw bags over their greatcoats and huddled about the fire, waiting for the morning.

That night there blew such a tempest that it seemed as if the end of the world had come. Fine snow swirled in through the cracks of the door and soon covered the floor. The wind shook at the houses until it seemed as if they would collapse any moment; it howled through the mountains and whipped the waters of the lake into a roaring frenzy.

"No one that went out in this storm would survive for one hour," Tokushima said to Tanabe.

"One hour? I'd be surprised if he lasted thirty minutes."

Tanabe pulled his straw bag farther over his shoulders.

"I wonder how the 5th is doing."

"You don't think . . . "

Tanabe shivered as he left the sentence unfinished. He and Tokushima stared at each other. By the light of the wood fire each was just able to make out the expression on the other's face. Tokushima felt that he and Tanabe were thinking the same thing. Taking all factors in consideration, the 5th should have left yesterday or today. If it was caught in this blizzard, how would the men cope with it? In his mind, Tokushima went over the map. If Kanda's men were surprised by a storm like this between Tamogino and Tashiro or between Tashiro and Masuzawa and if they were unable to reach shelter by nightfall, what would happen to them?

"*We* will cross the Mount Hakkōda divide on the final day of the exercise, so we've kept the most difficult part for last, but the 5th's got to face it at the very beginning. They aren't used to the snow yet. They're bound to get in trouble," said Tokushima.

Corporal Saitō was having a similar conversation with Saikai.

"I'm almost positive the 5th left today," said Saitō, staring at the fire.

"Did your brother tell you they would?"

Saikai broke some twigs and threw them on the fire.

"No, he didn't, but I just have this feeling. Who knows? Maybe he's lost his way and is wandering around this very moment, in this storm."

The other corporals told Saitō he was imagining things, but he continued to gaze into the fire. There was a haunted look in his eyes.

5

Toward dawn the blizzard still showed no signs of abating. It seemed absolutely impossible to leave in weather like this. The men in their billets were expecting at any moment a notice from Tokushima that that day's march was canceled. The orders they received, however, told them to look for someone who seemed capable of guiding the platoon across Inubō Pass to Herai, and to take him to the captain. For a while, the men found it difficult to believe that Tokushima was in earnest.

The village elders unanimously declared that in this storm no one could reach Herai, not even the army. Later, after the weather had cleared up, the elders said, someone would take the men over the mountains. Not one person volunteered to guide the platoon.

At this point a woman named Sawa Takiguchi spoke up. "Well, if they can't find anyone else to guide them, I will," she said. "I was born in Herai and take that road several times a year when I go to see my parents. I've done it in winter, too—twice no less—so if this storm doesn't get any worse I don't think I'll lose my way."

Sawa's husband was not at home; he had gone to the silver mine to earn some money in the winter months. But they had two children—eight and five years old respectively. Sawa's father-in-law, Denzō, introduced her to Tokushima.

"Sawa here has offered to be your guide, General," he said. "But please, Sir, promise me this one thing: if on the way she should tell you it is impossible to cross the pass, listen to her and turn back." And he joined his hands as if in prayer.

"General" Tokushima looked none too pleased at this request, but finally he accepted Denzō's conditions. He would let himself be guided by Sawa's advice and not force her to go ahead.

So, in spite of the blizzard, the Tokushima Platoon set out for Inubō Pass, with Sawa—in her baggy trousers, straw boots, and straw coat—leading the way. The people of Utarube came out and stood shivering in the snow to see them off.

The path to the pass led through a gorge filled with snowdrifts, so from the very beginning the platoon had to swim for it again. They had prepared themselves for a snowstorm, but this was worse—this was a snow frenzy. The wind blew from all directions at once and pulled down a curtain around them that cut off all visibility. Whirlpools of snow seemed intent on swallowing these human beings. The blizzard was so bad that no one was able to see the person in front of him: they had to bind around their waists the hemp ropes they had brought along for this purpose and proceed as a human chain. Now Corporal Matsuo's sprained ankle really became a burden to the platoon, for they had to take turns supporting him, and the men who carried his rifle and equipment needed to be relieved too.

At the head of the line, Sawa was going much faster than might have been expected. With light steps she skipped across the drifts, but when the wind made all progress impossible her body suddenly seemed to sink down into the snow. She went stop-and-go, stop-and-go, but there was a rhythm to her movements—the rhythm of the storm. The platoon could not keep up with her. From time to time Tokushima lost sight of her and was forced, much to his disgust, to call out her name.

They knew that they were moving in the general direction of the top, but how much progress they had made or how long they had been on the move they had no way of telling. They had no time to think; it was all they could do to keep up with Sawa. As they came closer to the top, the wind became a little steadier. It no longer threatened to knock them off their feet with its sudden gusts, but gradually settled in the west. They could not speak because of the cold, and they had lost all sensation in their fingers and toes. Then Sawa disappeared again. But a few seconds later she suddenly rose up before Tokushima and told him that they were almost at the top.

Almost! The men had to crawl on all fours to get there, for the wind was too strong to stand up in. This, they felt, really was white hell. Yet they were not afraid they might die, for the thought of Sawa gave them courage. As long as Sawa was leading them, there was hope! Sawa herself looked as if the blizzard did not bother her in the least. In the lulls of the storm, she would stand on a snow-covered stone and with a smile on her face look down on the men as they came climbing up, heaving and panting. Her red cheeks shone like a child's. Sometimes it seemed they heard her voice:

"Come on, soldiers, cheer up!"

"Captain, what *are* you doing?"

And when the wind died down, her impish laughter rose up from the snow.

It was Sawa who was leading the platoon. Sawa was in charge now, not the captain or his lieutenants. The men firmly believed that with Sawa to guide them they would escape from the white hell yet.

Under Sawa's command they crossed Inubō Pass. Once they were on the other side, the wind swooped down on them and knocked them headlong into the snow. But they drew courage from the fact that they were over the top. The farther they descended, the more the wind lost in force, and when they reached the Karezawa Valley, Sawa told them:

"The worst is over now, so why don't we have a bite to eat?"

It was far past the usual time for midday rations.

That morning they had toasted some salted millet cakes—gifts from the kind people of Utarube—wrapped them in oiled paper, and stored them close to the skin. Though the men were too exhausted to have much of an appetite, at Tokushima's orders they forced themselves to nibble on these. The temperature was 4°. The only one whose face still looked like that of a human being was Sawa.

On their way down, they met five reservists in army uniform who had come up from Herai to meet them. From then on it was no more than a walk. When they caught sight of some houses below them, Tokushima paid Sawa her wages—one fifty-sen coin—and shouted:

"Guide to the rear!"

"I see. You can do without me now, eh?"

This was her only reply, but the men who heard it were touched to the heart. They felt she had deserved better from them.

Tokushima ordered Kaga to blow his bugle, and thus the platoon marched into Herai, some 5 miles from that night's billets in Nakasato. The 15 miles between Utarube and Nakasato were almost behind them. Somehow they had survived the ordeal.

Throngs of people waving homemade flags welcomed the Tokushima Platoon to Nakasato, which lay in a narrow valley. A huge beacon burned on either side of the entrance to the hamlet. From the roofs of the houses curled the smoke of the fires on which the soldiers' meals were being prepared, and the delicious smell of cooking food made their mouths water. They had visions of bright lamps and glowing hearths—of a warm welcome to their billets; a hot bath; a hearty drink of saké; and tonight, at least, a long, sound sleep in warm bedding.

68

These dreams were rudely disturbed by the orders Tokushima issued after roll call.

"Tonight we'll hold a night-survival drill. All of us will have to get through the night as best we can around a fire, outside."

The men were truly exhausted. They had been unable to catch a wink of sleep in Utarube, and the hike across Inubō Pass had seemed to take the last breath out of them. They had not even been able to eat properly.

Tokushima followed the medical team's advice—reported through Lieutenant Tanabe—and allowed Matsuo with his sprained ankle to spend the night indoors. The people of Nakasato had made preparations to quarter the first soldiers to visit them in over twenty years, but on being told that the plans had been changed they brought food and saké out to the campfire. However, Tokushima warned the men that they were still on duty and forbade them to accept the saké.

It stopped snowing, but the evening was bitter cold. When night fell the cold became even more intense. The people who brought them food and firewood told them that it hardly ever got as cold as this.

Only the half of the body that was exposed to the fire received any heat; the other half almost froze. All night long the men kept turning now their fronts, then their backsides to the flames. But though the fire warmed them to some degree, they still had to stamp their feet all the while or they would have succumbed to the cold.

Some men, made drowsy by the heat of the fire, threatened to topple face first into the flames. Others were overcome with sleep and sat down in the snow. By then it was already past midnight. The wind had risen and chased down the temperature even lower. Tokushima saw that the men were losing their fight against sleep. He had to do something.

"All right, men, we'd better start digging," Tokushima announced. "We'll split up in three groups, and each group will dig its own shelter. The groups will take turns to provide two men to guard the fire. Lieutenant Tanabe will see to the formation of the groups, and Lieutenant Takahata will supervise the digging and construction of the shelters."

In a thick layer of snow, near the wood sacred to the hamlet's guardian deity, they dug their shelters, in the form of trenches. They did not hit soil until they had dug 8 feet. There was little they could do against the cold itself, which still bore down on them from above, but at that depth they were able to protect themselves from the gale that was blowing now. At least they were a little warmer than if they had remained around the fire.

6

It struck Probationary Officer Kuramochi that Corporal Saitō, who was walking right behind him, was not his usual self.

Kuramochi was in charge of the team that studied the problems involved in reading maps in snow-covered terrain, and since Saitō belonged to the same team, they had been working closely since leaving Hirosaki. The first time Kuramochi noticed that Saitō was behaving a little strangely was after they had left Nakasato. He could no longer hear him counting paces. The wind had been quite strong about dawn but had died down now, and the day looked as if it would turn out comparatively mild. The men were not wearing their hoods, so there was no reason why Kuramochi should not be able to hear Saitō, yet he could not.

Oh well, he thought, Saitō's never stopped counting, not even in the worst blizzard. He must be counting silently now. A look at his face will tell.

He looked over his shoulder. When Saitō caught his eye he suddenly began to count out loud, as if he had been startled from a dream.

He's sleepy, Kuramochi thought. Hell, I don't blame him, we're all sleepy. Under the circumstances, how could anyone expect him to continue counting?

But then he noticed that Saitō did not look sleepy, but pensive— like a man deeply lost in thought.

No, he's just sleepy, Kuramochi reassured himself. When you're sleepy, you sometimes look as if you're thinking. Who has ever heard of forcing men to go without sleep for two nights on end in a military exercise? I know we're supposed to be getting a lot of valuable information and all that, but there are limits!

Kuramochi looked at Tokushima, who was walking at the head of the line. That day, too, he was using a guide, though the road led simply from one village to another and so on to Sanpongi; a guide was not really necessary. Four men from Nakasato brought up the rear. They were pulling a big tub with Corporal Matsuo in it.

Kuramochi could not fathom the captain. How could someone so cautious that he used guides on a public highway have risked

Inubō Pass in a blizzard like yesterday's? Tomorrow they'd be starting on the most difficult part of the exercise, their assault on Mount Hakkōda. They should have had lots of rest, but instead they'd had to spend a sleepless night outside. Why?

He could hear Saitō counting again. Saitō's voice always sounded peculiar: very loud one moment, almost inaudible the next. When it reached 100, the voice would stop altogether and resume a moment later, from the count of two. This was because it took Saitō one step to move the soybean which marked 100 paces, from his left pocket to his right, and that step—the first of a new series of a hundred—was not counted out loud.

Now Kuramochi was wondering whether Saitō was timing these intervals correctly. Actually, they seemed to have disappeared altogether. It sounded as if Saitō jumped immediately from a count of 100 to a count of 2. The problem refused to leave Kuramochi alone, and the next time Saitō counted 100, the probationary officer looked around. Saitō's hand was not in his left pocket: he had forgotten to move the bean.

Then it struck Kuramochi that Saitō was not simply goofing off, but that his thoughts were occupied with a very serious problem. He looked worried—inexpressibly gloomy and cast down. Saitō, whose posture was always ramrod straight, now marched with his eyes glued to his feet. It was very strange. He looked as if he might fall flat on his face if someone suddenly shouted at him, so lost was he in his sad contemplations.

Kuramochi could not allow this to continue. He stood still. Now Saitō would have to halt too, and then perhaps he'd notice what he'd been doing.

As soon as Kuramochi stopped, he heard Saitō's voice cry out softly in what could have been an exclamation of surprise or of dismay.

Saitō was standing still, his face ashen. At his feet, its strap broken, lay his duffel bag.

"Zenjirō is dead," he said.

"Who is dead?"

"Zenjirō—my brother. He died just now."

Saitō made no attempt to pick up his bag.

"Where is your brother now?"

"He is orderly to Captain Kanda of the 5th Regiment."

Kuramochi had heard that Captain Kanda would probably be in charge if the 5th went ahead with the exercise. If his orderly was really dead, the implications were terrible.

71

"Come on, Saitō, you worry too much," said Corporal Izumidate, who had been walking beside him. "So your duffel strap broke. It happens all the time, but there you go and imagine all sorts of horrors."

His words had a reassuring ring to them, but they were not true. Duffel straps do not break all the time. They break very rarely. Izumidate picked Saitō's bag up from the ground.

"See? Here's a burn. It must've been too close to the fire last night, and it snapped where it got singed. Don't break your head over such things."

Deftly he tied the two ends of the strap together and returned the bag to Saitō.

"Anything wrong there?" shouted Tokushima from ahead.

"Broken strap, Sir. But we've fixed it," Kuramochi answered.

They marched on as if nothing had happened. Saitō soon resumed his counting, but because he clearly sounded upset, Kuramochi told Izumidate to take over.

Saitō had been thinking of his brother since the night they spent at Utarube. For no special reason he could imagine, the picture of Zenjirō wandering about in a blizzard would not leave him alone. Heaven knows how many times he had heard his brother's voice when the wind died down a few seconds. And a few minutes ago he had heard him again:

"Kichinosuke, ice flowers are blooming on my coffin!"

That very moment Saitō's duffel strap had snapped.

At Maida, Kuramochi used a long break for rations to ask Saitō why he had said that his brother was dead.

"You're tired, that's what it is. When people get exhausted, they often suffer from this sort of delusion."

When Kuramochi reported the incident to Lieutenant Takahata, Tokushima and Tanabe were standing close enough to overhear what was being said.

"In short, Sir, I think the men are plainly exhausted and absolutely should be allowed to get enough rest tonight."

"Weren't you in charge of map reading?" Takahata retorted. "I'll thank you to leave such speculations to the team that studies fatigue. Don't set yourself up as an expert in what you know nothing about."

But Kuramochi was not to be daunted so easily.

"Saitō belongs to my team, Sir, and as his team leader it is my duty to speak up when I have reason to be concerned about the health of one of my subordinates."

"Wait a second," Tokushima interrupted. "Didn't you just mention that Saitō's brother was Captain Kanda's orderly? What reason does Saitō have to believe the 5th has left barracks?"

"No reason at all, Sir. But he's got this fixed idea that the 5th left Aomori on the twenty-third. It's all in his mind, a delusion. He's too tired to think straight."

"Well, we'll make certain that he gets a decent night's rest in Sanpongi. Saitō's not the only one who's tired. All of us are."

But after Tokushima had dismissed Kuramochi, he lost himself in thought. Just suppose Saitō's delusion turned out to be the truth. The idea sent a shudder down his spine, and it was not a shudder of cold. Had Saitō really been hallucinating about his brother in the 5th? Or had he in fact seen the fate of the Tokushima Platoon?

Tokushima recalled the letter he had written to Kanda before his departure. Whose group would survive the blizzards of Mount Hakkōda—Kanda's, Tokushima's, or both? Was it not more likely they would all find their graves in the snow on its slopes? Oh, stop worrying, he told himself at last. There's no way you'll be able to see into the future.

The sky, which had been clear that morning, had clouded over again. It looked like snow.

From Nakasato to Sanpongi, it was 14 miles. The snow on the road posed no problems.

When they arrived at their quarters in Sanpongi, Tokushima summoned Private Fukumatsu Oyama, who had gone along to guide them from Sanpongi to Masuzawa, and told him he could spend the night with his family if he promised to be back in time the next morning. Overjoyed with this totally unexpected permission, Oyama rushed off to see his parents, who lived only a mile away.

The day's march might be over, but there was still work to be done. They now had to prepare themselves for the most difficult obstacle of all, Mount Hakkōda itself. All sorts of things needed to be stocked up on: straw boots, oiled paper, red pepper (to put in their boots as protection against frostbite), emergency rations, and so on. If anything was wrong with their equipment, they had only one night to fix it. Officers and probationary officers had to prepare reports on the data the various observation teams had collected since Kiriake, for the next day Matsuo would leave in a buggy for Numazaki Station, from where he would take a train back to Hirosaki. Once there, he would deliver the entire dossier to Regimental Headquarters.

73

Tokushima sent a telegram to Major Monma of the regimental staff to let him know they had safely arrived in Sanpongi and to explain about Matsuo. He asked the owner of their lodging house, Sadao Suzuki, to arrange for Matsuo's transportation to Numazaki.

Suzuki would be happy to see to this, but he had something to discuss, he said, and led Tokushima to a private room. There he gave him a note, a message from Major Monma, who had telephoned from Hirosaki:

A company of the Aomori 5th Infantry left barracks on January 23, at 6:00 AM. Captain Kanda is in command, and Major Yamada and eight members of his battalion staff went along as observers. They plan to stop at Tashiro and Masuzawa and to arrive in Sanpongi the twenty-fifth.

Tokushima scanned the note before he muttered a vague word of thanks. Just for this he needn't have called me to this room, he thought. But Suzuki made ready to speak again.

"To be honest, Captain, I'm worried about the 5th. If they were planning to spend the night in Tashiro the twenty-third, in Masuzawa the twenty-fourth, and in Sanpongi the twenty-fifth, they should have been here already. But a few minutes ago some man who'd just come from there told me that by 2:00 PM today there still hadn't been any sign of the 5th at Masuzawa."

"The twenty-fifth is today," Tokushima reminded him. "I suppose they were delayed by one or two days. You can't always travel exactly according to your itinerary, you know. And on the twenty-third and twenty-fourth the weather *was* very bad." He recalled the blizzard at Inubō Pass.

"Exactly, Captain. And that's why I am worried."

If Suzuki said more than this, he would be meddling in army affairs. So he left it at that.

Tokushima told no one what he had heard from Suzuki. It wouldn't do to get the men upset, he thought.

7

At six the following morning the platoon left Sanpongi for Tashiro, where Tokushima was planning to spend the night. Private Oyama would be their guide as far as Masuzawa. Their road followed the Kumanosawa River, a tributary of the Oirase, and led them through such tiny communities as Kumanosawa, Nagasawa,

Yomogihata, Nakamura, Ishiwatari, Fugane, and at last Masuzawa. The weather was comparatively good, though there was
snow on the road, and Oyama beamed with pride as he guided the
platoon through his native land.

They arrived at Masuzawa on schedule and made for the ele-
mentary school, at the entrance of which a sign had been posted:

REST STATION

AOMORI 5TH INFANTRY   HIROSAKI 31ST INFANTRY

The village headman and the headmaster were waiting with the
schoolchildren to welcome the platoon. Tea was served by the
housewives of the village, who had come flocking to the school.
The smell of cooking pervaded the air, and the suspicion that saké
had been prepared did not seem unwarranted.

"I'm sorry. We really appreciate your kind intentions, but we
have to push on toward Tashiro today, so I'm very much afraid we
can't accept your hospitality," Tokushima apologized to the headman, whose name was Ujiya. "Still, you would do us a tremendous
service if you could find us some guides. We need them in a hurry."

Ujiya exchanged glances with the other village leaders before he
answered.

"You want to go on to Tashiro? Today? I'm sorry, Captain, but I
honestly think you ought to reconsider. From here on the snow
gets so deep, you'll be lucky to reach Tashiro if you start out early
in the morning. If you leave now, you'll still be on the road by
nightfall, and in the dark it's quite impossible. Also, for that sort of
enterprise it won't be easy to find guides. On days when it snows,
people should be off the roads after noon. So take my advice, please.
Spend the night here, and leave tomorrow morning early, and I'll
see to it that you'll have your guides by then."

Tokushima could feel that the headman was speaking sincerely.

"In the army it's a terrible thing if you're one day behind
schedule," he told Ujiya in a voice that was virtually a whisper.

"Maybe so, Captain, but the 5th Regiment is now two days late
already. They must have started later than scheduled, I suppose, for
we had a terrible blizzard here the twenty-third and twenty-
fourth." Ujiya thought for a moment. "If they left Aomori on
schedule in spite of the weather, they're probably stuck in Tashiro.

Still, the fact that they're two days late *is* strange. All of us are hoping that nothing bad has happened to them."

"All right then, we'll change our plans and spend tonight in Masuzawa, but I'm afraid I must ask you to find us quarters—and guides." The captain bowed to the headman.

After quarters had been found, Tokushima summoned Lieutenants Tanabe and Takahata and all the probationary officers, including the doctors.

"I suppose you'd better know," he began. "After we reached Sanpongi I was given a telephone message from Major Monma, to the effect that a company of the 5th had left Aomori on the twenty-third. Their plan was to spend the night of the twenty-third at Tashiro, the twenty-fourth at Masuzawa, and the twenty-fifth at Sanpongi. Now they're two days late and still haven't reached Masuzawa, so it's beginning to look as if something might have happened to them."

Tokushima had said "something," not "accident," yet the men started. Silently they waited for him to continue.

"But even if something has happened to the 5th, that doesn't mean our platoon will change its plans. There is no reason why we should. We will leave Masuzawa early tomorrow morning, as scheduled. If something did happen to the 5th, we must be prepared to assist in their rescue. Now some of the lower ranks who saw the sign at the school entrance may have drawn their own conclusions as to why the 5th hasn't shown up yet. Fortunately Mr. Ujiya, the headman, and the other villagers seem to be taking the view that the 5th delayed its departure because of the bad weather we had the twenty-third, so I am asking all of you present here not to mention the contents of Major Monma's telephone call to anyone. The men have enough to worry about as it is, with our departure tomorrow."

The faces confronting Tokushima expressed an emotion akin to anger. So for all we know, the 5th got wiped out on Hakkōda, some were thinking, and tomorrow it's our turn to go up there. Others worried whether the 5th was safe. Yet others were determined that they should get through where the 5th had failed. Everybody thought something else, but one feeling was shared by all: what lay ahead of them was more terrible than they could possibly imagine.

One source of general concern was that, between Utarube and Inubō Pass, they had been unable to use their compasses. This meant that, without guides, a mountain march in the coldest part of winter was impossible. They knew that the reason their compasses had failed had something to do with the low temperature, but the weather had been so bad they had not had an opportunity to pinpoint the exact nature of the problem.

All looked grave. Under these circumstances it took some courage to be the first to speak up.

"But why has Regimental Headquarters in Aomori made no attempt to check if their men arrived in Masuzawa?" wondered Kuramochi. "All they'd have to do is telephone the police in Sanpongi and ask them to send out a runner or a horseman, and they'd know right away."

Everyone agreed. This march was so difficult you'd expect Headquarters to worry about their men even if they'd been delayed by only one day.

"Yes, I see your point," said Tanabe. "Mr. Ujiya has said nothing about inquiries from Aomori, so it could be that Major Monma's telephone call . . . "

Tanabe did not finish the sentence. He was going to suggest that the major's information had been incorrect or that the 5th had left but turned back because of the blizzard but then he realized that, if such had been the case, Monma would surely have called again.

"No, Major Monma's message was clear, and Mr. Suzuki, who took it, is absolutely reliable. I'm afraid there's no reason to question the accuracy of our information," Tokushima said in answer to Tanabe's unspoken question.

"Then what is Aomori up to, for heaven's sake?" Kuramochi wanted to know. "Are they trying to hush things up, do you think?"

"Well, supposing something did happen," began Takahata. "There is something to be said, I guess, for avoiding publicity and dealing with it within the army only. . . . "

He did not quite know how to go on, for he recalled that recently there had been an inordinate number of documents stamped "Secret" floating about. Although relations between Japan and Russia had deteriorated dangerously, Takahata was nevertheless of the opinion that all this secrecy could be carried too far.

Tokushima folded his arms.

"At any rate, we'll have to ask our Headquarters as soon as possible to inform Aomori of the situation."

77

8

As a matter of fact, Headquarters in Aomori was worrying whether Kanda and his men had arrived safely in Sanpongi. Early in the morning of that very day, there had been a telephone call to the Sanpongi police. The person placing the call was a sergeant named Noguchi, who was acting on orders of an adjutant of Lieutenant Colonel Tsumura, the regimental commander. Noguchi did not know that Sanpongi also lay on Tokushima's route and had merely asked the police to check if "a unit of soldiers on winter exercise" had spent the previous night there, assuming that this description could only refer to Captain Kanda's company. Noguchi had also assumed that there was no need to explain army movements to a civilian.

The Sanpongi police called Noguchi back almost immediately to confirm that such a unit had indeed arrived about 4:00 PM the twenty-fifth and had spent the night in lodgings—a literal answer to the question asked. During these calls, the regiments' numbers were not mentioned once.

Noguchi reported to the adjutant that Sanpongi had confirmed that the soldiers had arrived safely at 4:00 PM, January 25. The "safely" he threw in for good measure.

On getting this information, Tsumura checked—just to make certain—the itinerary of the Tokushima Platoon, which he had lying on his desk. On finding that Tokushima too had planned to reach Sanpongi by the evening of the twenty-fifth, the colonel ordered his adjutant to call the Sanpongi police himself.

In answer to the second inquiry, Sanpongi reported that the soldiers of the 31st had spent the night in Sanpongi and had left for Masuzawa early that very morning. His face ashen, the adjutant reported back to the colonel.

The 5th Regiment launched its rescue operation that morning, January 26.

9

That same day Tokushima asked Gonzō Kobara, a young man from Masuzawa, to run to Sanpongi and send a telegram to Colonel Kojima, the commander of the 31st. The cable stated no more than the facts:

Tokushima Platoon arrived Masuzawa January 26. Planning to begin ascent Hakkōda tomorrow morning. Note 5th Regiment was due here on twenty-fourth, but so far no trace.

With the text of this telegram and the money to pay for it, Tokushima gave Kobara fifty sen for his trouble—the same amount he had paid each guide since leaving Hirosaki.

Ujiya the headman visited Tokushima's quarters after dark.

"I've been looking for guides, Captain, but this year there's a lot more snow around than normal. I'm afraid I haven't found anyone willing to go. They're saying that, if they get caught in a storm on the way to Tashiro, they'll die for certain, and as for Tamogino, they say that's absolutely out of the question."

"But if the weather is good, is it possible to get to Tashiro?"

"I think so."

"How many men are there who could guide us?"

"If we put all men with hunting experience together, I suppose there'd be, oh, about seven, I'd say."

"Good. Then I'd like those seven to be our guides. Please tell them they need take us only as far as it is possible to go."

"As far as it is possible to go?"

"You heard me. As far as it is possible to go."

Tokushima's mouth was grim as he glared at Ujiya. His face was terrible now, the face of a man who would refuse to take no for an answer, who at the least attempt to argue would roar out that army orders were to be obeyed. Ujiya nodded silently.

The wind howled through the mountains. Masuzawa itself lay comparatively sheltered, but outside the hamlet the weather was awful. Ujiya wondered if he should tell Tokushima that at this time of the year storms raged continuously on Mount Hakkōda, by night and by day. But the captain looked so fierce that he merely wished him good night and left.

By then, the lower ranks of the platoon were fast asleep. except for Kichinosuke Saitō, who kept seeing his brother Zenjirō's face. It was frozen stiff and the color of a wax candle.

PART THREE

LOST

JANUARY 21, 1902, WAS A BRIGHT AND SUNNY DAY.
The upshot of Major Yamada's discussion with Lieutenant Colonel Tsumura on the twentieth had been that the Hakkōda Company would consist of five platoons: one each from the E, F, G, and H Companies of Yamada's own 2nd Battalion, plus one special platoon made up from career corporals serving in the 1st and 3rd Battalions, so that it might be said that the whole 5th Regiment participated in the exercise. All the enlisted men were to be experienced soldiers, not raw recruits. Captain Kanda would be in command of the company, but Yamada and a number of officers of his battalion staff would go along as observers.

On the afternoon of the twenty-first, after having made a thorough study of the plans Kanda had submitted, Yamada issued the following orders to all company commanders:

On January 23, the day after tomorrow, a company consisting of seasoned soldiers of the 2nd Battalion will march to Tashiro and spend one night there. Close attention must be given to the points listed below.

Then followed five paragraphs with details concerning the composition of the company, its equipment, where it would assemble, and so on. Considering clothing and luggage, the major wrote:

All men will wear field uniforms, greatcoats as protection against the cold, and straw galoshes. Lower ranks will carry mess tins, small duffel bags hung from the shoulder, and water canteens. Backpacks will contain three sets of normal daytime rations and parched rice, as well as six rice cakes per person; other luggage is optional.

It cannot be said that Yamada had given much thought to the equipment with which he was sending the company out into the

83

cold that reigned on Mount Hakkōda. He merely gave the participating officers their orders in writing, with an added oral instruction that they should seriously consider ways to protect their men against the low temperatures, in case they had to bivouac somewhere during the exercise. Perhaps everyone had better carry pocket heaters, he suggested—metal boxes filled with smoldering ashes and carried near the chest. Like Yamada, the medical officer discussed the prevention and treatment of frostbite in only the most general terms.

Since the plans for the exercise were published the twenty-first and departure had been fixed for the morning of the twenty-third, each company was busy selecting participants. As the officer in charge, Kanda called all platoon leaders together and gave them detailed instructions concerning clothing and equipment: "Tell the lower ranks to bring two greatcoats against the cold and to bring red pepper to put in their shoes and oiled paper to wrap around their socks, against frostbite."

This order was duly passed on to the men. However, since red pepper and oiled paper were not issued with the rest of the equipment but were considered optional luggage, very few took the trouble to go to the PX to buy some.

Galoshes were issued on the afternoon of the twenty-second. They were of the variety the local people called *tsumago*: overshoes made of straw, much shorter than straw boots, which reach almost to the knee. There was a good deal of clowning when the men tried to fit these galoshes over their army boots. None of them had any idea how terrible the following day would be.

One of those who bought red pepper and oiled paper—and old newspapers too—was Corporal Murayama. As the son of a charcoal burner in the mountains of Iwate Prefecture, he knew very well how to protect his body against snow and cold. Murayama had been told that Mount Hakkōda consisted of eight peaks: Maedake, Tamoyatsudake, Itodake, Ishikuradake, Akakuradake, Takada Ōdake, Ōdake, and Kodake. But as seen from the barracks, Mount Hakkōda looked like one gently sloping high mountain that was occasionally covered by wind clouds. "Wind clouds" was a term that the charcoal burners in Murayama's village used a lot. It referred to the puffy sort of cap clouds like balls of cotton that have been pulled out and twisted a bit. They are called wind clouds because their appearance is an unfailing omen of storm on the mountain.

Whenever he saw the wind clouds over Mount Hakkōda, Murayama remembered the village of his birth. Oh no, the mountain's getting the wind up again, he would say to himself. It looks so innocent, but I bet it's hell there when it storms.

"The more innocent a mountain looks, the more it should be feared," his father always used to say, adding that this held true for Mount Iwate and for Mount Fuji as well. Not that his father had ever seen Mount Fuji, but he had decided it was a fearsome mountain. So when Murayama saw how innocent Mount Hakkōda looked, he recalled his father's words and felt that here, too, was a mountain that deserved to be feared.

As Murayama was leaving the PX, he ran into Corporal Fusanosuke Etō.

"I see you stored up on red pepper and oiled paper, too," said Etō, and he asked what the old newspapers Murayama had in his hands were for.

"They'll keep you warm when the wind is cold," Murayama answered.

Etō nodded. "I guess I'd better get some too, then," he muttered to himself. "Can you believe it? Everyone seems to think this is going to be a piece of cake. Some of the men are suggesting that we'd better wear one shirt instead of our normal two because we'll sweat a lot on the way up, and I've heard others say that they won't wear regulation boots but heavy socks under their galoshes. They're asses, the lot of 'em. They've got no idea how cold it can get, deep in the mountains."

Etō went into the PX.

The tendency among the lower ranks to make light of the coming exercise was partly caused by the fact that Major Yamada's order had made it sound so simple: they would "march to Tashiro and spend one night there," that was all. Another reason was that the plans were made public on the afternoon of the twenty-first and departure was fixed for the early morning of the twenty-third. In that short interval everyone was much too busy to exchange accurate information about conditions on Mount Hakkōda or about the hardships they might expect. The officers had no time to assemble the lower ranks to enlighten them on such matters. And, unfortunately for the 5th, Kanda's practice march to Kotōge on the eighteenth had suggested that the roads were as easily negotiable as in summer. Because the weather had been good there and there had been virtually no wind that day, almost all soldiers had taken off

85

their greatcoats, and the transportation squad, pulling their burden, wore no more than a single undershirt. These facts had gone the round of the regiment, which explains why so many soldiers regarded the exercise as something of a lark.

On the afternoon of the twenty-second, the composition of the Hakkōda Company was announced. It would consist of 10 officers (one of them an army surgeon), 4 warrant officers, 2 probationary officers, 34 career NCOs, and 160 enlisted men—a total of 210 men, including 9 observers from the staff of the 2nd Battalion. Company commander was Captain Kanda; Lieutenants Katō, Nakahashi, and Ono were in charge of the 1st, 2nd, and 3rd Platoons, respectively; Second Lieutenant Suzumori led the 4th, and Lieutenant Nakamura, the Special Platoon. The delegation from the battalion staff consisted of Major Yamada, Captains Okitsu and Kurata, Medical Officer Nagano, Warrant Officers Imanishi, Tanikawa, and Shindō, and Probationary Officers Tanaka and Imaizumi.

Finalizing the roster had involved a dizzying round of activities. For serious preparations almost no time was left.

Now that the company was formed, Kanda suggested to Yamada that the men be assembled on the parade ground to hear the major advise them concerning the exercise on which they were to depart the following morning. The major would speak a few words, as a matter of protocol, and then Kanda, as the officer in charge, would address the men. There were a number of things he wanted to tell them. He already knew what he was going to say:

"Some of you seem to take this exercise rather lightly. I want it to be clear to everyone that this is not going to be a march across the Aomori Plain. Our enemy, the snow, lurks out there somewhere, storms lie waiting in ambush, and the cold is a bandit who will creep up on us and steal the warmth from our bodies."

He wanted to tell them that they should take lots of extra socks and gloves so that they could change them when they got wet; that apart from the two undershirts they would be wearing they ought to carry at least one more; that they had better bring pocket heaters; and that they should under no circumstances forget to wrap oiled paper around their socks and put red pepper in their shoes if they wanted to prevent frostbite. They should also know what he had heard from Sakuemon in Tamogino: that it could get so cold saké would freeze and that twice in the past people from Tamogino had tried to cross Mount Hakkōda in the snow, at the cost of twenty lives. Kanda imagined that if the lower ranks were aware of all this, they would not fail to take proper precautions.

He looked at Yamada. Yamada seemed unconvinced.

"With our departure tomorrow, everyone will be busy packing today. No, I think it's better not to assemble the men. If there's anything you absolutely want to tell them, you can always do so through the platoon leaders," he said coldly and got to his feet.

This put Kanda at a loss. He was worried about tomorrow. If he, the officer in charge, had to ask Yamada permission for every little detail, things were going to be difficult indeed.

When Kanda got home that evening, he asked Zenjirō Hasebe, his orderly, if he had finished packing.

"Yes, Sir, and seeing as we'll be staying at the springs at Tashiro, I didn't forget to put in some soap."

Kanda had really meant to ask whether Hasebe had finished his own packing, but his question had been misunderstood.

"We'll be leaving early tomorrow morning, so why don't you hurry off and pack lots of socks, gloves, and shirts for yourself. You'll need them."

After sending Hasebe back to barracks, Kanda fell to wondering why there was such a gap between the men's ideas about the coming march and their commanding officer's.

Is there anything else I could have done, he wondered. He felt like an engineer who finds a defect in his engine but has no time to fix it. The defect was obvious: none of the participants in the exercise took it seriously enough.

Kanda considered postponing their departure for another two or three days, but immediately there appeared before his eyes the image of Tokushima and his platoon, advancing steadily through the snow.

No. Further delay would jeopardize the reputation of the 5th and his own good name as a soldier. Postponement was out of the question.

"Bunkichi, what is it?" asked Hatsuko, his wife. "Your face . . . "

"What about my face?"

"You look so worried."

"Because I bear a heavy responsibility for tomorrow."

At first Hatsuko did not seem to get his meaning, but when his words sank in, she asked:

"Isn't there anything special I can do for you? If the burden is as heavy as you say, you must allow me to pull my weight." She smiled. "For whatever it's worth."

She wanted to take her husband's mind off his brooding, but the expression on Kanda's face did not soften.

"There is. You could pack me a pocket heater and ashes—enough for five or six days."

"Five or six days?"

Hatsuko stared at him with wide-open eyes. The exercise was scheduled to last only three days. Had he not told her that they would reach a highway on the third day, so that only the first two would be really difficult? Why then should he now ask her to pack enough ashes for five or six days? She could not understand.

"We're crossing Mount Hakkōda in the snow. Who knows what may happen. . . . " said Kanda, looking at his wife.

Here was a husband whose eyes always seemed to declare to his wife that he was going to show everyone. He might be no more than a commoner's son who had never graduated from the Military Academy, but he was going to be a major, that much he knew he had in him! But now his eyes told a different story. Now Hatsuko saw in them a dark shadow she had never seen there before. When he was sent to the front in the war against China or when he went to Taiwan, his eyes had never looked like this.

"Oh!" she exclaimed and sank to the floor. It was not her husband's eyes that had frightened her, but the dark shadow that was moving inside them.

2

On the twenty-third of January 1902, the dark grounds of the 5th Infantry barracks in Aomori crackled with activity. A steady stream of orders pierced the cold air and mixed with the tramping of soldier's boots double-timing through the snow. By 6:00 AM, the Hakkōda Company was lined up as scheduled.

The enlisted men were dressed in blue duck-cloth uniforms, over which they wore khaki greatcoats of plain wool. One more khaki greatcoat, intended as protection against the cold, was tied to each backpack. The only difference between the NCOs' uniforms and those of the enlisted men was that the NCOs' were made of wool. The officers wore black woolen uniforms under greatcoats of the same color and material. The footwear of the lower ranks consisted of boots with spats and leggings and, over these, straw galoshes. As for the officers, most wore long leather boots under their straw galoshes. A few wore the rubber boots that had lately become fashionable in the cities. The leaders of platoons and squads carried small lanterns, which cast an eerie light on their white-gloved hands—the only white visible in the darkness.

The snow fell softly down on the parade ground as the 210 men waited for the signal to depart.

Captain Kanda summoned the platoon leaders and passed down the order of the day:

1. This company will march to Tashiro today as scheduled.

2. The platoon commanded by Lieutenant Katō will lead the way, followed by the platoons under Lieutenants Suzumori, Nakahashi, and Ono, and the Special Platoon under Lieutenant Nakamura, in that order. The rear will be brought up by the baggage train.

3. The front platoon will wear snowshoes and widen the road to facilitate the passage of the baggage train. Every fifty minutes there will be a short break, during which the front platoon will fall back and the other platoons move up one place. No snowshoes need be worn until Kōhata.

4. During the march, discipline will be maintained as a matter of course. The sanitary and health precautions explained yesterday will not be neglected.

5. I myself will march at the front of the line, with the trail-breaking platoon.

The "sanitary and health precautions" had been communicated to the company by the medical officer and they consisted of the following points:

Unscheduled breaks not to last longer than about three minutes, and soldiers to massage their fingers while waiting; trousers to be buttoned up at all times; leftover food not to be thrown away, and saké to be consumed in small quantities only; when bivouacking in the snow, dozing off to be avoided; in case of frostbite, the affected part to be rubbed first with snow, then with cloth, but not to be exposed to fire unless the skin refuses to turn red.

It was so obvious that physical contact with damp or wet clothes caused frostbite that it was hardly necessary to warn the men to keep their socks and gloves dry.

Little by little the night sky turned bright.

At 6:55 AM, in light snowfall, the Hakkōda Company marched out the barracks gate. The sound of the company bugle cut through the frosty air. The temperature was 21°.

They marched in double file, one platoon following the other. In the rear was the baggage train—fourteen sleds, pulled by four soldiers each.

From barracks it was almost 2 miles over level ground to the village of Kōhata, which they reached at 7:40 AM. Here they took a fifteen-minute break to make the necessary adjustments to their clothing. The forty men of the front platoon put on their snowshoes.

Kōhata lay at the southern end of the Aomori Plain. From there on, all was mountains. There the road began to climb, and the snow got deeper. By the time they reached Tamogino, 2 miles farther, the snow was 5 feet deep. Nevertheless, the forty men with their snowshoes did such a thorough job preparing the way that the rest of the column was hardly inconvenienced, although the soldiers pulling the sleds of the baggage train had begun to lag.

At Tamogino the company took a short break to give the sleds a chance to catch up. The villagers came out and stared at the soldiers, their faces showing their amazement at how much bigger and better equipped this group was than the one that had visited them before.

Together, Sakuemon and Genbei walked to the chestnut tree under which the battalion staff sat resting.

Sakuemon unwound from his face the towel he had wrapped around it for warmth. "We are looking for the captain who was here the other day," he said.

"Captain Kanda is somewhere over there," answered one of the officers, pointing to the front of the line. "Why do you want to see him?"

"Well, the other day he asked for guides to take him to Tashiro, so if he still wants them, I think we may be able to help him somehow."

"Did you say Captain Kanda asked for guides?" Yamada demanded.

One look at Yamada, and Sakuemon realized that here was someone higher in rank than the captain he had seen five days before.

"Yes. . . . That is to say, he asked if we had people who could serve as guides. He didn't exactly ask for them."

"Of course not! The idea!" Yamada snorted.

"But I think you ought to know that there's very little chance you'll reach Tashiro without guides. So far, twenty people from our village have got lost and died in the attempt, and they knew the way. Also, tomorrow is the feast of the mountain god, and that means bad weather for sure."

While he was speaking, Sakuemon tied the towel back around his face. It was getting colder.

"Are you saying it's impossible to reach Tashiro without guides?"

"I think so. This time of year there are snowstorms up there every day, and there are no landmarks on the moor you have to cross before you get to Tashiro."

"And how many guides does your village have?"

"I suppose we could find about five," said Sakuemon, looking at Genbei over his shoulder.

"That's right. Five men for sure," Genbei confirmed. Then he exclaimed, "Ah, there's the captain we talked to last week!"

He had spotted Kanda, who came hurrying back from his position up front. At Genbei's exclamation, Yamada looked around. His eyes met Kanda's.

When Kanda saw that Sakuemon and Genbei had gone straight to the battalion staff, he cursed his bad luck. He had intended to summon these two immediately on arriving in Tamogino and not to report to Yamada until they had helped him find guides. The major could not very well object to the officer in charge taking such a step. But now Sakuemon and Genbei had gone straight to Yamada.

"You're just saying that because you want a reward!" Yamada barked, so loudly that Kanda could hear him. Startled, Kanda slowed down his pace.

"This is an *army* exercise! You know what that means? It does *not* mean that the army will hire a guide for every mile of the way, but that it will solve its problems by itself. The army has guides that are a lot more reliable than local people, for they're not in it for the money, like you. You want to see one of our guides? This, my friends, is a compass!" Yamada took a compass out of his pocket and showed it to Sakuemon. "With compasses and maps to help us, we don't need guides!"

Sakuemon and Genbei bowed their heads. Their faces showed they knew the matter had been settled.

Kanda realized that Yamada's angry scolding of the two village elders had really been directed against himself, the officer in charge. Yamada had in effect ordered him not to use guides and had thus interfered in the chain of command.

"Those two were claiming it's impossible to reach Tashiro without guides. What utter nonsense! They just want to earn a few coins," said Yamada, looking at Kanda as if to make certain he had been understood.

Kanda got the message. He could only be silent, for even if he managed to make a case for how necessary guides were, Yamada would hardly give him permission to go and hire some now.

After inspecting the sleds in the rear, Kanda resumed his position at the front of the line. The snow was still coming down the way it had when they left barracks, but it seemed as if the wind had risen. From time to time the snow showed signs of drifting, but it would fall back to the ground almost as soon as it had started moving.

Kanda looked up at the sky. What a drab white hue it was. He took a deep breath, as if to suck that drabness from the white sky and transform it into the order to fall in. But as he was about to utter the words, he heard Major Yamada from behind.

"Fall in!"

Yamada's stentorian voice was famous throughout the 5th. The order he had just given had been audible to everyone in the company, wherever he happened to be. The enlisted men, who had stacked arms and were resting, took their rifles and fell into line, and the soldiers at the sleds picked up their ropes. The moment they heard Yamada give the order, they sensed something was wrong. They were participating in the exercise as a company, and companies were commanded by captains—in their case, Kanda. The battalion staff had gone along merely as observers, so to hear orders from the mouth of the major was the last thing the men had expected. When the order was issued from the rear, most of the lower ranks looked to the front, wondering what had happened to the captain.

"Forward, march!"

On hearing Yamada give this order, too, most of them concluded that for some reason or other the command had shifted to the major. And as far as the lower ranks were concerned, it really made no difference who was in charge.

Lieutenant Katō of the First Platoon noticed that Kanda, who was standing in front of him, looked as if Yamada's voice had knocked the wind out of him. For a moment, Kanda seemed petrified, incapable of interpreting Yamada's order. The captain looked around and signaled to Katō with his eyes, his chin drawn in just a little. Katō took this to mean that Kanda was giving him permission to go ahead.

Katō shouted: "1st Platoon, forward!"

But Katō felt a little strange. Worried, really.

The platoon began to move. One after the other, the leaders ordered their platoons to march, and the Hakkōda Company advanced up the road as if nothing were wrong.

3

Before Tamogino they had seen footprints in the snow, but once beyond the village any signs that people used the road ceased completely. The accumulated snow had erased every trace of the path that Kanda's company had beaten here five days earlier. Still, they could clearly distinguish the road, which stretched through a thin forest toward Kotōge. The snowshoe squad had to be relieved a number of times. As they drew closer to Kotōge, the snow increased rapidly in depth. It was a fine, granular snow, in which sometimes even soldiers wearing snowshoes got stuck. Kanda was filled with amazement and fear when he saw what changes nature had wrought in only five days.

When the front platoon got bogged down in a drift, Major Yamada's loud voice would come from behind to order a rotation. And when he saw that the baggage train could not keep up, he would shout at some lieutenant to get his men to help pull the sleds.

This way, Yamada's status was no longer that of a mere observer; he had clearly become the *de facto* officer in charge. Instead of being led by its captain, as had been planned, the Hakkōda Company found itself under the command of a major.

This change in authority meant that the other eight officers from the battalion staff were no longer observers either; they had to assume the capacity of aides to the major. Thus Yamada would tell one of the warrant officers to go to the front to speed up the relief of the trailbreaking platoon or order one of his probationary officers to the rear to see what was delaying the sleds.

The nearer they got to Kotōge, the stronger the wind blew, until they were moving in what was practically a snowstorm. Their circumstances had changed incredibly since they left barracks, and they threatened to change even more.

The company reached Kotōge at 11:20 AM. The men stacked arms and rubbed their hands and stamped their feet while they waited for the sleds, which did not arrive until ten minutes later. The soldiers of the transportation squad had pulled their burdens into Tamogino with heads steaming and coats off, but now, as they dragged the sleds up to Kotōge, all coats were tightly buttoned up.

The baggage train arrived just when it was time to eat. From their duffel bags and backpacks the soldiers took the rice balls that were supposed to be their meal. They found them frozen hard as stones. Some men split them open with their bayonets and ate them this way, but others threw them away in the snow, complaining that they couldn't possibly eat such stuff. Instead, they tried to nibble on rice cakes, but those were just as frozen, so it made little difference. Because all they had with them were rice balls and rice cakes, not eating these meant not eating at all.

Although Second Lieutenant Nagano was on the battalion staff, he was no mere observer, for he would have joined the Hakkōda Company anyway as its medical officer. And as a doctor, he could not turn a blind eye to what the men were doing. He sought out Kanda and advised him to forbid the men to throw away their food. The men ought to know that, on a winter exercise, food was precious, Nagano said. It might not be pleasant to eat frozen food, but if they did not put up with it and eat something, they would lose their strength.

Kanda stood munching on a piece of bread, an idea of Hatsuko's, who had thought that in the cold of the mountains bread might be better than rice—though the boiled egg she had put in with the bread was a piece of marble. When he heard Nagano's report, Kanda interrupted his meal and told the platoon leaders to warn the men.

"Anyone who threw away his rice balls, pick them up and keep them for later. You can warm them up when we build a fire!" shouted Lieutenant Katō.

But it is not so easy to recover rice balls from under a cover of snow.

Corporals Murayama and Etō were obviously enjoying their rice balls. They had wrapped them in oiled paper and kerchiefs and carried them under their uniforms, so the rice had not frozen. Some of the men had used the same method, and others had suspended their rice balls from their belts and kept them under their greatcoats. These precautions had not been inspired by any suggestions from higher up, but were entirely the result of individual ingenuity, mostly on the part of men from the mountains, who knew from their work how cold it could get there. Soldiers who had allowed their rice balls to freeze to the core received their share from men who had been more sensible.

But the weather affected them more than hunger. It was so cold that it was almost unbearable to stand around for long, particularly for the enlisted men in their duck-cloth uniforms. Their two greatcoats were not enough to stop them from shivering, and many began to have their misgivings about the rest of the exercise. They tried to encourage each other with stories about the saké they would drink after a nice hot bath in Tashiro that night, but where the hell Tashiro was nobody knew. Their worries were not diminished by the impenetrable snow curtain that hung beyond Kotōge. During the break they also got to hear how the major had refused to hire guides at Tamogino.

"If you ask me, we ought to call off the exercise and return to barracks," Nagano remarked to Kanda.

"Return to barracks? Maybe you're right. The weather's getting worse every minute."

Kanda agreed with Nagano. In fact, he had just concluded, in view of the snow drifting over the road before them, that they were not going to make it without guides.

"But what reason can we give?" he asked Nagano. To persuade such a muleheaded character as Yamada, they would have to come armed with ironclad arguments.

"For one thing, the weather has suddenly changed: we're in for a terrible blizzard. For another, our clothing is insufficient for a march in this extreme cold, especially the enlisted men's—their uniforms are made of duck cloth, and they ought to be wearing wool. Also we need rations that won't freeze. Right now, one-third of the men have not eaten any food. Under these circumstances it'd be dangerous to go on."

Nagano had spoken urgently, not bothering to pause for breath.

"Yes, those are certainly convincing reasons. Now all we have to do is see if they convince the major." 95

Side by side, Kanda and Nagano walked up to Yamada and pleaded with him to call off the exercise and return to barracks immediately. But although Yamada did feel worried about the change in the weather, he was not about to follow their advice so easily. Instead, he called the platoon leaders together.

Standing in the snow, they deliberated what they should do: go on or turn back. The fact that this question was being discussed at all was strange. If Kanda, the officer in charge, agreed with Nagano, the decision to return had already been made; all he had to do was report it to Yamada. If Yamada found that decision inappropriate, he should try to convince Kanda to change his mind. Or, if he considered that he himself was in command, he should state his opinion and decide one way or another. But to call all the officers together and hold a strategy meeting in a snowstorm was tantamount to admitting before the assembled lower ranks that there was a lack of unity in the command of the company.

Nagano explained why he was so certain the weather had changed:

"When I visited the meteorological station in Aomori last night to ask what sort of weather we might expect, the director told me that a strong low-pressure area was moving north long the coast of the Pacific. If this depression approached the coast of northeast Honshu, there would be heavy snowstorms in the mountains, but whether it would actually come this way or not he couldn't tell until today about noon—in other words, until now. But what he could tell me was that if on reaching Kotōge we found a strong northwestern wind, we ought to assume the depression was on its way. And in that case, he said, we'd better turn back. Well, the weather is behaving just as he said it would. It's blowing harder every second, and the temperature is plummeting. For that reason alone I think we ought to return as soon as possible. But we have other problems, just as grave: the duck cloth of the enlisted men's uniforms is much too thin, and one-third of the men have not eaten because their rations were frozen."

Nagano had spoken quite forcefully, and most of the officers supported him. They seemed especially impressed by his explanation about the weather. These officers thought that if Captain Kanda was resolved to call the whole thing off, then the question was settled. Some even wondered why Major Yamada had thought it necessary to call this meeting at all.

The next to speak up was Warrant Officer Shindō. Although he was not quite an officer, Shindō was not an NCO and he was on the battalion staff; he could not be denied the right to speak.

"Lieutenant Nagano says that the rising wind and falling temperature are caused by that low-pressure area, but I wonder if that's the only possible explanation. This close to a high mountain it would be strange if there were no wind. And while it's true that the men's uniforms are made of duck, they are also wearing two greatcoats, so I don't see that they are that much worse off than we are."

Nagano retorted frostily: "As medical officer I am responsible for the health of the men. I have considered the matter objectively, professionally, and come to the conclusion that it is impossible to proceed. This conclusion is based on solid facts, and I hardly think this is the time or place to indulge in futile argument. While we are dawdling, the weather is only getting worse."

It was as Nagano said. The wind had gradually picked up and seemed to have locked the Hakkōda Company in its snowy grip.

"May I request permission to speak, Sir?"

Outside the circle of NCOs that had formed around the circle of officers, a strapping corporal stepped forward and saluted Yamada.

"With respect, Sir, Lieutenant Nagano has just said that it is impossible to continue, but is it not in the nature of the Japanese Army to make the impossible possible? All of us NCOs wish to continue toward Tashiro as planned."

These words created a general stir among the NCOs. There were shouts of agreement. Two or three others showed signs of wanting to step forward.

Yamada realized the situation threatened to get out of hand. All at once he drew his sword and pointed it toward the blizzard:

"Advance!"

It was a truly bizarre scene: Yamada had called for a meeting, but here he broke it off and announced of his own accord that the exercise would be continued. It could be argued that circumstances had forced his hand; it could also be argued that he had forgotten his responsibility as a commanding officer and caved in to pressure from a group of NCOs. The order to advance itself was strange, and the drawn sword seemed pure theater. Kanda turned pale, and Nagano made no attempt to hide his anger.

But all was over. The decision had been made. They would advance.

The officers returned to their posts and the NCOs to their places in line. The enlisted men, who had watched these proceedings with chattering teeth, took up their rifles. The squad leaders held

97

roll call and reported to the platoon leaders, who in turn reported to Kanda. When the formalities were finished, the 210 men of the Aomori 5th Infantry marched into the oblivion of the snowstorm. It was 12:15 PM, January 23, 1902.

The official report issued by the 5th Regiment on July 23, 1902, would state:

> At 11:30 AM the Hakkōda Company reached Kotōge. The men stacked arms and paused to wait for the arrival of the baggage train and to eat their rations. The wind grew gradually stronger and the cold correspondingly worse. The rice they had brought along to eat was frozen solid and white as snow. The men formed groups of two or three and ate their food crouching or standing, often without taking off their gloves. About twenty minutes later, the march was resumed, but the progress of the baggage train was greatly impeded by the increasingly deeper snow and steeper slope. In one hour the men covered no more than 1½ miles.

4

In the deep snow of the mountains, a progress of 1½ miles per hour is not all that slow. The distance from Kotōge to Tashiro being slightly over 4 miles, the Hakkōda Company could have reached its destination in just about three hours. The men's dreams of a hot bath followed by a few drinks of saké could have come true. But things did not work out that way.

When the company set out from Kotōge, the baggage squad, in the rear, found that every single sled—each sled carrying about 220 pounds of provisions and fuel—had sunk into the snow and refused to budge. In the front, the snowshoe squad found it impossible to clear a path, because after Kotōge the road became quite steep and the snow not only grew deeper, but was feather-light and fluffy. Occasionally their snowshoes sank into the snow and turned from a help into a handicap.

As a rule Kanda was to be found at the front of the column. To march with only a map and a compass to go by was disheartening work, he thought, but he could do it if he set his mind to it. He would use his compass to find his direction, fix on a suitable landmark out that way, and proceed toward it. If he then recorded on the map the distance and direction traveled, he might reasonably expect in due course to reach his destination. But this was possible only under certain conditions: good weather, enough visibility to choose a distant landmark, and a landscape with topographic features conspicuous enough to be included on the map.

On this particular day, the snowfield that lay before the Hak-kōda Company was shrouded in drifting whiteness. Visibility was bad and the wind strong—the worst possible conditions for such exacting actions as getting out the map, setting the course with a compass, and recording the route on the map. Yet Kanda had to do these things, or they would never reach Tashiro.

To make up for what nature refused to provide, Kanda used people. He set his course with the help of several NCOs, who would count paces, walk ahead to function as landmarks, or go out to reconnoiter the lay of the land. Because of the furiously drifting snow it was impossible to see very far; only during occasional lulls did visibility improve somewhat. Kanda used such opportunities to see if he could recognize the natural features of the terrain on his map, to make certain that he always knew where he was.

Beyond Ōtōge lay a vast, snowbound plateau. There was hardly a tree in sight; only here and there did the branches of a black alder stick up through the snow, its shriveled black berries rattling in the wind.

The compass was Kanda's only guide. What would he do if, as Tokushima had told him sometimes happened, the extreme cold caused it to malfunction and he could no longer use it? He felt like praying. To be absolutely safe, Kanda had put his compass close to his pocket heater and took it out only when absolutely necessary.

It had become more and more obvious that the baggage train could not keep up. Each platoon had sent men to the rear to help pull the sleds, but even so they were unable to catch up with the main force. Finally, on reaching the Sainokawara Plain, Kanda went up to Yamada and suggested that the sleds be abandoned and the luggage divided among the platoons, each man to carry his share. If they did not do so, the train would only lag farther behind, until the whole company was forced to wait. Since the highest authority now lay with Yamada, Kanda could not take such measures without first consulting him.

But Yamada rejected the idea out of hand.

"You can't just go and abandon the sleds! I'll admit they're in a bit of a rough spot now, but for all we know they'll be gliding along smoothly in a little while. No, we'll deviate from our plans only if there's no other way." 99

A dense cloud of snow carried by the ever-stronger wind seemed to hang over the frozen plain, like a pall of white smoke. This snow did not come falling from the sky, but was blown up from the ground, which explains why visibility improved when the wind died down. To most of the lower ranks it might seem as if they were merely walking in a straight line through the blinding drifts, but Kanda remained alert and never missed the slightest change in their surroundings.

During one lull in the storm, the shape of a mountain to their right became partly visible through the drifting snow. Kanda barely managed to stifle a shout of joy. That could only be the Maedake, the front peak of Mount Hakkōda. This confirmed that they were still on the right course. Not unnaturally, he was filled with fresh courage.

He had to share his joy with someone and told Corporal Etō, who was walking beside him:

"Look, that's the Maedake!"

Etō stared in the direction Kanda was pointing and said, in a voice that clearly showed his astonishment:

"My god! That mountain is huge!"

But before the words had left his mouth, a screen of snow had hidden the Maedake from sight again.

It became more and more obvious how exhausted the lower ranks were. Their faces, whipped raw by the blizzard, had turned purple. They would purposely wade through waist-high snow or swim through chest-high drifts to escape from the cold.

Whenever he heard Yamada order a relief of the front platoon, Kanda's lips quivered nervously. Until that day he had had confidence in the major, had even respected him. He had considered him an exemplary soldier. But Yamada's behavior on this march was so extraordinary as to be beyond comprehension. In Yamada's eyes, Kanda was no more than the officer charged with leading the way, and Kanda felt compelled to remind himself that all this giving of orders meant Yamada had taken over the command. I suppose I'll just have to be content functioning as one of his aides, Kanda thought.

The Hakkōda Company marched through the drifting snow in a deep silence that was broken only by someone exclaiming that it couldn't be far to Tashiro now. Likely, the speaker was one of the lower ranks, never an officer, trying to encourage his comrades. The men wanted to stay in this white hell not one second longer than was absolutely necessary.

When we get to Tashiro I can soak in the springs, and I wouldn't be surprised if they allowed us two or three flasks of saké each, they told themselves as they slogged on through that desolate snow desert—across the Ōtaki Moor and the Sainokawara Plain, and past two low mountains, the Yasunokimori and the Nakanomori. The front of the column reached the hulking Umatateba, 2,402 feet high, at 4:10 PM.

The Umatateba is the highest hill on that undulating plateau, unmistakable in summer and especially in winter, when it wears a carapace of ice. The locals called it the Ice Mountain.

Kanda consulted his map. Not until he had made certain that the ice mountain before him was indeed the Umatateba was he willing to accept the idea that Tashiro was now only a mile away.

So we made no mistake on those 3 miles from Kotōge, he said to himself. It was a gratifying thought.

He led his men to a hollow on the other side of the hill, where they were more or less out of the wind, although still within reach of the really strong gusts. Here they took a break, during which Kanda sent out some men to see what had happened to the baggage train.

They reported back that the sleds were well over a mile behind. As company commander, Kanda now had to act fast. He had to see to it that the sleds linked up with the main body and that everybody was safely on the way to Tashiro before it turned dark. Because night was falling already, he told Lieutenants Suzumori and Nakahashi to take their platoons back to help the train. This meant that the men, who had imagined that they would soon be relaxing in the hot springs, had to put down their rifles and backpacks and go all the way to the rear to help pull the sleds.

Kanda also sent fifteen men—under Sergeant Major Fujimura, who said he had walked this road in summer—toward Tashiro to prepare for their arrival. Among them was a bugler, with orders to blow a signal as soon as the squad reached Tashiro.

Soon after Fujimura and his men had disappeared behind the snow curtain, the weather, which had given them occasional breathing spells, turned even worse. The change was so sudden that it seemed as if an avalanche had come down before them. The wind shrieked through the mountains, and a driving snow swept into their eyes until they could hardly see. They were now on the Hakkōda Massif, where the wind never blows steadily but comes from all directions, in sudden gusts that create whirlwinds of snow everywhere. In this awful weather, the blizzard raging about them,

101

the main body had to wait for over two hours before the sleds managed to catch up.

By then it was completely dark. Nothing had been heard from Fujimura's squad, but even if the men had reached Tashiro, how could they have communicated this to Kanda? The sound of the bugle would have been drowned out by the storm.

"Captain Kanda, you will detach yourself from the company and reconnoiter the route to Tashiro," Yamada ordered, thus demoting Kanda from officer in command of a company to high-ranking scout. In addition, the order split the company into three groups; the main body, Fujimura's squad, and Kanda's squad.

In the dark and the blizzard, which still raged with unabated fury, the main force under Yamada now descended from the Umatateba toward the Narusawa Valley, which lay to the south, according to the map. It was a simple idea: just go south until you reach Tashiro. However, part of the Narusawa Valley was a gorge so deep that it would be very difficult to get out of and, to avoid this danger, the company proceeded gingerly.

Just when the head of the column had reached the valley, Fujimura's squad linked up with the rear. In the dark the men had lost their direction and wandered through the snow until they stumbled on the main body again.

The moon was exactly two weeks old. Under a cloudless sky, the landscape would have been quite visible. But in this snowfall it was almost impossible for each man to see the person walking in front of him.

Yamada ordered the men to abandon the sleds and to distribute the baggage among the transportation squad. The order made little difference. With or without the baggage, the sleds were unable to advance by so much as a hairsbreadth.

The snow at Narusawa reached up to the chest. The men had to shout to each other as they worked their way forward.

Now Yamada ordered Lieutenant Ono forward to reconnoiter the route to Tashiro—the second time he used an officer as a scout. Ono soon reported back:

"Our way is intersected by a steep slope and the snow gets deeper all the time. Further progress looks difficult. I suggest we find a suitable place for a bivouac and wait for dawn before we try to find our way out."

This report persuaded Yamada not to go farther that day, but where they were then was no "suitable place" to pitch camp. For this, they would need a level and sheltered site.

Kanda and his squad had discovered just such a spot, 650 feet east of Narusawa. The area was known as Hirasawamori, although of course no one was in a position to consult a map and ascertain its location or its name.

Yamada issued orders for the company to prepare to bivouac on the site Kanda had found. He told the battalion staff to remain where it was, and he ordered the cooks to prepare a meal there. He told the platoons to preserve their present positions in the line, and he sent Lieutenant Nakahashi and fifteen men to assist the transportation squad and guide them to the campsite.

By the time Nakahashi's men had guided the transportation squad to the camp with their lanterns, it was 9:00 PM.

On the site selected for the bivouac, there stood some beech trees—tall, but ineffective as a windbreak. Therefore, using spades, the platoons dug trenches in the snow: 6½ feet wide, 16 feet long, and 8 feet deep. But because the snow lay as deep as 16 feet, they were unable to dig all the way down to the soil. One such trench was to accommodate an entire platoon, including its leader. Instead of the hot bath and the saké they had been looking forward to, the men had to satisfy themselves with a hole in the snow, but no one had enough strength left to complain.

Every platoon was allotted one and a half bags of charcoal; each man, three rice cakes and one can of beef.

In addition to the trenches for the platoons, they also dug a trench for the combined use of the battalion staff and the kitchen squad. In its center stood a big flat copper kettle with a capacity of ten gallons. Around this, a wider area had been cleared so that the cooks had room to walk about.

When they tried to light the charcoal underneath the kettle, everyone realized exactly how difficult it was to prepare a meal in a snow trench. When the kitchen squad finally managed to light a fire, with the help of some burning charcoal bags, the snow promptly melted and extinguished it. If there had been dead trees about, they could have gathered branches for firewood, but now there was nothing for it but to start another fire on top of the wet, extinguished charcoal. But the hotter the fire, the faster the snow underneath it melted; the floor of the trench sank lower and lower. The tripod supporting the kettle was in constant danger of tilting over and spilling its load.

Yamada and the other eight officers of the battalion staff sat in a circle around the kitchen squad, who were desperately trying to produce a meal. It took a long time for the rice to boil, but the cooks used a lot of charcoal, which enabled the staff officers to dry their wet things and toast some rice cakes.

The men were trying hard to get fires started in the other trenches too. But when they succeeded, the number able to warm themselves was very small. The platoon leaders allowed ten men to stand around the fire for ten minutes, after which they had to make way for others. Those whose turn it was could place rice cakes on top of the charcoal or warm up their frozen rice balls. Among them were some who had not eaten at noon; for these men, their toasted rice cakes were both lunch and dinner. Ten minutes was a very short time—too short to grill a rice cake, let alone to dry wet clothes. When they returned from the fire to their old corner in the trench, the men felt the cold even worse than before.

Those who had served in the transportation squad that day were particularly to be pitied. Though their underwear was soaked with sweat, they had brought no change of clothing, and the fire was not hot enough to allow them to strip and dry their things.

As the night wore on, the blizzard grew worse and the temperature dropped amazingly. The cold penetrated the two greatcoats and the uniforms until it reached the men's sweat-soaked shirts. It was hard to bear. From every trench arose cries:

"Don't sleep!"

"If you fall asleep, you'll die!"

But the men were deadly tired. Several dozed off in that mind-numbing cold.

At 1:00 AM each man received one ration of half-boiled rice. This revived their spirits for a while, but the cold that assaulted them immediately after their meal was so intense that it seemed impossible to endure. They sang marching songs and stamped their feet, but their voices sounded plaintive and feeble.

5

Major Yamada feared something terrible would happen if he did not get his men out of this predicament fast, so he called Kanda and ordered him to tell the platoons to prepare for an immediate return to barracks.

"With respect, Sir, I think that under the circumstances it is not advisable to leave so soon," Kanda objected. "By now the blizzard will have wiped out the tracks we made from the Umatateba to this campsite and, if it hasn't, they'll be indistinguishable in the darkness. We don't even know exactly where we are, so I consider it extremely risky to move now. Why don't we wait until dawn? We can send out a few men then to check out the terrain, and leave when they have made certain of our way back. I know the men are cold, but in the trenches they are at least out of the wind. If they leave shelter, they'll be exposed to the full force of the storm and develop frostbite before you know it. So, Sir, please wait until dawn!"

But Yamada refused to listen to this advice.

"To waste more time like this would mean sending the men to their deaths. If we leave right away, we'll be able to go back the way we came a few hours ago, but if we wait until morning, all the men will suffer so badly from frostbite that they won't be able to move. No, we'll leave immediately!"

Kanda was in no position to disobey this order, so he called the platoon leaders and told them to have their men ready to return to barracks by 2:00 AM. He also instructed each platoon to accept a few of the soldiers of the transportation squad.

"We're leaving at two?"

Whoever's idea it was, the platoon leaders thought the order so absurd that they could not believe their ears. Here they had dug trenches and found shelter from this awful blizzard. They had at last had a warm meal—only half-cooked, to be sure, but warm. The thing to do was to wait in the trenches for morning and to leave as soon as the weather showed even the least sign of improvement. But now? It was so dark you couldn't see a hand before your face. Several lieutenants passionately demanded some sort of answer.

"Major's orders, I'm sorry," was all Kanda told them. What would be the use if he mentioned that he had beseeched Yamada to wait until dawn?

At 2:00 AM the platoons climbed out of their trenches and lined up. When the men felt the wind whip about their bodies, they began to shiver uncontrollably. Many complained of the cold.

After they were assembled, roll call was held. No sooner had the order to depart been given than there was a howl like that of a wild beast. A soldier dashed out of the ranks and leaped into the soft, deep snow around the campsite, screaming like a madman, the words indistinguishable. In his frenzy he threw down his rifle and duffel bag and began to tug at his clothes, all the while forcing his way through the snow with incredible vigor. Other soldiers tried to restrain him, but to no avail. With desperate strength the demented man knocked them down. He tore off his uniform and shirt and threw them away. Then the screaming stopped. The soldier sank down in the snow.

"What's going on? What happened?" Kanda shouted.

Lieutenant Nakahashi reported that a soldier had gone berserk.

"Have him taken care of right away. Call the medical officer." But the soldier was already as good as dead. By the time they had finished putting the clothes back on to the naked body they had lifted from the snow, he lay motionless in their arms.

Such an incident right before their departure cast a gloom over the whole company. Kanda went to report the soldier's death.

"It looks as if the exposure to the extreme cold after leaving the shelter of his trench drove him crazy."

Hoping that this death might induce Yamada to change his mind, Kanda briefly outlined the progress of the soldier's madness. The previous day he had worn himself out pulling one of the sleds. The one shirt he wore was soaked with sweat, and the sweat had spread to his duck-cloth uniform, which was frozen stiff. In the trench already he had shown symptoms of advanced exhaustion and frostbite. He had been so tired that he had even been unable to eat the half-cooked meal they had received.

"So because one man goes berserk, I have to change my order?" Yamada forestalled Kanda.

Obviously, it was now too late for that.

By the light of a small lamp held by Corporal Etō, Kanda consulted his map and his compass to find their way back. The tracks they had made only a few hours earlier had disappeared completely.

The men plodded on through the chest-high snow. Kanda had fixed on a northwesterly course, which would take them to the edge of the gorge at Narusawa. They had to work their way around it and climb a steep slope, but then they would be on the Umatateba.

Swimming through the snow, they made extremely slow progress. Their lines were ragged, and the weakest were showing signs that they might not be able to keep up.

It took them two hours to reach the gorge, exactly according to Kanda's schedule. They would not descend into the gorge, but would backtrack about 330 yards and turn west. The slope that would then become visible would lead straight up to the Umatateba. This judgment was based on the information provided by the map.

Kanda paused a few seconds, then ordered a 180-degree turn. He was right.

That Kanda had been able, in spite of the darkness, to lead his company to this spot was entirely due to his cool head and sound judgment. However, when the men behind him saw that they were doubling back, they received the impression that their guide had lost his way. They were tired. Although they did not understand the situation, the eyes they turned toward Kanda were filled with accusation.

"What does Kanda think he's doing?" asked Yamada, who was walking in the rear.

Warrant Officer Shindō, right behind him, said, as if in answer, "We seem to have taken the wrong road."

This was the extent of their conversation, for a while.

Kanda's figure came toward them through the darkness, a lantern in its hand. He was creeping, rather than walking, through the snow.

Suddenly Shindō said to Yamada, "Sir, I have been this way to Tashiro before."

"When was that?"

"Last summer. I remember this beech forest, and I could swear that if we turn to the right here, we'll get to Tashiro."

It was impossible to see a thing in the darkness. From the one or two trees he could make out by the light of the lanterns, it was highly unlikely that Shindō was able to tell the road to Tashiro. And it was not as if he had a map with him. He was merely recalling the previous summer, when there had still been snow on the road and in the beech forest through which it led. This had somehow given him the notion that Tashiro lay somewhere to their right. The piercing cold and lack of sleep had muddled his head.

"Why the devil didn't you tell me sooner that you knew the way?"

"I was not quite certain, Sir."

"But now you are?"

"Yes, Sir. I remember positively that tall beech tree over there. It stood on the right-hand side of the turnoff to Tashiro."

Shindō pointed at the tree with his lantern, but it had disappeared in the snowstorm.

"Well, go and make certain. If that is the tree you saw on your way to Tashiro, you'll be our guide from here on."

Shindō turned back through the snow to the tree and shone the light of his lantern on it. Because the snow was over 6 feet deep at this spot, its trunk was hidden from sight, but its branches were sticking up through the snow. One branch, about 8 inches thick, had been cut off with a saw.

"This has got to be the road to Tashiro, Sir. That sawed-off branch tells me."

"You mean people have been working here?"

Now Yamada himself waded through the snow toward the tree. By the light of his lantern he could clearly see that one branch had been sawed off. This was nothing strange in the area, merely a sign that some charcoal burner had found a branch of the right size.

But when Yamada saw the stump left by the saw, he imagined there must be people living nearby. He believed what Shindō was saying was true.

"All right!" he shouted. "We'll change our plans and proceed to Tashiro. Shindō, lead the way!"

Kanda came running back, covered from head to foot with snow. When he saw that the members of the battalion staff had gathered under a beech tree and were studying it by the light of their lamps, he halted. This boded no good.

"Ah, Kanda! We've found the way to Tashiro, all right! Shindō here knows it, and he is going to take us there. Pass the word to the platoons."

Kanda stood aghast. The same Yamada who had been unable to wait until dawn before starting on the way home now wanted to cancel his earlier order before it was light.

"Sir, you *must* allow me to be the judge of that," Kanda protested. "I know where we are. All we have to do is trace our steps back for a short distance and we'll be on our way to the Umatateba and home." He was begging now, frantically. "We can be back at barracks today."

"But the men are tired. Remember that soldier who went berserk and died? The sooner we get them to safety the better, there isn't a second to lose. And now that we've found the road to Tashiro, it stands to reason we'll take it."

"But, Sir, if you want to go to Tashiro, we should go exactly the other way. Shindō must have made a mistake."

When Kanda turned to Shindō to explain to him, map in hand, why he thought he had been mistaken, Yamada grabbed Shindō's lantern and shone its light on the stump of the branch.

"Look, someone cut a branch off this beech to mark the road to Tashiro. Now, go quick and tell the platoon leaders that we've found the way there. That ought to cheer up the men."

Kanda had been unable to get a word in. He stood still. A wave of despair washed over him.

6

The Hakkōda Company, now guided by Warrant Officer Shindō, greeted the morning of the twenty-fourth in a forest of sparsely growing beeches. That is to say, it was morning, but because of the blizzard the day never got any brighter than a moonlit night. Yet the men followed Shindō without complaining, for they believed that before long the lights of Tashiro would shine out through the darkness.

The number of men suffering from frostbite in their hands had increased, and orders were given to tie the rifles to the backpacks so the men could keep their hands in their pockets. Even so there were men who failed to recover any feeling in their hands, though they warmed them against their bodies or rubbed them together. Many others complained of numbness in their toes. Fatigue and cold caused more and more men to fall behind, and because they could not be left to themselves, the lines gradually became longer.

The soldier who was carrying the kettle suddenly collapsed in the snow. He was pulled up, but his lips twitched violently and he was unable to speak. Another soldier took over his burden, but he too collapsed before he had walked 100 yards. There was nothing for it but to abandon the kettle.

So far they had proceeded over a plateau, but now they began a descent that rapidly became quite steep. When they reached bottom, after much slipping and sliding, they were confronted with a river—the Komagome. They marched along its bank until they found themselves in a dark ravine, with a river before them and a sheer cliff to their left, unable to advance another step. It was 8:30 AM. By this time Yamada had lost his faith in Shindō's capacities as a guide, but it was already too late: Shindō had led them into a hopeless situation.

Yamada called another strategy meeting. He had done the same at Kotōge, but this time he seemed to feel responsible for the plight he had brought on by his acceptance of Shindō's story. This awareness was clearly visible from the way he peered over the map. The storm tugged at its edges and would have carried it off if it had not been held firmly at each corner, and the ever-falling snow made it necessary to wipe the map continuously. When Yamada took his compass out of his pocket, the needle refused to move. Kanda had carried his own compass on his skin and with its help they finally established their direction. But even Kanda's compass froze within three minutes. It was frightfully cold.

"I believe we are right here, on this spot," said Kanda. "To get out of here I don't see any alternative but to go westward along this tributary of the Komagome and to turn off toward the Umatateba on the way."

He had traced in pencil the route they had come the previous day and scribbled notes here and there, as a result of which diligence the map had become smudged and dirty.

The meeting was soon over. None of the officers raised objections, for most of them believed the main reason they were in such a predicament was that, since Kotōge, Yamada had never ceased interfering with Kanda's command.

"I suppose we'd better do as Captain Kanda suggests: go west along the brook and look for a way to reach the Umatateba."

The speaker was Captain Kurata, one of the observers on the battalion staff. He had, at Yamada's suggestion, decided to join the company only the day before its departure, so he knew very little about the plans for the exercise. For this reason he had so far refrained from comment. The fact that this officer, after Yamada the ranking member of the battalion staff, decided to speak up now did not go unnoticed among his colleagues.

Kurata's support for Kanda's plan was decisive. From then on Yamada and Kurata, who had so far walked in the rear, marched with Kanda at the front of the line. They had reached the point at which further progress was impossible unless the leading officers worked closely together.

About this time, order in the ranks began to disappear. It had become increasingly difficult for the lieutenants to keep their platoons together. One soldier after another fell behind, and whenever this happened another soldier of the same platoon had to carry the straggler's rifle and backpack. But because he already had his hands full with his own luggage, that soldier in his turn would fall behind.

The snow and the cold became progressively worse. Visibility was less than 30 feet. The footsteps of a man in front disappeared before the eyes of the man walking behind him.

They followed the stream, until its banks suddenly narrowed and disappeared. They could go no further. If they wanted to continue in the same direction, they would have to wade through the brook, and everyone knew how dangerous it would be to get wet feet.

"It's unavoidable," said Yamada. "We'll have to climb this cliff."

"Wall" would have been a more appropriate choice of words. Without the trees and shrubs on the face of the cliff, the snow would have had nothing to cling to.

Since the half-boiled rice they had been given at 1:00 AM, the men had eaten nothing. Their stomachs were empty, their hands frozen. Soldiers fell down because their fingers were too numb to grab hold of the trees. For every two steps up, they would slide one down. The ascent took two hours.

When at long last they made it to the top, they were welcomed by a gale that cut off their breaths. Even in the gorge the wind had been bad, so it stood to reason that it was much stronger on the exposed heights. The mercury in Medical Officer Nagano's thermometer stood at $-4°$.

Because of the headwind their progress was slow, and because of the swirling snow they could not see what lay ahead. Now that they had struggled out of the gorge, they at last had time to eat something, at an hour too late for breakfast and too early for lunch. They munched on the rations of parched rice they had received on their departure from Aomori, but they had to wash it down with snow, for the water in their canteens was frozen.

Forward again. The officers up front desperately tried to get their men on the way back to barracks, but not only was there almost no visibility, the terrain was also extremely complicated. Frequently they merely wandered about, without a clear idea of their course. Yet the company gradually worked its way westward, against the wind, and reached the Narusawa Valley. At least they were moving in the right direction.

Ice stood on the eyebrows of the lower ranks. The soldiers who suffered most were those with frozen hands. When they had to urinate, they were unable to unbutton their flies; when they were finished, they could not button themselves up again. On such occasions they had to ask for the assistance of men who still had the use of their hands. Many of the lower ranks suffered from frostbite on hands and feet. Several of the men hastened their deaths by tearing off their buttons in their urge to urinate, thus allowing the cold wind to blow into their trousers. Other men urinated without opening their flies at all, the result being that their trousers froze, the lower part of their bodies grew cold and numb, and they became unable to walk.

Most of the lower ranks shuffled along like sleepwalkers. They unthinkingly followed the man in front: if he stopped, they stopped too. Fatigue, lack of sleep, and cold had made the soldiers hopelessly drowsy. Some actually did sleep while they walked, and they would topple headlong into the snow, without warning—never to get up. These men were not stragglers, but the fatigue and exposure were taking their toll. If the soldier walking in front collapsed, the man behind him would collapse too, as if tempted by the example.

Some men suddenly broke out in horrible screams, ran about frantically, dove headfirst into the snow, and died. Others sat down in the snow, cackling hoarsely. Yet others started babbling nonsense and stripped themselves naked.

The situation had become desperate. There was no help for these soldiers—they were dying. For the others, the only hope was to find a sheltered place where the wind was a shade less strong.

Suddenly, Lieutenant Ono of the 3rd Platoon collapsed. His orderly tried to raise him, but he did not get up.

"Lieutenant! Lieutenant!" the orderly shouted, but only the storm answered.

"Lieutenant, please! Get up, Sir!" The orderly was close to tears.

Zenjirō Hasebe heard him and fixed his eyes on Kanda, who was walking in front of him. As Kanda's orderly, he had to remain by Kanda. He must not fall behind. He imagined Lieutenant Ono's orderly would probably sit by his master until he died. Then the orderly would fall asleep, by the lieutenant's side. This seemed natural to Hasebe, who strangely enough felt no fear of dying, despite all the men he had seen collapse about him.

Hasebe was walking right behind Kanda because the company was no longer marching in formation. The platoons were mixed up.

From first to last, the members of the transportation squad were the most to be lamented. They had to carry the rice, the charcoal, the cooking utensils. This was no ordinary toil: many of them fell and died in the snow, their burden on top of them.

Toward nightfall the company reached Narusawa Hollow, where it was decided to lay out a second bivouac. Efforts were made to collect the stragglers, but many of them were now covered by the snow and could no longer be found.

At roll call it became clear that forty men had disappeared. Almost all the survivors were suffering from frostbite.

7

When they wanted to start digging trenches, it turned out that there were no spades. The soldiers carrying them had fallen down on the way, as had the men carrying the charcoal, who had collapsed under their bags and died where they lay.

That night the survivors banded closely together around their officers and stamped their feet until dawn. It was cold sitting down, and it was cold standing up. To sleep was impossible, and if one opened one's mouth to speak, the cold struck to the very core of one's teeth. Many thought back with longing to their first bivouac.

The lower ranks tried to eat some parched rice, but many of the men could not bring the food to their mouths with their frozen fingers. They had to be fed by those whose hands still functioned. It became dark, but the storm showed no signs of abating. The cold grew ever more intense, and the number of soldiers who died in their sleep increased gradually.

"You'll die if you sleep! Sing a song, and huddle close together, so you can warm each other with your bodies."

They all heard the orders, but they were in no spirit to sing and lacked the strength to huddle.

In the darkness, the blizzard raged.

Occasionally a plaintive cry was heard:

"I've got to take a leak! Someone help me with my buttons!"

But there would be no answer. The men's heads were fuzzy with cold and sleep; they could not get up the energy to see to the needs of others. But those who shouted that they had to urinate were still in comparatively good shape. Others never uttered a word but simply let the urine run into their trousers. The extreme cold also caused sudden attacks of diarrhea, and often enough the victim's frozen hands prevented him from lowering his trousers. The legs of those who thus befouled themselves began to freeze immediately, until the men toppled over in the snow like logs, dead. The company's suffering had ceased to be pathetic; it had become gruesome.

Zenjirō Hasebe was standing next to Kanda. As his orderly, he felt he had to do something to help the captain, but there was nothing he could do. Hasebe's body was screaming for rest. He fell asleep on his feet.

"Hasebe, are you asleep? Come on, man, pull yourself together! If you sleep, you'll die!"

Kanda's voice dragged him back to consciousness, but soon he was overwhelmed by a craving for sleep even more irresistible.

There was Kichinosuke, his brother, walking toward him in a blue woolen uniform with brass buttons down the chest and red shoulder patches that bore the number "31." The badges on his collar were a bright scarlet, and on the sleeves of his uniform glittered the two golden stripes that indicated he was a sergeant.

Kichinosuke! When did you get promoted?

They made me a sergeant for taking part in this exercise.

You mean they gave you an extraordinary promotion?

Yes, for distinguished service.

Distinguished service?

Yes. When the Tokushima Platoon crossed Mount Hakkōda, we found your company in one hell of a mess. But we got you out, never fear. I got my promotion because I saved your Captain Kanda.

Really? You saved the captain?

Tokushima was right, you know. He had this hunch that you people might be somewhere around here, so we started searching.

And there you were!

So what happened to me? Who saved me, eh?

Look Zenjirō, I'm really sorry I've got to tell you this, but you were dead.

Dead? Me? Like hell I died! I'm still alive! Zenjirō Hasebe is still alive, you hear! Alive and kicking!

With a loud cry Hasebe opened his eyes.

"You hear? Zenjirō Hasebe is still alive, and don't you forget it!"

"Hey, Hasebe!" came Kanda's voice out of the darkness. "What's wrong with you? Were you having nightmares?"

"Yes, Sir. I dreamt I saw my brother."

"Your brother? That would be the one who serves in the 31st, right?"

"Yes, Sir. He joined Captain Tokushima's platoon. I dreamt that he came to save us."

"And were we saved?"

"Yes, Sir. You were, but my brother told me I had died."

"Oh, come on, Hasebe! Don't you see that's the sort of dream you get if you depend too much on others? Do you really think someone will come to our rescue? In a place like this? If you can't help yourself, man, what *can* you do?"

Kanda's angry voice drove away the last bit of Hasebe's drowsiness. The cold hit him at once, so hard that he feared he would freeze to the marrow of his bones. He had lost all sensation in his feet a long time before; now he was losing the feeling in his ten fingers. He felt that he might die soon, as his brother had predicted. What would Kichinosuke say if he died before he got here to save me? Hasebe nodded off again.

"Hasebe! Wake up, man! Tomorrow we'll find our way back to barracks. If you die here, your brother will laugh at you," said Kanda, shaking Hasebe's shoulder.

"Do you think Kichinosuke would laugh if he found my body, Sir?"

"He will. You bet he will. Because he'll see that you died like a dog, for no good reason."

"But Sir, do you really think he'd laugh if he found me dead?" Hasebe asked again.

In spite of the darkness it seemed to Kanda as if he could read the look in Hasebe's eyes.

He must be under tremendous strain, Kanda thought. This means a lot to him.

"No. No, he won't. He'll cry, I'm sure. So pull yourself together, come on! Or do you want your brother to shed tears for you?"

Hasebe gazed into the darkness, from whose edges he imagined he could hear death's footsteps drawing near. His head ached with cold. Yes. If Kichinosuke found his dead body, he'd cry. He tried to imagine his brother weeping, but could not. All he saw was an angry scowl.

"Come on, Hasebe! Don't fall asleep now! Stick it out till morning!"

But Hasebe did not hear. His knees buckled, and slowly he sank to the ground.

"Hasebe! Get up, Hasebe!"

With great difficulty Kanda managed to pull Hasebe to his feet. He slapped him with the flat of his hand until at last the orderly regained consciousness.

Some of the men died screaming, others silently, yet others while cursing their pain. If they stayed here any longer, not a soul would be alive by morning. Kanda shouted at Yamada, who was the hub of the human circle:

"Please, Sir! If we mark time like this, we'll end up losing most of the men. We'll have fewer casualties if we move on. Let's not wait for the morning, but leave right away. We know we're at Narusawa Hollow, so the Umatateba has to be to the north of us. We have only to go north and we're on our way back!"

Kanda was almost begging. But Yamada refused.

"What are you talking about? How can we find our way back in this darkness and this snow? No, wait till dawn. We'll leave as soon as it gets light. Have you forgotten last night? We got into this predicament because we left camp in the dark. Do you want us to make the same mistake twice?"

"But, Sir, the situation is completely different! Last night it was better to wait for morning, but tonight it is better to keep on going. Please, Sir, let's leave!" Kanda shouted, putting all he had into his appeal.

"Come, Kanda, keep your head," came the calm voice of Captain Kurata. "I know very well how you feel, but under the circumstances I believe we'd better do as the major says."

Kanda turned toward the speaker. He could not see his face, but he sensed the authority in that composed voice.

"It's highly unlikely we'd find our way back in the dark," Kurata continued. "We'd much more likely end up wandering about in this blizzard. Think of that. No, let's wait for dawn. By then the wind may have died down a bit, too."

Kurata had spoken so persuasively that Kanda felt his resistance melt away.

Kurata's right, he thought. What came over me? The cold and the fatigue must have gone to my head.

Kanda did not raise the subject again. Listening to the voices and the sounds of men rushing to their deaths in the darkness of the night, he recalled the letter Tokushima had sent him. If he remembered correctly, the men of the 31st would be coming this way from Tashiro tomorrow or the day after, and if it was tomorrow. . . . He remembered how Tokushima had told him that it was impossible to cross the mountain without guides. So maybe Tokushima would come guided by some local people who could find their way in the snow. What would he think if he found the pitiful remnant of Kanda's company? Still, Kanda wished he'd come as soon as possible. If he did, they might yet be saved.

It became a little brighter. The wind calmed somewhat, but the cold showed no signs of abating. Kanda looked at his watch. It was 3:00 AM. The brightness was only snowlight, but it was a sign that the sky had cleared.

Yamada gave orders to break up camp. It was just before dawn, and in this brightness he judged the company could make some progress.

Kanda held roll call. In one night, thirty men had died, making a total of seventy dead—one-third of the company. The remaining two-thirds were in extremely bad shape.

When he went to check his map and compass before departure, Kanda found that two of his three lanterns had disappeared. The last one was bound to Corporal Etō's backpack. Kanda ordered someone to light a candle, but everybody's hands were frozen. No one had enough strength left even to strike a match, except for Kurata, who wore knitted woolen gloves. With his help they finally managed to light the lantern.

Kanda and Kurata consulted the map and came to the conclusion that, if they wanted to find the road to the Umatateba, they should move due north.

8

The voice with which Yamada ordered the men out had lost its usual vigor. The first night Yamada had spent near the comparative warmth of the cooking fire, but this second night the cold had sapped his strength. He left the command to Kanda and Kurata and followed the ranks, supported by his subordinates. When the column set itself in motion, one or two more men collapsed. No one tried to help them up. The company moved forward in deadly silence.

About one hour later they found themselves on the edge of a cliff and were forced to turn back to their campsite and try the opposite direction.

There was no doubt they were at Narusawa. The road they had come the evening of the twenty-third had to be somewhere around here. And in fact, there were a number of clues, even in the deep snow, that might have helped them find it. At one point between the Umatateba and Narusawa, the road ran through forest, and there the gap between the trees clearly indicated its course. Where the road swung around the Narusawa gorge, it was cut out of the

mountainside, and its location was betrayed by the steplike formation of the snow. One more landmark could have been provided by
the sleds and unnecessary luggage they had abandoned the first
night. But they did not discover these signs until dawn, when it
was bright enough to see. By snowlight it was impossible.

Next their path was blocked by a mountain. Again they had no
choice but to return to their campsite.

"Heaven has abandoned us!" Kanda broke out in despair as he
struggled through the snow. "We're all going to die! Why don't we
just go back and lie down in the snow next to our comrades who
went before us!"

The storm had calmed down and, in the quiet among the trees,
his words were audible to all. They felt as if a huge fist had struck
them in the chest.

Zenjirō Hasebe had heard him too. Hasebe revered Kanda with
an awe that bordered on the idolatrous. To him, Kanda was an
almost superhuman hero: a commoner who had not graduated
from the Military Academy and yet reached the rank of captain. If
one had asked Hasebe for his opinion, he would have said that it
was not Kanda's fault that the company was now in these desperate straits, but Yamada's, for having whittled Kanda's command
away from him. Still, he had felt that as long as he stayed near
Kanda he would survive, even if all the others died. Every time
Hasebe had dozed off and fallen down that night, Kanda had woken
him up and kept him alive till the morning. But now this same
Kanda was saying that they might as well give up and die. It was a
terrible shock to Hasebe. That one outburst of his captain de-
stroyed his hope to live.

A mist closed before his eyes. The snowy plain disappeared, and
Kichinosuke's face floated up in its stead. Kichinosuke was crying,
crying as if his heart would break. I was right, Hasebe thought.
Kichinosuke would cry if I died. Funny he should cry, though. I
don't feel dying is at all terrible.

Hasebe fell down in the snow, and as he did so, his rifle was
thrown from his backpack. An NCO who was walking near him
kicked him about the shoulders with his straw galoshes and yelled
at him to get up, but Hasebe did not stir. Instinctively, automat-
ically, the NCO picked up the rifle, for every day of his military life
it had been hammered into him that a soldier's rifle is more
important than a soldier's life. Once he had it in his hands,
however, he realized how heavy it was. His own rifle was almost
more than he could carry; he wasn't going to be bothered with

118

someone' else's. He turned the rifle upside down and stuck it in the snow, by Hasebe's head.

After Kanda's outburst, Hasebe had been the first to fall, but his example was followed left and right by others, all of them soldiers who had trusted their officers absolutely and obeyed them in everything. For a moment it looked as if Kanda's lament might be the death of the whole company.

Captain Kurata averted this danger.

"I found the way!" he shouted. "I looked at the high ground near our bivouac and now I know exactly where it was we camped. If we turn back that way and get to the Umatateba quickly, we can reach barracks today. Look, the weather's getting better too!"

Kurata's voice rang loud and clear. To the officers and lower ranks, so confused that they no longer knew whether they were alive or dead, it seemed no less than miraculous that Kurata still had so much energy. His words shook the lower ranks out of their lethal despondency, at least for a while.

The second time the company returned to its campsite, it was 5:00 AM. During the two hours they had wandered since moving out, some thirty men had died, bringing the total number of dead to half the company.

During those two hours, Yamada had lost consciousness. Kurata, now senior officer, collected the backpacks of the dead soldiers and with them lit a fire to warm the major. The provisions in the packs were pooled and divided among those who had run out of food. The backpacks burned fiercely, as if fueled by the bitter spirits of their dead owners. Hoping Yamada would come to, the men stood around the fire to shelter it from the wind. The burning backpacks not only revived Yamada to the point where he could stammer a few words, but also gave new strength to the officers, who were standing close to the fire. But the enlisted men, who were too lowly to be near the flames, did not receive any of their warmth.

Some of the men ate rice cakes they toasted over the fire, but others would not touch the cakes, even when offered some. Despite their empty stomachs, everybody had lost his appetite. Instead, they suffered from an unslakeable thirst. When the melting snow began to form puddles near the fire, some of the men went down on all fours and lapped up the water like dogs.

The fire died soon. The only things left to burn would have been the greatcoats of the dead, but it seemed too cruel to strip the bodies of these. No one even tried.

119

The day began to dawn. The storm had abated and visibility had improved, but the cold grew ever more intense. Yamada lost consciousness again. Kanda had lent him his pocket heater, but had forgotten to give him hot ashes to fill it, an indication of how Kanda's mental faculties had weakened.

"I need volunteers to find the way to Tamogino," shouted Kurata. He had realized that there was no sense in wandering about and that the best course of action was to send out a reconnaissance team.

Twelve NCOs stepped forward. All of them suffered frozen hands and feet to the same degree, yet they snapped to attention before Kurata as smartly as if they had just left the barracks gate.

Kurata divided them into two groups: one, under Corporal Watanabe, was to explore the direction of the Komagome River; the other, under Corporal Takahashi, was to reconnoiter the high ground to the northwest.

"If you find the way, one man will immediately report back to the main body, and the rest of you will continue to reconnoiter toward Tamogino," he instructed. "We will wait here until we hear from you."

As it grew lighter, the snowfall decreased and it became possible to examine their surroundings. The view from the thin forest at Narusawa was bleak indeed: an undulating plain of snow, with beeches stretching their bare branches to the sky, and here and there a fir tree, its top bent down with snow. From the way the plain ahead seemed suddenly to stop in midair, they could tell they were near the edge of a steep cliff. To the north, row after row of mountains had become visible. Among them had to be the Umatateba.

Kanda and Kurata were studying the map, when suddenly a soldier shouted:

"A rescue team!"

The men looked in the direction he was pointing, and to many of them it did seem as if they saw a group of soldiers, in double file, marching down the hill toward them.

"A rescue team! A rescue team!"

Now they were all shouting.

"Oh, I can see Mother again!" a soldier exclaimed.

His cry was immediately taken over by others. All these soldiers, from different prefectures of northeast Japan, were calling for their mothers in their native dialects, some of them with tears streaming down their faces. Mother was all they had left now. If

Mother were here, she would know what to do. To survive meant to see Mother again.

But Kurata did not see any rescue team, nor did Kanda. They looked at each other before they returned their gaze to where the men were pointing. The branches of the trees stirred in the wind. Kanda realized that, by fixing his eyes on the snow that drifted sideways, he could trick himself into believing that the trees themselves were on the move. By some fluke, the trees on the slope facing them grew in double rows, and this had led the men to believe that they were seeing a rescue team of approximately platoon strength.

Kurata felt the blood freeze in his body. For a moment he was afraid that the one half of the company that was still alive had collectively taken leave of its senses. At the Military Academy he had heard about a whole platoon suffering from mass hallucinations brought on by exhaustion. That platoon had opened fire on an imaginary enemy. Now his men were hallucinating too.

"Blow a signal!" he shouted, in an attempt to call the men back to reality. He hoped that the stirring sound of the bugle would break the spell.

The bugler put his instrument to his lips, but he was unable to produce any sound except a few eerie low notes that seemed like groans rising up from the bottom of hell. At these ominous tones the men realized that they were seeing no more than a winter landscape. With sighs of despair, babbling incoherently, one soldier after another sank down in the snow.

One corporal went up to Kanda.

"Captain, I think the best way to get back is to build a raft and float it down the Komagome. I'll go and cut some wood right away." He had got this idea because the Komagome River flowed past the Aomori barracks.

"Don't be silly!" Kanda told him. "The Komagome is much too shallow and has lots of rocks and waterfalls. A raft would be dashed to pieces. Wake up, man!"

The corporal did not seem to have understood, for he turned and ran off into the snow and lunged at the beeches with his bayonet. But a bayonet is not an axe; he did not cut so much as a single branch. As if flung back by the trees, the corporal sank down in the snow. He did not get up.

Some men announced that they would go look for the way and plunged into the snow; others issued orders for the kitchen squad to assemble. There were soldiers who suddenly struck out at their comrades near them. Several demented men died in rapid succession.

At 11:30 AM, Corporal Takahashi came back, alone.

"I've come to report that we found the road, Sir. The other five crossed the Umatateba and are on their way toward Tamogino."

Takahashi seemed in full possession of his senses. His information was accurate, too. Kanda and Kurata were overjoyed at the news that, near the top of the Umatateba, the road was still distinguishable, be it ever so slightly.

"We found the way! Fall in!"

At the sound of Kurata's voice, even soldiers who had collapsed earlier got back to their feet.

Kurata noticed that over half the men were too weak to carry a rifle. Marching through the snow fully armed had been extremely hard on the men, but because they had been told so often that a soldier's rifle is his soul, many had refused to abandon their rifles, even in death. Kurata ordered the remaining soldiers to stack arms. Of the roughly seventy men who were still alive, half complied; the other half continued to carry their rifles.

Guided by Takahashi, the company extricated itself from the labyrinth of Narusawa and emerged on the road to the Umatateba.

Now that they were on the way back, the men had calmed down considerably. The steep climb up the Umatateba was very difficult, but there was comparatively little wind and visibility was good. By encouraging each other with shouts that they were not going to die now that they were on the right road, they made it to the top. There they discovered a coil of rope that had been discarded during their ascent two days earlier.

It was 3:00 PM at last. The men had found their way, but already night was approaching. The wind, which appeared to have died away, picked up again. Major Yamada fainted a third time. They divided into two groups: one carried Yamada, and the other, led by Kanda and Kurata, tried to find the way. In this way, the company slowly made its way northward.

The attention they had to lavish on the unconscious Yamada was becoming a danger to the men. Two soldiers might put their arms under his shoulders, but after 300 feet through the deep snow they would fall down—and Yamada with them. Yamada would be picked up right away and given to some other soldiers to carry, but the fallen men remained lying where they were. To save one major, one soldier after another sacrificed his life. Yet no one found this at all ironic. Everyone was convinced that Yamada's death would spell the doom of the entire Hakkōda Company. Yamada had to live, whatever the cost in lives.

They passed the slope of the Nakanomori and entered the Kayaidosawa Valley. Here they could go no farther. Their third night was awaiting them.

Fifty survivors placed themselves around Yamada. They had no fire and no wood, nor did they have the energy to collect the backpacks of dead soldiers to make a fire. Thirst plagued them more than hunger. They ate snow, though they knew they should not.

All of them were in a daze. That night twenty men died, but this time without ranting or raving. When their strength gave out, they simply slumped down at the feet of their comrades and embarked on their last journey as if they were falling asleep. The soldiers who formed the outer wall of the human circle that shielded Yamada went first. This night, too, the men died in the order of their ranks. No one warned the others against the dangers of falling asleep, and no one tried to huddle close to his neighbors to defend himself against the cold. They were mentally and physically exhausted. All they could do was wait for death.

9

The morning of the twenty-sixth it snowed furiously. When the time came to leave, the soldiers who had died during the night lay buried under snow. The best that could be said of this day was that there was comparatively little wind.

The thirty survivors were covered from head to foot with ice. These ice wraiths in human shape swam through the snow, most of them only one stroke ahead of death. None but a few, such as Kurata and Kanda, were still able to think rationally.

There was no order to leave, no roll call. When Kurata and Kanda split up to find the way—the one going right, the other left—the others simply followed, without knowing what they were doing.

From the moment Yamada had lost consciousness, Kurata had acted in the awareness that he, as senior officer, had to assume the responsibilities of the battalion commander. As for Kanda, he had never lost sight of the fact that he was the one who had drawn up the plans for the exercise and who was in command of the company.

The snow was falling when Kurata and Kanda parted ways. When they met again, after wandering about for several hours, it was still falling. Neither Kanda nor Kurata had any confidence left in his ability to lead the men out.

Because of the heavy snowfall, visibility was so bad that they could not even establish their present position, for after Kanda had given his pocket heater to Yamada, his compass had frozen and was completely useless.

About 9:00 AM it stopped snowing, and the darkness suddenly gave way to broad daylight. Aomori Bay became visible through a gap in the clouds. Kurata and Kanda got out the map and were able to ascertain that they were at a point north of the low mountain Yasunokimori. Their relief at the knowledge that they were still on the right road was plainly visible on their faces. Now that the weather had improved and they knew where they were, it seemed possible to reach Tamogino if they kept up their present pace.

Two hours later these hopes were dashed. The sky darkened, and a true blizzard descended on them—extremely heavy snow combined with a northwester gale that blew straight into their faces. The men froze in their tracks. They were lost again. Kurata and Kanda had to resume their position at the head of the line, for when the two captains moved, the men would follow.

With their route hidden from sight by the blizzard, a growing number of men collapsed in despair. As before, the fall of one man would prompt others to follow his example. They toppled over like a row of dominoes. After falling down, those who were still alive would pick themselves up and walk on. They had no idea whether it was Kurata or Kanda who was leading the way. They merely followed, it did not matter whom.

Kurata led his group downhill, toward the gorge of the Komagome River. Virtually dragged through the snow by a number of soldiers, Yamada followed at the rear. In the gorge the snow lay deep, but there was very little wind. They followed the Komagome downstream until the gorge narrowed and sheer cliffs on either side made further progress impossible.

Kanda was progressing with confidence. He had verified his direction when the sky was clear, and he was convinced that if he continued on his present course he would not fail to reach Ōtōge, and so Tamogino. He imagined that at present he was somewhere near the Sainokawara Plain. His group had dwindled to just a few hangers-on. Corporal Etō followed him like a shadow.

Night fell, but the dusk seemed like the dawn to Kanda. In the darkness he saw the lanterns and heard the shouts and laughter of a rescue team. Hallucinations all. He no longer knew whether he was walking or standing still. The blustering of the storm sounded like the breaking of huge waves. Kanda was walking along a sandy beach by a dark sea and wondered why he had so much trouble moving over such a surface. White shells, washed ashore by the waves, lay piled on the beach like heaps of snow. On closer inspection, these white heaps also contained red, green, even pink shells. He reached out to pick up such a pink one, when all at once it grew in size and exploded into flames.

Fire! Fire!—someone shouted.

People were shouting, running up and down the street. Red flames ascended from a red-brick chimney. When the red flames turned into black smoke, he heard the voice of General Tomoda:

The Hakkōda Exercise is especially important because we assume there will be war with Russia.

But that war has already blazed up around us—came the voice of Colonel Nakabayashi.—Look at that fire!

Something will have to be done about that fire—said Colonel Tsumura of the 5th.

And Colonel Kojima of the 31st Regiment said—I wonder if the 5th can put it out!

"I can, and I will. Please leave the fire to me!" Kanda shouted. The sound of his own voice brought him back to reality.

He shook his head hard. As he did so, he heard something rattle inside it. The rattling grew louder and turned into the tramping of many boots. Amazed, he opened his eyes and saw Tokushima's platoon come marching toward him in double file, each man carrying a lamp. It looked for all the world like a lantern procession.

It's all right—Tokushima told him.—All your men are safe. You can stop worrying.

And Tokushima clapped him on the shoulder.

All are safe! Thank you! Thank you, from the bottom of my heart.

He bowed to Tokushima. But when he lowered his head, everything disappeared except for the darkness and the roaring of the storm.

Kanda had slumped to the ground. He tried to get up. He had to get up. If he didn't report the danger they were in, the whole company would perish. But he could not get back to his feet.

"Etō! Etō, where are you?" Kanda shouted into the darkness. Etō's answer came from right behind him. The corporal seemed to have fallen asleep on his feet.

"Etō, you go ahead to Tamogino as fast as you can, get some people, and come back here to help us," Kanda ordered him loudly.

But Etō had not quite taken in this sudden order and asked Kanda to repeat it.

"I can't move any more, Etō, so you go to Tamogino and get some people."

Kanda's voice was much softer now than a moment before.

"Captain, don't give up, please! It's almost morning. When it gets light, they'll certainly come looking for us. Don't give up!" Etō tried to help Kanda to his feet, but Kanda could no longer stand up.

"Etō, if you don't go ahead, the whole company will die. Quick now. Go to Tamogino and get help. Quick!"

Kanda must have lost consciousness then, for he kept repeating the same words, over and over again. Sometimes, when his voice had faded to an almost inaudible whisper, the urgency of his orders seemed to recur to him and he would start again.

"Yes, Sir, I understand. I'm to go to Tamogino and get help," Etō repeated the order.

"Good, Etō. Go now."

And Etō went, Kanda's voice still in his ears. In the dark, he could not see where he was going. He made his way downhill on sheer guts.

After he had sent Etō away, Kanda slept for a while. Some monster was running around inside his head. He awoke in the cold just before dawn. It was getting brighter, though it was still snowing. He had lost all feeling in his lower limbs—they were frozen. He could not feel his hands anymore either, but his head was strangely clear. He knew perfectly in what situation he found himself. The reasons why the exercise turned into such a disaster were neatly arranged inside his brain: they had not hired guides at Tamogino, they had given in to the NCOs at Kotōge, they had broken up their first bivouac too early, and they should never have listened to Warrant Officer Shindō. It was all perfectly clear.

But I, Kanda, was the one who made the plans. They were full of oversights. I underestimated the severity of the climate. I procured the wrong sort of equipment. My preparatory studies were totally insufficient.

"The whole responsibility is mine," he tried to whisper, but the words did not come out.

Maybe Etō will reach Tamogino. Then the rescue team will come. But they won't find the others. The others are dead. All they'll find is me.

He thought of Yamada.

If he'd only left everything to me. If he hadn't taken my command away from me. These things might not have happened then. But it's too late to complain. I was the one who made the plans. I was the officer in charge. I had to make the decisions if something happened. If I survive, I won't be able to shirk that responsibility. Of course I can forget about further promotions. I might even be dismissed from the army. And if I can no longer be a soldier, after giving my whole life to the service, what is left for me?

He had lost all desire to live. Death was all that was left to him. But he had lost the use of his hands and feet. There was only one way to find death: by biting off his tongue.

Captain Kanda bit down, but his jaws lacked the necessary strength. He could not bite through. Slowly, the blood welled up inside his mouth.

10

At 6:00 AM on the twenty-seventh of January, a rescue team of over sixty men, commanded by Second Lieutenant Mikami and accompanied by several guides, left Tamogino to find out what had happened to the Hakkōda Company. From Tamogino on, they were hindered by deep snow, and between Kotōge and Ōtōge there blew such a terrible snowstorm that even the guides hesitated about going on. With Mikami cursing them and cajoling them in turn, they finally reached the Ōtaki Moor about 10:00 AM.

Suddenly the guides, who were walking up front, stopped and pointed ahead. Something was standing in the snow. Something that looked like a common wayside statue of the guardian saint of children. Except it was too tall. A real statue would have been invisible, covered by the snow.

DEATH MARCH ON MOUNT HAKKŌDA

They pressed ahead, and Mikami strained to identify the mysterious still object.

It was a soldier, buried to his chest in the snow.

Mikami drew nearer, making his way with a kind of overarm stroke. The soldier's hood was frozen solid. The face inside it was frozen too. The eyes were wide open, but they were not the eyes of a living person.

Captain Murakawa, the medical officer, came running up and gave orders to dig the soldier out. Holding up blankets, the men formed a tent to shelter him from the wind. Others stamped down the snow until it was hard enough and deposited the frozen soldier on a bed of blankets.

"Oh, no! It's Etō!" shouted one NCO.

"We may be able to save him," Murakawa said as he arranged Etō on the blankets. He had noticed that rigor mortis had not yet set in.

Etō's clothes were frozen through, but when Murakawa peeled off his tunic and trousers and wrapped him in dry blankets, he found that Etō's body was still warm. When Etō was properly bundled up, Murakawa and three orderlies began to massage him, the sixty men of the rescue team standing around them like a human windbreak. Gradually the color returned to Etō's face, little by little his vital signs became stronger. Ten minutes after Murakawa began his administrations, Etō showed a faint reaction when someone shouted his name in his ear. Then he moved his eyes. His mouth moved. He was trying to say something, but he could not get the words out. Lieutenant Mikami put his ear to Etō's mouth in an attempt to catch what he was saying.

". . . Captain . . . Kanda . . . "

All Mikami heard were fragments of sentences.

"Captain Kanda is somewhere around here. Quick! See if you can find him!" he ordered his men. Then he shouted into Etō's ear, "Where are Major Yamada and the rest of the company?"

"All . . . dead . . . " was the answer.

When Etō had recovered and realized that he was the only one with the rescue team, he had not unnaturally assumed that the whole company had perished.

128

"They're all dead? Are you certain? Are there no other survivors?"

"Maybe one . . . or two."

Etō closed his eyes. Attempts were made to revive him, but his life hovered on the brink.

Mikami ordered his team to search the vicinity and told Sergeant Major Hiromura to run back to Regiment with the news about Etō and the company.

About one hour later they found Kanda, buried in the snow not far away. When they moved him, blood flowed from his mouth. His body was still warm, so Murakawa and his orderlies tried giving first aid, but they could not bring him back to life.

Next, they found Corporal Oshikawa, but his body was frozen hard and no attempts to revive him were made.

For two hours Mikami scoured the area, but then he decided that it was impossible to continue the search under such conditions. In the snowstorm and the cold, one member of his team had collapsed and half of his men suffered from frostbite in their hands. The rescue team returned to Tamogino, its members taking turns carrying Etō on their backs.

Ordered to report the tragic news to Regiment as soon as possible, Sergeant Major Hiromura ran as fast as conditions allowed. In Tamogino he found a support team under Lieutenant Furukawa, which had just arrived there. When Furukawa heard Hiromura's report, he ordered Corporal Hanada to take over from Hiromura, who was exhausted from his run through the snow.

Hanada, too, ran as fast as he could. When he arrived at the Aomori Headquarters, he had almost no breath left in his body.

"They found Corporal Etō on Ōtaki Moor," he was able to pant out. "He was almost dead, and when they revived him he said the whole company had died. The rescue team is still searching the area."

This, the first news of the disaster, reached Regimental Headquarters at 2:30 PM.

The barracks of the 5th was in an uproar. Thirty minutes later, 150 men, under Captain Shioda, marched through the gate to help in the search. It made little sense to send out all these men, but Colonel Tsumura had to do something.

Next it was reported that Kanda's body had been found.

After dark, Lieutenant Mikami visited Tsumura at his official residence, where all officers from the rank of company commander upward had assembled. Mikami looked deadly pale. He had not eaten anything since that morning, and he suffered from a slight case of frostbite in his fingers.

"I'm sorry, Sir, but unless this search is organized very, very methodically, we will only lose more men," was the first thing Mikami told Tsumura.

129

And step by step he broke it to them how appalling the conditions were on that snow-swept upland. He told them how they had found Etō and Kanda. He told them how, after two hours of searching, over half of his sixty men had lost the use of their hands, and how one man had collapsed in the snow.

The faces of the officers grew hard.

By this time, the 4th Brigade had passed the news of the disaster down to the 31st Regiment. Colonel Kojima wired Sanpongi, ordering Tokushima to call off the exercise and return to barracks. But in the early morning of that day, the Tokushima Platoon had left Masuzawa for the haunted slopes of Mount Hakkōda.

PART FOUR

FOUND

I

THE MORNING OF JANUARY 27, the Tokushima Platoon got up at
2:00 AM and left Masuzawa soon afterward.

Seven guides from Kumanosawa led the way. They were dressed
in snug warm trousers, tight-sleeved jackets with cotton padding,
fur jerkins, and, over it all, long straw coats with pointed hoods. On
their feet they wore straw boots, and around their calves they had
wrapped rags to serve as leggings.

These guides were not volunteers. They had agreed to go along
at the special request of their village headman, but when they
noticed on leaving Masuzawa that they were in for bad weather,
they whispered to each other that they would never get through to
Tashiro. For in winter the Tashiro Moor is one vast snowfield
where in a blizzard visibility can be so bad that all progress is
impossible. The guides knew this very well, and what they were
really telling each other with their whispers was that they should
wait for a good opportunity to convince Tokushima to turn back.

The platoon moved in a northwesterly direction through the
valley of the Kumanosawa River, over a road covered with snow.
Past Dorobuchi, just over a mile outside Masuzawa, it began to get
light. They were walking on the bottom of a ravine, with steep
mountains rising up close on either side. The snow now became
rapidly deeper.

The leading guide was relieved regularly, though it really made
little difference to the others. No matter who broke the trail, the
snow was still deep and the going hard. Tokushima followed right
behind the guides, at the head of his men. From time to time the
guides stopped to listen to the ever-louder blustering of the storm
and to observe the sky, from which the black of night seemed to
have repelled the light of dawn. Some would use that chance to
steal a furtive glance over their shoulders; others turned all the way
around to stare into Tokushima's face.

They saw a face that gave nothing away, except one obstinate idea: Let it snow as hard as it likes, I'm going on.

They struggled up the slopes of the gloomy Kitamasuzawa Valley, but once at the top they found the weather even worse. The snow reached to their waists, at places even to their chests. At the midway point, six miles out of Masuzawa, they stopped without sitting down to eat their midday rations, but they found that their rice balls had frozen into lumps of ice.

Tomekichi Sawada, the oldest of the guides, said to Tokushima: "I'm sorry, Captain, but I'm afraid that in this storm it's impossible to reach Tashiro. We'd better head back now and try again when the weather's better."

At this, Tokushima flew into a rage.

"How do you know it's impossible until you've actually tried it?" he shouted. "What sort of guides are you, to let yourselves be frightened by a little bit of snow?"

The guides were struck dumb. When they left Masuzawa, they had seen Tokushima chatting amiably with the village headman, like the sort of officer who is strict to his men but kind to civilians. But now this same captain was heaping abuse on them! Sawada decided he had better let the matter drop, although he really felt like telling Tokushima that they were the guides and he, Tokushima, the one being guided, and if he didn't like their work, he knew what he could do with it. But he kept his mouth shut. "How do you know it's impossible until you've tried it?" That, Sawada supposed, was logic of sorts.

But in this storm . . . Sawada looked up at the sky.

"Stop dawdling there! Get a move on!" Tokushima shouted again.

Sawada got a move on. A pretty mess they had landed in! This captain and his band of soldiers would be the death of them yet. He cudgeled his brains to find a way to make Tokushima see they simply had to turn back, but everything returned to the unanswerable question of how you knew something was impossible until you tried it.

They continued. The storm got worse, visibility became terrible, and more than once they lost their way. On such occasions, the seven would stick their heads together and argue which direction was best.

From the guides' deliberations, Tokushima had understood that, of the seven, Torasuke Ōhara knew this area the best.

"All right, you lead," he told him. "Keep your eyes peeled, and look sharp! Seven big men, and they can't find their way about! What's wrong with you?" he demanded angrily.

Ōhara turned and glared at him, but spoke not a word as he went and took his place at the head of the column.

It was terribly cold. The water in the canteens had frozen a long time before. The guides and the soldiers ate snow while they walked. When they reached the Ōnaka Moor, the blizzard became yet worse.

"Watch out for frozen fingers!"

When Tokushima shouted out an order, it was passed down the double file in which the platoon was marching. Soon after leaving Dorobuchi, the lower ranks had taken their rifles off their shoulders and slung them across their backs. They were now able to rub their hands as they walked. Since leaving Hirosaki, they had learned very well how to protect themselves against frozen limbs. The cold bit their fingers, but their feet were not so bad. Experience had taught them that two pairs of socks, sprinkled with red pepper and wrapped in a double layer of oiled paper, worn inside straw boots, were an excellent precaution against frostbite in their toes. The snowstorm did not frighten them either, for they remembered the blizzard that had attacked them when they were crossing Inubō Pass.

Compared to Sawa, who had walked at their head as briskly and effortlessly as if the snow did not bother her at all, these seven guides had for some reason seemed dispirited all along. Those who doubted their guides' enthusiasm soon found their suspicions confirmed.

Almost at the exact center of the Ōnaka Moor, the seven lost their way, and then the men began to realize exactly how difficult this route was. They could not see 30 feet ahead. Not a tree grew on this snow plain, except for an occasional beech that appeared to have found its way there by mistake.

"A thousand apologies, Captain, but we can't go a step farther," said Ōhara, who had walked up front all the time. "I'm afraid we're unable to guide you beyond this point."

"Nonsense! You promised to take us to Tamogino, didn't you? Do you want to go back on your word now? You're afraid of a bit of snow, that's why you can't see the road ahead! You're not really trying. How about setting your mind to it? That might work!"

"When we left Masuzawa, the headman told us to take you as far as we could and to turn back when we thought it was impossible to go any farther," Ōhara sputtered. "He did not tell us we absolutely had to guide you all over the place!"

Some of the words did not come out very clearly, for Ōhara was shivering with cold.

"Are you saying that you decline the honor to function as guide to this Special Platoon of the Hirosaki 31st Infantry? That is a treasonous act against the Imperial Japanese Army, my friend. Did you know that?"

Tokushima too found it difficult to speak in the cold, but he was also so angry that he seemed almost to choke on his words.

Faced with the threat of treason, beset both by the cold and by the Imperial Japanese Army, Ōhara began to tremble like a leaf.

"Please, Captain, don't mind Torasuke. He doesn't know what he's talking about. I'll take the lead from here on," said Yoshihei Sawanaka, taking a step forward.

"Good, that sounds a little better. Look alive now, and remember that in the long run it's better to confront a problem squarely than to avoid it. And I might as well give it to you straight: you'd better get used to the idea that you will stay with us until it's all over. Together we'll brave this weather and reach the Aomori Plain, or together we'll find our graves in the snow."

After these words, the guides had no choice but to forget about turning back. Now it was a matter of reaching Tashiro before dark, if they wanted to save their lives.

But already the day was drawing to a close. Because of the storm, it had never really become broad daylight. Now, about three in the afternoon, it was rapidly growing dark.

Relying almost entirely on his intuition, Sawanaka led them from the Ōnaka Moor to the Tashiro Moor, which they knew they had reached when the landscape leveled off. But the Tashiro Moor was even larger than the Ōnaka Moor. To find the way to the hot springs in this vastness was an almost hopeless undertaking. Constantly hailing each other in the storm, the seven guides searched the snow for landmarks. It became a race against the night. They had to find the way, or die.

Then someone shouted:

"Here! I found Good Fortune Rock!"

When the platoon moved in the direction of the voice, they saw a huge boulder shaped like a trapezoid. It was covered with snow,

136

but because it was an important landmark, the local people recognized it easily.

"Captain, now that we've found this rock, we know where we are, but I don't think we can get to Tashiro before it becomes completely dark," said Sawanaka. "The best thing would be to dig a hole in the snow and spend the night in it. But I know there's a shed nearby on Narita's old pasture. While your men dig a shelter, we'll go see if we can find it."

Tokushima agreed this was a good idea, but instead of allowing all seven guides to go, he told four of them to stay and sent six NCOs along in their place.

"There are two of you for every one of them. Don't let them out of your sight for even a second," he warned.

Tokushima took this measure because he believed only half of what Sawanaka had told him. After the guides found the rock they had started whispering among each other, without ever taking their eyes off Tokushima and his men, who were still some distance away. Tokushima had noticed this and suspected they might be planning an escape.

Using spades, the men dug a hole in the snow. The practice they had had in Nakasato now stood them in good stead. Their shelter was circular, with a diameter of 13 feet and a depth of 9 feet— enough for them to be out of the wind when they crouched on the bottom.

The guides who had gone out to look for the shed came back unsuccessful. In their fear of losing their way in the snowstorm, they had not dared to go too far.

The men had not eaten since they left Masuzawa that morning at two. Their clothes were wet and frozen, their bodies chilled through. At Tokushima's order, everybody, including the guides, crept into the hole, which was barely large enough to hold them all. Shouting rhythmically, they then began a kind of pushing contest for the warmest spots at the center. Anyone who dozed off during this game soon ended up on the outside, where the cold woke him up. The men did what they could to conquer a place in the center.

After midnight the storm died down, and the glitter of the snow took the edge off the darkness. Captain Tokushima prepared 137 lanterns and sent out four NCOs with Sawanaka and Kyūzō Ujiya, who seemed to know this region best, to find Narita's shed.

About 6:00 AM, Ujiya and two NCOs were back.

"We've found the shed!" they reported. "And there's fire-wood, too!"

When the men in the hole heard this news, their spirits rose. Guides and soldiers clambered out of the shelter and followed Ujiya through the freshly fallen snow. By the time it got so light they no longer needed their lanterns, they reached a tiny shed. The only part of it that stuck out above the snow was the roof.

A fire welcomed the platoon on its arrival. Around it stood the remains of an old fence, which had been dug out and split into kindling with the help of a hatchet that Sawanaka carried on his belt.

Tokushima now divided his men into two groups, one to wait its turn while the other had a chance to warm up and eat something inside. At last they were able to eat. Once the fire was burning well, they placed their frozen rice balls in the flames, where they were heated to the core. The men were also able to dry their wet clothes. The two meals they had brought with them from Masuzawa were more than enough to still their hunger, and the chance to warm themselves at a fire almost restored them to their original spirits.

Tokushima noticed how the guides toasted rice cakes and stuck them under their stomach bands. When he asked why they did this, he was told:

"To keep warm, of course. If you put hot cakes there, your belly won't get cold and your cakes won't freeze either. Nothing beats hot rice cakes if you have to go out in a snowstorm."

So Tokushima told his men to eat their rice balls now, but to toast their rice cakes, wrap them in a double layer of oiled paper, and put them under their stomach bands to save them for later. Those who had already eaten their cakes were told to scorch their rice balls until they were crusted black and to carry these under their uniforms.

The break lasted for only two hours, but the men had been able to eat a solid hot meal and to drink some warm water from their canteens, so they felt quite recovered.

The storm gradually abated, as if it recognized its defeat.

2

It was 9:00 AM, the twenty-eighth of January, when Tokushima ordered the men out again.

"No matter what happens, we must reach Tamogino today, and because we will pass right through the center of the Hakkōda

Range, I want every man to inspect his clothes and equipment one more time," Tokushima told the platoon before departure. He paused briefly before he added, "And on the march today, let me know the moment you see anything unusual."

"Anything unusual." They all knew what he was thinking. The men of the 5th had been expected in Masuzawa on the twenty-fourth but had not yet arrived by the twenty-sixth, and since it was certain that they had left Aomori the twenty-third, this delay could only mean that something had happened to them.

Tokushima had hardly given this order when he recalled how nervous Kanda had looked. Kanda, who had humbled himself by mentioning that he had not graduated from the Military Academy, but had come up from the Training Corps. Tokushima hoped that this inferiority complex hadn't got Kanda into trouble. In a military world in which almost all officers were of samurai origin, Kanda's exaggerated awareness of his commoner's roots might affect his performance. Even if Kanda himself had not been so sensitive about his record, there was always the danger that his fellow officers and superiors might judge his performance with eyes prejudiced by their own feelings of superiority. Tokushima had heard that Kanda didn't get along too well with his immediate superior, Major Yamada, and, according to Major Monma's telephone message, both Yamada and Kanda were taking part in the exercise. This worried Tokushima. According to Monma, Yamada had enormous confidence in his own judgment, and if, for example, he should decide not to use guides, there was little Kanda would be able to do about it.

"Guides! That's right, it had almost slipped my mind. We have to decide who will lead the way. From here we were planning to go to Tamogino via Narusawa, the Umatateba, the Nakanomori, the Yasunokimori, Ōtōge, and Kotōge. Who knows that road best?"

The guides turned their eyes to Tetsutarō Fukuzawa, who was standing at the back of their group, eyes to the ground. He was the youngest of the seven.

"That would be Tetsu," said Tomekichi Sawada. "His aunt is married to someone in Kōhata, the village next to Tamogino, and Tetsu has walked that way more than once in summer."

"But never in winter?"

"Why should he? We've got trains now, don't we?"

Sawada's repartee so amused the guides that they burst into laughter, which shows how much their spirits had revived. But their laughter seemed to rub Tokushima the wrong way.

"I'll thank you not to make any more stupid jokes. Just answer the questions you're asked," he flared up. Then he turned to Fukuzawa.

"Mind you do a proper job!"

His eyes frightened the young guide.

As soon as they left Tashiro, the weather turned bad. They were hindered in their progress by the same type of snowstorm that had delayed them the day before. Fukuzawa cursed his ill fortune from the moment he took his place up front. The route from Tashiro to the Umatateba led through a labyrinth near Narusawa and was so complicated that even in summer travelers ended up in the gorge if they were not careful. One may imagine how difficult this road was in winter. Now, in the storm, it was completely unrecognizable. The wind, too, was of little use to set a course by, for it was as treacherous and unreliable as the terrain over which it blew.

To find the way, Fukuzawa ran about as if his life depended on it. He asked the other guides to check the beeches for the light-green moss that grows on the shadow side, or the north side. But a sample of one tree was not enough. The guides had to check many trees, and only those that grew on a location typical of that terrain.

If they took the wrong road in this maze and ended up at the bottom of the gorge, they would lose precious time climbing back to the top. It began to seem very likely that the Narusawa Valley, which had already led the 5th astray, might now be the death of the 31st.

Tokushima followed Fukuzawa like a shadow, but he never interfered. When the guides lost their way, he would merely tell his men to wait in double file and leave it at that. The seven crawled through the snow, doing all that lay in their power to extricate themselves from this dark valley. When, at about two in the afternoon, it stopped snowing for a while and visibility improved, Fukuzawa discovered the road. Covered with snow, to be sure, but still recognizable as a cut through the forest.

They had just crossed a sparsely wooded hill and emerged on a fairly flat plain studded with clumps of beech trees, when Fukuzawa cried out. He had found a rifle stuck upside down in the snow.

"It's the 5th! The 5th got caught!" one of the men exclaimed.

Kichinosuke Saitō broke out of the ranks and ran forward, plowing through the snow to get closer to the rifle, beside which the tip of the hood of a greatcoat was visible. Removing the snow with his hands, like a dog scratches with its paws, Saitō dug out the body of a dead soldier.

140

"It's my brother! I knew it! I knew it was Zenjirō!" he exclaimed, apparently not surprised at all by this truly miraculous coincidence.

He took the body in his arms and lifted it out of the snow.

"Zenjirō! I'm sorry, Zenjirō! I came too late!" he sobbed while he clung to his brother's corpse, which was frozen as stiff as a plank. Zenjirō had died with his eyes open: their sockets had filled up with snow.

Nine feet away, Saikai the journalist discovered the snow-covered corpse of a bugler, his hands still holding on tightly to his rifle.

"Captain, will you give me permission to carry my brother's body away from here?" asked Saitō.

"Saitō, I know how you feel, but I'm afraid it's impossible. If you carried your brother, you yourself would collapse. And if you collapsed, someone would have to help you, and he'd collapse in his turn. There'd be no end to it. I really am sorry, but I see no way but to leave your brother's body here and come back for it later."

One could hear a pin drop. Even the storm seemed to be holding its breath.

Saitō burst into heartrending sobs.

"Then please let me at least take his rifle with me!"

Without waiting for Tokushima's answer, he picked up his brother's rifle. Tokushima's mouth moved, as if he were going to say something, but at that moment Probationary Officer Kuramochi reached out and took the rifle out of Saitō's hand.

"Here, let me take care of this. You already have a rifle, I don't. Two rifles are too much for one man to carry. But don't worry, your brother's rifle is in good hands."

Tokushima closed his mouth again. He looked as if he had wanted to object but had thought better of it.

"By joining all of you on this exercise, I have become a soldier, too," Saikai said as he bent down over the dead bugler. "I will carry this rifle."

But the corpse refused to release the weapon. One of the NCOs bent back the stiffened fingers and handed the rifle to the journalist.

The men were overcome with horror. They looked about, but everything was shrouded in snow, no other bodies were visible. They stared at their feet. Were they not trampling on dead bodies? If they waited much longer, hands might reach out at them from underneath the snow.

141

Tokushima gave the order to leave and added, in a ringing voice: "From now on there will be no talking in the ranks!"

The disaster that had befallen the Hakkōda Company was not to be discussed.

3

Deeply downcast, the platoon followed Fukuzawa through Narusawa. Not until he pointed out the Umatateba did the men finally believe they might actually reach Tamogino. The Umatateba towered up before them, its wind-polished ice cap glittering in the sun.

Since they were on the right road now, they stopped to take a group picture and have an overdue midday meal. The rice cakes they had placed under their stomach bands had completely cooled off but were not frozen. On splitting open the charred rice balls the men found the insides still warm. The water in the canteens was frozen, however, so they ate snow. It was a cold lunch.

"Well, with this our food has run out, so we simply have to get to Tamogino today," Tokushima said as they were about to leave.

Actually, they still had emergency rations: parched rice and ordinary rice, of each enough for two meals. Tokushima had been thinking of rice balls and rice cakes. About the 5th he said not so much as a word.

The ascent of the steep slope of the Umatateba took unexpectedly long. It was already past four in the afternoon by the time they reached the top, and it was snowing lightly.

On their way down to the Yasunokimori Plateau, they found sleds loaded with sacks of charcoal. The sleds stood pointing toward the Umatateba and had obviously been abandoned while the 5th was on its way to Tashiro.

By the time they reached the Yasunokimori, night had fallen. They had had mild snow flurries all the way, but there was comparatively little wind and the thin clouds in the upper atmosphere allowed enough snowlight for them to find the way.

Fukuzawa's pace began to slow. He was young and strong, but guiding the platoon through that terrible stretch between Tashiro and the Umatateba had exhausted his mind and body. They had finally got as far as the Yasunokimori, true, but Fukuzawa had no confidence in his ability to lead his charges to Tamogino in the dark. He thought he might have managed in daylight, but how were they going to cross that vast, desolate, rolling snowfield by night? A wave of despair washed over him.

He knew that if they turned to the northwest after leaving the Yasunokimori Plateau and followed the mountain ridge as they descended the gently undulating upland, they would come out at Ōtōge. But if they took the wrong road, they would end up in the gorge of the Komagome River. This was a terrifying prospect. Once in, they would never be able to get out again.

But he could not tell exactly where they should make that turn. The snow continued to fall in flurries, and the night turned pitch black—the clouds in the upper atmosphere had grown thicker. Fukuzawa stood still. He was no longer certain of his position. His sense of distance was confused too, for instead of keeping up a normal walking pace, as on a summer road, he had had to swim through snow.

When Fukuzawa stood still, the platoon halted too. The men understood very well how their guide could have lost his way. To hide their own apprehensions, they continued to stamp their feet.

Then someone uttered a cry:

"Look! Lost souls!"

Ahead of them they saw a slowly moving cluster of little flames, a chain of souls. They did not travel at a steady speed, but hesitantly, waveringly. The flames appeared to have arranged themselves into a procession that came toward the men, but it was impossible to tell how far away they were, or how near.

"Yes, they're souls! The souls of the 5th!" the men shouted to each other.

To those who believed this, it seemed as if the flames had suddenly materialized out of nothing and now came flying their way.

"It's my brother! Zenjirō's come back to guide us out of here!" cried Saitō, and he dashed off toward the flames.

"They're *not* souls!" thundered Tokushima. "Those are the lights of the train from Aomori to Hachinohe. If you look carefully you'll see they're far away. Those lights are the windows of a train!"

The souls disappeared. The train was lost from sight.

Quickly, Tokushima issued orders:

"Until I give you permission to do otherwise, everyone will remain standing in his present position, facing the direction of those lights. No one will move! Lieutenants Tanabe and Nakahata, light your lanterns and join me here."

Their lanterns were not special army models; they could be bought in any store. The ones the platoon used burned candles rather than kerosene. Lighting a lantern is very difficult with hands that are nearly frozen. When at long last both lanterns were lit, the men appeared to have calmed down a little.

Tokushima opened his map, shone the light on it, and told his lieutenants, "Since it's possible to see Aomori Bay from the Yasunokimori, it should also be possible to see the lights of a train running along the coast."

He handed one lantern to Fukuzawa.

"Here, Fukuzawa, turn the beam of this lantern in the direction where we saw those lights a minute ago. Good. Now your beam is pointing toward Aomori. Remember that well. If you follow a course a little to the left of your beam, you will reach Ōtōge."

To be on the safe side, however, Tokushima sent out some men to explore the lay of the land nearby. After they came back, he studied the map again, the reconnaissance team by his side. Only then did he take out his compass, which he had kept under his stomach band next to his pocket heater. Hastily he established which direction was north.

"Good, we are on the Yasunokimori Plateau, that much is certain. Fukuzawa, if you go this way, you'll soon reach Sainokawara and the Ōtaki Moor, and later Ōtōge and Kotōge."

Tokushima made a slight correction in the direction in which Fukuzawa was shining his lantern and told the men to line up on the beam, in front of Fukuzawa. Tanabe stood next to Fukuzawa to check the men's position and warned them not to deviate from the line of the beam. The men advanced a number of paces until they were ordered to a halt, after which it was Fukuzawa's turn to advance until he reached the last man in the line. This process was repeated a number of times, and great care was taken that the beam shone at all times in the right direction.

When it was clear that the men understood the routine and they were proceeding in good order, Tokushima remarked to Tanabe:

"If this had been the same kind of storm as we had last night, it would have been all over with us. Tonight may be cold, but at least the wind has died down. There's only one thing that worries me: we can't go very fast in this deep snow, so we might run out of candles."

"How much longer do you think our supply will last?"

"Oh, not more than a few hours."

"Then everything depends on how far we can get in that time."

Fukuzawa, who had heard this conversation, deemed it unlikely that they would reach the Ōtaki Moor in less than five hours if they kept walking at their present speed. And once there, how were they to continue?

Their progress slowed to a snail's pace. The previous day they had got up at two in the morning and they had been unable to sleep at all in their hole in the snow near Tashiro. The men were overcome with fatigue. Some looked as if they might doze off on their feet.

After they had passed Sainokawara, snow began to fall again. Following the light of the beam became difficult.

"Sorry, Fukuzawa, but I'm afraid you'll have to walk in front again," said Tokushima, "We can't possibly wait here until morning."

"It's not very far now to the Ōtaki Moor. I can do it," Fukuzawa answered. With him in the lead, the seven guides once more preceded the platoon.

They were groping their way through the dark. After two hours or so, the wind dropped and it became quiet. I wish it would also get a little lighter, Fukuzawa thought, but the clouds were as thick as ever and the darkness showed no signs of lifting.

Suddenly they heard a deep, mournful sound: "HWOOOOOO!" The echo lingered for quite a while.

"That's the siren of the ferry in the harbor of Aomori!" shouted Fukuzawa. He had heard that sound before, on approximately the same spot.

"We're on the right road, no mistake about it!"

He turned in the direction from which the sound of the siren had come. Soon it began to snow again. About an hour later, Fukuzawa thought he had stepped on something hard.

"That's funny! Seems like there are footprints here!" he said.

They lit their last candle: footprints were everywhere.

"Now why should there be so many footprints in a place like the Ōtaki Moor?" Fukuzawa wondered aloud. But Tokushima immediately guessed that the prints had something to do with the 5th Regiment.

By and by the prints converged until they formed a clear track. All the platoon had to do from here was simply to follow this path down the hill.

When they had walked for another hour, Fukuzawa announced, "We're at Ōtōge now. Just below us lies Kotōge, and beyond it, Tamogino."

Tokushima asked him if he was certain. On receiving an affirmative answer, he checked this information against the data provided by the team that had kept the log of their march. After verifying that they must indeed be at Ōtōge, Tokushima addressed his men:

"Our platoon has successfully completed the most difficult part of this march. Tamogino lies right before us. Now, it is very likely that in the village we will find a 5th Regiment rescue team for Kanda's company, but I strictly forbid anyone to discuss in any way the things we have seen. If there is any reporting to be done, I will do it. Everyone else will keep his mouth shut."

He turned toward the guides.

"By guiding us all the way from Masuzawa, you have been of extraordinary help to us, and we thank you from the bottom of our hearts. We will part from you here, but you must not mention to a soul that you know what happened to the men of the 5th Regiment. If you do, it's possible that you will be dragged back to Narusawa. And that's not all. If you say anything untoward, chances are you will spend the rest of your days in a dark hole. Under no circumstances must you reveal the things you have seen these past few days. If you value your lives, be silent—even to your closest relatives! And you had better not remind anyone that you accompanied us either. If anyone asks you questions, play dumb. I will now give each of you fifty sen for your services, but be careful: if you lose too much time in Tamogino, you may fall into the hands of the 5th Regiment. You'd best go on straight to Aomori Station and take a train home from there."

With these words, Tokushima handed each guide his wages.

The seven felt that, after risking their lives, fifty sen per person was much too little, but they kept silent. Speaking out did not seem advisable. Tokushima's threat about spending the rest of their lives in a dark hole had become a new source of fear. They were also afraid that the rescue team of the 5th might be waiting for them in Tamogino.

Fukuzawa dropped his coin in the snow. He wanted to look for it, but it was too dark to see, and if he had found it, he would have been too tired to pick it up. Of the seven, he had carried the heaviest responsibility, and now, the very moment he was released from it, Tokushima's words had given him another burden. He felt confused. His head swam, and all strength seemed to flee from his body. He sank down in the snow.

The platoon departed, the guides were left behind. Not one soldier spoke a word of farewell to the seven.

"Hey, Tetsu, come on!" shouted Yoshimatsu Nakamura. "Pull yourself together! You've got to guide *us* now. What are we to do if you leave us in the lurch?"

And Katsutarō Komura reminded him, "Tetsu, you got married just two months ago. Your bride is waiting for you! What's to become of her if you die in this place?"

But even the thought of the wife he loved did not raise Fukuzawa to his feet. Finally Nakamura and Komura put their arms under his shoulders and dragged more than carried him toward Tamogino.

It was snowing hard again.

"Soldiers! All they can think of is themselves! To them, we are no better than worms!" Tomekichi Sawada said bitterly in the direction the platoon had disappeared.

But the soldiers had been swallowed up by the darkness. Not even the sound of their footsteps was audible any longer.

4

The Tokushima Platoon arrived in Tamogino on the twenty-ninth of January, at 2:00 AM. At the entrance to the fourth house in the village hung a wooden sign: "MORTUARY." Tokushima stood still and gazed at the characters, which the light of his lantern revealed as being freshly written. He felt as if he were a spirit returned from the other world to see his own grave. His men saw the sign too. They could imagine what had happened to the 5th Regiment's Hakkōda Company.

Lamps were lit in every house, and in front of every door lay piles of objects that were immediately recognizable as army supplies. It appeared as if each family had taken in a large number of soldiers.

When Tokushima knocked at a house near the center of the village, a sentry came out, but he dashed back inside without being able to say a word. He obviously thought that the ice-covered soldiers standing at the door were the ghosts of the lost Hakkōda Company.

"It's them, Sir! I tell you it's them!" they heard the sentry shout as he shook awake his sleeping NCO.

At this point Tokushima went inside, accompanied by Tanabe and Takahata.

"Tokushima, 31st Regiment," he introduced himself. "I have over thirty men waiting outside. They may not all fit into this house, but I'd appreciate it if you would let in as many who do."

The NCO, wide awake now, saluted and asked: "From which direction did you get here, Sir?"

"From Sanpongi, via Tashiro."

"What? Did you really, Sir?"

Obviously amazed, the NCO went off to wake the owner of the house. The other soldiers billeted there woke up too, and the NCO, who had his wits about him, ran off to report Tokushima's arrival to the commander of the 5th Regiment rescue team, Major Kinomiya.

While housing arrangements were being made, the Tokushima Platoon was told that the whole Hakkōda Company had been lost. Tokushima's men were served hot soup and millet rice, but the terrible news had spoiled their appetites. They ate their meal in silence, then retired to four houses in the neighborhood that were willing to serve as temporary quarters.

Major Kinomiya sent orders that Captain Tokushima was to report to him at once. Different regiments or not, rank was rank.

Kinomiya looked at Tokushima's haggard figure.

"You must be exhausted," he said. Then he inquired about the route the Tokushima Platoon had followed.

Tokushima was prepared for this and gave Kinomiya dates and hours without having to resort to notes.

"So? You came via Tashiro?" Kinomiya asked. "Isn't that interesting. You know, close to 210 men of our regiment left barracks for Tashiro the twenty-third and are now missing. On the twenty-seventh we found Corporal Etō on the Ōtaki Moor. He was unconscious, but when he came to he told us more or less what had happened."

Kinomiya did not say that it looked as if the whole company had perished, but Tokushima had already heard this from the NCO who had welcomed him.

"Is Captain Kanda missing too? He was the officer in command."

"Captain Kanda's body was found on the Ōtaki Moor the twenty-seventh. He had bitten his tongue. He killed himself to take responsibility for his inadequate planning."

"Inadequate planning, Sir?"

"Yes. Not enough preliminary studies, not enough equipment."

148

"Surely that conclusion is a little premature, Sir. As far as I know, Captain Kanda was a meticulous planner. He even came to Hirosaki to ask me about our ascent of Mount Iwaki."

"Did you know him well?"

There was an ominous glitter in Kinomiya's eyes.

"Yes, I did."

"And did you by any chance compare notes with him before you left?"

"No, Sir, I did not."

"Oh, but you must have! The 31st had a fairly detailed knowledge of our plans. There must have been a leak somewhere. Not that it matters, mind you. Our regiments belong to the same division. But to my next question I want a direct answer." Here Kinomiya raised his voice. "Did you see anything on the way?"

"How do you mean, Sir, see anything?"

"Don't try to wriggle out of it, Tokushima. It stands to reason that you passed the site where the Hakkōda Company got lost. You followed the same route from the opposite direction. There is no way you could not have seen something!"

Kinomiya had spoken in the haughty, overbearing tones of someone who knows that his rank makes him superior to the person before him.

Tokushima could not forgive Kinomiya for blackening Kanda's character—Kanda, who had bitten his tongue. Inadequate planning, indeed! Tokushima had himself just crossed Mount Hakkōda in a blizzard and knew only too keenly the despair his dead colleague must have felt. If Tokushima's men had had to struggle against such snow for two days on end, they might have perished too. And he, Tokushima, would certainly have bitten off his tongue!

"Well? Don't just stand there, Tokushima! I asked you a question. Did you see anything, yes or no?"

"No, Sir. I saw nothing. We may have passed close by the site of the accident, but it was snowing so furiously you could hardly make out the man in front of you."

This was the first lie Tokushima told in his professional life. Of course he was irritated by Kinomiya's arrogance, but what had really made his gorge rise was the way Kinomiya had in the same breath reported Kanda's death and blamed Kanda for the disaster.

"Really? You saw nothing, eh? Well, then I have no reason to keep you any longer. Thank you."

149

Tokushima was dismissed.

No sooner had he stepped outside than he stood still. He had just remembered those two model '97 rifles that Kuramochi and Saikai had carried back.

I'm tired, he thought. That's why I got so riled at Kinomiya. I can't say we saw nothing: we brought those rifles.

He considered going back in to apologize for the lie he had just told, but when he recalled Kinomiya's high-and-mighty attitude he could not persuade himself to do so. The following morning he would tell everything. First he had to calm down a bit.

Tokushima returned to his quarters. His head was throbbing, his whole body hurt. He sat down by the hearth and drank some warm water. There was still some time until dawn. He used it to dry his wet things before the fire.

The matter of the two rifles weighed heavily on his mind.

5

Supported by his friends, Tetsutarō Fukuzawa stumbled through the snow. There was little danger that they would wander off the trail, which had been tramped out and hardened by so many men. On the other hand, they had no lanterns. In the darkness, they could hardly see where they were going, but fortunately the snow came down in flurries only. During lulls the faint light that shone down from gaps in the clouds gave them a vague idea of the outlines of the terrain. If now they had to face a real storm and the trail of footsteps was erased, they would unquestionably lose their way.

All of them muttered curses against the army, especially against Tokushima, who had simply dumped them in the middle of nowhere when he no longer needed them.

"Come on, Tetsu, hang in there!"

"Hey, Tetsu, don't even think about dying! If you die now, all Japan will laugh at you!"

Although these encouragements were addressed to Fukuzawa, they were in reality meant for themselves.

"Come on, Tetsu, just a little farther and we'll be in Tamogino. And just below Tamogino is Kōhata, where your aunt lives."

The seven wanted to reach Kōhata as soon as possible. The tips of their fingers and toes had already grown numb, and they knew very well that if they continued like this for another two or three hours they would lose the use of their hands and feet. So they huddled together and, slipping and sliding, descended toward

Tamogino. The trail became clearer all the time and in some places was marked by parked sleds and heaps of charcoal in bags, indications that the 5th Regiment rescue team was very close.

Below Kotōge it stopped snowing. In the hushed silence of the forest, they heard a dog bark.

"There's Tamogino!" shouted Tomekichi Sawada, voicing both his relief at being safe and his fear at the new danger that now lay waiting for them. When he heard the barking of the dog, he recalled how Tokushima had told him that the 5th might take them back to Narusawa if they were found. The others were thinking exactly the same thing.

"If we meet soldiers of the 5th and they ask us where we're from, we'll tell them that we got lost in the snowstorm on our way back from Tashiro to Masuzawa. Don't let on that we know what happened to their Hakkōda Company!" Sawada warned.

No one familiar with the terrain would fall for this story. Sawada knew this very well. Such an error would mean that they had made a 180-degree turnabout. But it was the only idea that occurred to him—which goes to show to what extent fatigue had muddled his thinking.

"Right, that's what we'll say if they ask us. I don't want to spend the rest of my life in some dark hole," said Torasuke Ōhara, in whose mind Tokushima's warning had assumed increasingly fearsome proportions.

The lamps of the village came into sight. By the light that fell through cracks in the doors, they could make out piles of military baggage under every eave. It looked as if there was no house without soldiers staying in it.

Frightened though the seven were of the 5th Regiment, a greater source of fear was the captain who had abandoned them some two hours before. If Tokushima bumped into them now, he'd certainly curse them as a bunch of miserable laggards. That in itself wouldn't be so bad, but much more terrible things would be in store for them. They knew all this, yet when they saw the light of the lamps, they badly wanted to ask for help. In their present shape, they couldn't possibly make it to Kōhata—two more miles through the snow. Tetsu would collapse if they tried.

"All right, I'll see if I can't find a house where they'll let us rest a while," said Katsutarō Komura.

He told his comrades to wait and went into the village, hoping to find a house that did not have any soldiers billeted in it. This turned out to be impossible. The more than 200 men of the rescue team

151

had been divided among all the houses, every one of which was bursting with people. Komura returned soon and suggested that the most remote house was probably their safest bet—or so he felt. "There'll be soldiers there, I suppose, but there're sure as hell not going to be any officers there."

The seven dragged themselves to the house Komura had in mind and halted by its door. From inside came the sound of someone stirring. The door was not locked, so Komura opened it a crack and peeped inside. A man who looked as if he might be the master of the house was at work in the entrance hall.

"Excuse me," whispered Komura. He placed his hands together in a gesture of supplication and pointed at his comrades waiting outside.

The man was amazed at Komura's appearance. At one glance he could see that Komura had only barely managed to escape from a fearful mountain storm. Quickly he checked the inside of the house and came out, shutting the door behind him.

"What's the matter? Where on earth do you people come from?" "We're from Masuzawa," Sawada answered. "We must have lost our way as soon as we left Tashiro, but we didn't know it until we found ourselves on the Umatateba. So we decided that as long as we were there we'd better continue in the same direction, and that's what we did, all night long. Tetsutarō here has an aunt who lives in Kōhata, and we figured she might help us, you know. . . . But when we got here, we found we were too tired to move on. . . . We hate to bother you, but would you be good enough to let us rest here until we've dried our things?"

Like Komura earlier, Sawada placed his hands together.

"You have relatives in Kōhata?" asked the man. "What might their name be?"

Because Tamogino and Kōhata were neighboring villages, many families in the area were related by marriage.

"My aunt's name is Kesa, Gentarō Suzuki's wife," said Fukuzawa.

When the man heard this, his attitude changed immediately.

"Oh, if you're a relative of Gentarō's . . . " And drawing closer to the seven, he whispered, "You can see for yourselves what it's like: there are so many soldiers here that there's hardly room even for us to lie down. I wish I could ask you in, but it's plain impossible. Tell you what, though. I'll make you a fire in the yard, so you can warm yourselves."

He woke up the other members of the household. They brought live coals from the house and firewood from the shed and built a blazing fire in the yard. A pan of hot soup was produced from the kitchen, enough to give the seven a bowl each. They felt as if a bright lamp had suddenly been lit inside their chilled bodies.

Keeping a close eye on the soldiers in the house, their host told them that a whole company of the 5th Regiment had died on Mount Hakkōda.

"Didn't you see anything on the way?" he asked.

"Of course not," said Kyūzō Ujiya. "It was snowing so hard I was happy if I didn't lose sight of the man in front of me."

The commotion by the fire had awakened some of the soldiers. A voice rang out and asked who was there.

"We're much obliged to you," Sawada whispered to their host as he signaled his comrades with his eyes. They got up from the fire and melted into the darkness.

After 60 feet they looked back: soldiers were searching the yard with big lanterns of the type railroad workers used.

The seven fled, Fukuzawa leading the way. He was tired, but the bowl of soup and the heat of the fire had restored his energies somewhat and the thought of the 5th taking him back to Narusawa was unbearable to him.

Outside Tamogino the road was pitch black again, but they knew that dawn could not be far off. Their host had been busy preparing the soldiers' breakfast, and the temperature had suddenly dropped—sure signs that it was close to daybreak.

Because their wet clothes had had no chance to dry, the cold air soon made them as stiff and hard as they were before.

"When we get to Kōhata, we'll be OK," they told each other.

The sky was beginning to turn brighter, but Fukuzawa was again having trouble walking.

"Hey, Tetsu, don't give up. We're almost at your aunt's now. Once we get there, we'll have nothing to worry about."

But Fukuzawa shook his head quite vigorously.

"The barracks of the 5th is right next door to Kōhata. If we rest at my aunt's and they catch us, what'll we do then?"

Here was one more reason to be afraid.

"But Tetsu, can you walk all the way to the train station? Suppose you can't make it?"

Fukuzawa set his jaw.

"I'd much rather die in the snow than be picked up and killed by the army."

Their greatest concern was that they might be pursued. If armed soldiers caught up with them and ordered them to halt, it would be all over. The army, they thought, was capable of anything.

Once they passed through Kōhata, they were on the Aomori Plain, right by the barracks gate of the 5th Regiment.

The sun had risen, but there was as yet no traffic on the road. The seven split up in a group of three and one of four. This was an idea of Sawada's, who felt that seven people walking down the road together might look suspicious. He was even worried about the way they walked.

Don't look about," he warned. "Look straight ahead, and act as innocent as you can."

As they drew closer to the barracks, they could hear orders being shouted on the parade ground. A little closer again, and they saw a large group of soldiers lining up, preparing to march out of the gate. Escape to one side or the other was impossible, for the snow lay so deep that they had to stay on the road.

"Hurry up! We've got to get past that gate before it's too late!"

There was no question now of walking in two groups. Supporting Fukuzawa on both sides, they dragged him past the barracks gate as fast as they could. The sentries stared at the scarecrows passing by, but did not attempt to stop them.

The seven were hardly past the gate when two lightly equipped companies marched out and turned off toward Tamogino.

The guides hurried through the awakening city to Aomori Station.

"Near the station there'll be a place where we can eat. We're not going to make it without something in our stomachs."

"Yes, we've got to eat, but suppose we get there and the train's just about to leave. Doesn't the train come first?"

After some discussion they agreed that getting on the train was more important even than getting something to eat.

When they consulted the schedule at the station, they found that they still had lots of time, so they looked around for a restaurant. There was one that had just opened up for the day, but its stove was already red hot.

"Where have you people been?" asked the owner as he poked up the fire. "You're all sopping wet!"

"Oh, we lost our way," Ōhara answered evasively.

6

Once on the train, the seven breathed a bit more easily.

"Well, the 5th didn't get us after all!"

"Don't say that too soon! The army only has to send one telegram or make one phone call to the police, and someone will be waiting for us when we get off at Numazaki and ask us to step over this way, please."

"But why the hell do we have to be so afraid of the army? We guided those soldiers of the 31st, and that was bloody good of us. It's not as if we've done something wrong, is it?" one of the guides complained angrily, wiping his tears away with his knuckles.

"We found out what happened to the Hakkōda Company. That's what we did wrong! When we get home, we mustn't say a word to anyone, except maybe that we parted from the 31st at Tashiro and made it to Tamogino by ourselves."

By the time the train arrived at Numazaki, the guides had worked out how they should behave.

It was snowing when they got off. As fast as they could, they walked to the town of Shichinohe, a distance of some six miles over a snow-covered road. Their clothes, which had never dried completely, grew wet again and froze. But they were on their way home, to the only place where they could feel safe. Since they could not trust anyone from outside their village, their greatest fear was that strangers might ask them questions. For if anyone let drop a hint of what he knew, chances were that none of the seven would ever see the light of day again. When one of them remarked that army jails were said to be even worse than ordinary jails, the others began to tremble as if they were already on their way there.

It was past noon when they reached Shichinohe, so they went first to a noodle shop for lunch. Because they had not expected to guide Tokushima beyond Tashiro, none of them had taken any money with him when he left home. All they had between them was the three yen they had received as their wages, Fukuzawa having dropped his share in the snow. From these three yen they had had to buy breakfast, train tickets, and, in Numazaki, straw boots. So, after each had finished two bowls of noodles, all their money was gone.

They left Shichinohe in a bad snowstorm. It was seven miles to Kumanosawa, for the snow had made all shortcuts impassable. The closer they got to home, the deeper the snow became and the harder the storm blew. They were the only ones on the road.

When they had come to within a few hundred yards of their village, Sawada called the other six together.

"Don't tell anyone—not your parents, not your wives—that we know what happened to the Hakkōda Company. If only one person lets it out, all of us will end up in jail. We parted from the 31st at Tashiro, that's our story. Everyone understand? We reached Tamogino by ourselves. All right?"

They all agreed on this.

And here Fukuzawa's feet refused further service. By sheer willpower he had forced himself to walk this far, but now he could not take another step. His comrades had to carry him into Kumanosawa.

It was 4:00 PM. The worried people of the hamlet streamed out of their houses to meet them, some shedding tears when they saw the wretched condition the seven were in.

When some people asked if they knew what had happened to the soldiers of the 5th Regiment, the guides repeated over and over again, in what almost sounded like a scream of despair: "No, no, nothing! We left the 31st at Tashiro and walked to Tamogino by ourselves."

The villagers suspected that they were hiding something, but they did not probe any deeper.

Even when Fukuzawa had been carried inside his house by his relatives and been laid down by the fireside, he did not move. He could not move. Tsuru, his young wife, clung sobbing to Tetsutarō's motionless body. For this she was loudly scolded by her mother-in-law, Tatsu:

"Stop sniveling and spread the bedding, quick! And mind you use two quilts!"

With scissors, Tatsu began to cut the frozen clothing from her son's body. After she had peeled off all the clothes, she massaged his whole body with a dry cloth. She also tried to feed him some soup, but he had not enough strength left to swallow. With eyes closed, Tetsutarō lay as powerless as a newborn babe. They carried him into a quiet room and placed him in the bed Tsuru had made.

Tatsu looked at her daughter-in-law.

"Come on, Tsuru, take off your clothes and get into bed with him!"

Tsuru looked puzzled.

"Yes, you heard me. When someone is almost frozen to death, the best thing to bring him back to life is the heat of another body. Tetsutaro may well die if you don't warm him up. So, if you want to keep your husband, get in with him and make him as warm as you can."

Now Tsuru understood. In front of the other relatives, she undressed and stark naked got into the bed and took her husband in her arms. But Tetsutarō appeared unaware that Tsuru lay beside him.

The seven guides from Kumanosawa survived. After they had recovered, their relatives and neighbors asked them all sorts of questions, but the seven stubbornly refused to answer. Even when the village headman visited them and with a smug look on his face suggested that surely they could tell him privately, they stuck to their story: they had guided Tokushima as far as Tashiro, and from there on they had been on their own. Not one of them so much as breathed that they had seen two dead soldiers of the Hakkōda Company.

All seven refused to go outside, but locked themselves inside their homes as if they had been frightened out of their wits. And when they heard news of a stranger in the village, they would be sick with worry.

"It looks like that awful blizzard has driven them crazy. Isn't it sad?" the people said to each other.

When at last the facts about the Hakkōda Incident became known, the villagers told each other in whispers that this might well explain the seven's mysterious silence. But they only whispered this among themselves. Toward outsiders, the whole village closed ranks with the guides and kept silent.

7

Almost as if in pursuit of the seven guides, the Tokushima Platoon had left Tamogino early the same morning the guides did. The men marched up the road to Aomori, where the Shioya and Kagiya inns were evidently expecting them, despite their late arrival.

Before setting off, Tokushima had sent a probationary officer and an NCO ahead with orders to cable Colonel Kojima of the 31st Regiment in Hirosaki, telling him the platoon was on its way.

The Shioya and Kagiya welcomed the men with steaming hot baths. As they sat soaking in their tubs, the soldiers finally began to feel how good it was to still be alive.

Accompanied by three subordinates, Major Monma arrived at eleven o'clock on the train from Hirosaki to welcome the Tokushima Platoon in the name of Colonel Kojima.

"Congratulations! You were superb! Superb!" he greeted Tokushima. In a voice breaking with emotion, he continued:

"Where the 5th Regiment's Hakkōda Company failed so tragically, our men of the 31st were brilliantly successful! Really, I don't have words enough to praise you."

He then inspected the platoon and spoke a few words to each man.

The 5th and the 31st were always being compared. The 5th had fought with distinction in the war against China, but the 31st was a much younger regiment and had as yet nothing it could be proud of. Both regiments understood very well why Division Command liked to play them off against each other, and their proximity made the competition inevitable.

This time, the 31st had come out on top! This elated not only Monma, but the whole regiment, from Colonel Kojima down.

But when Monma inspected the ranks, he noticed that the platoon had really been only one step ahead of disaster. He would tell a man that he had done splendidly or congratulate him on his excellent performance, but none of the answers he received sounded particularly happy or proud. Earlier, many of the men had barely managed to take off their uniforms before they collapsed on their beds, and not a few had fallen asleep in the bath. Almost all the men suffered from frostbite in their hands and feet. The gaunt, wasted faces of the lower ranks and probationary officers told Monma how grueling an exercise this had been.

The plans had been for the platoon to proceed to Hirosaki via Mount Bonju, but in their present condition this seemed out of the question. Monma placed a telephone call to Hirosaki and suggested to Colonel Kojima that Tokushima be ordered to change his plans and to march home over the highway.

Kojima not only agreed immediately, but added, "Tell Tokushima to spend one night in Namioka on the way."

For the battle was won. The 31st had scored a complete victory. The 5th had been routed. It would be senseless now to force the men any harder. What they needed more than anything was a leisurely march home and a chance to let their victory sink in.

When Monma conveyed the colonel's new orders, Tokushima did not show displeasure, but he did not seem particularly happy, either. Monma was puzzled about why Tokushima did not look more cheerful after his splendid achievement, but attributed it to fatigue.

"You must be exhausted. Have a good night's rest," he told Tokushima. "Of course I'm dying to hear how difficult it all was, but I'll reserve that pleasure for some other time. I have to take the next train back to prepare for your victory parade."

"No, Sir. Please listen to my report before you leave."

And Tokushima let it all out. He outlined their journey from Hirosaki to Sanpongi and explained how they lost one day in Masuzawa because they had to find guides. Here his eyes began to glitter, and when he told Monma that at Narusawa they had discovered the frozen bodies of two soldiers of the 5th plus their rifles, his voice sank to a whisper. He seemed worried he might be overheard, though he and Monma were the only two persons in the room.

"I had planned to hand those rifles to the 5th's rescue team in Tamogino, but I changed my mind."

He related how Major Kinomiya had summoned him and gave a detailed account of their conversation. He explained how angry he had been at the way Kinomiya had put the entire blame for the tragedy on Captain Kanda's supposedly inadequate planning and insufficient preparation, and had glossed over Kanda's suicide. Tokushima had found this unforgivable.

"So I answered that I had not seen a thing. We never gave them the rifles. They're with us here in Aomori."

Now that his story had been told, Tokushima heaved a sigh of relief.

"Yes, yes, I see," said Monma. "I understand perfectly how you must have felt. Major Kinomiya has behaved badly, no matter how you look at it. He did not behave as a soldier should. He ought to have welcomed our men of the 31st a bit more warmly, especially after that harrowing ordeal of yours. And the way he summoned you and grilled you is downright amazing. If there were things he wanted to ask, why didn't he go to you and ask you politely? Heavens, man, I got angry myself, just listening to your report! If it had been me there instead of you, I'd have told him the same thing."

This was very kind of Monma, but to the question of how to dispose of the two rifles he could not immediately think up a good answer. They could not simply destroy them, because they had always told their men that a rifle was a soldier's soul. Two missing rifles were more serious than two missing soldiers.

159

"Anyway, the big question right now is how we're going to get those damned rifles to Hirosaki," said Monma.

He mulled over the problem for a few minutes; then he slapped his knee.

"I've got it! The two NCOs who came with me are on official business and therefore they didn't bring their rifles. They can take yours. If we tell them the rifles belong to two of your NCOs whose frostbite is so bad they can't carry them themselves, I'm certain my men won't object. That way your whole platoon will be properly armed when you enter Hirosaki the day after tomorrow, and nobody will notice any discrepancy in the number of your rifles except for those NCOs of mine. And you can trust me to find some business to send them out on the day of your return."

Monma had sounded quite casual as he described his plan.

"About the rest we'll worry later. Division Command has already issued orders that all units should prepare to assist in the search for the Hakkōda Company, so I imagine our regiment will soon be sent out, too. At that time we can always ask for permission to return the rifles to Mount Hakkōda."

Monma smiled, apparently well pleased with this ruse.

"We really shouldn't hide the fact that you found those two bodies and took their rifles, but now that you've brought the rifles this far, I think we'd better. We don't want to worry the colonel more than is necessary, do we?"

Monma returned to Hirosaki that very day. He told his NCOs to carry the rifles and saw to it personally that these were taken straightaway to the armory. Sergeant Sasaki, who kept its keys, was ordered to watch over them until Captain Tokushima collected them in person.

Now that the crossing of Mount Bonju had been converted into a march down the highway, Saikai, the correspondent from *Tōō Nippō*, decided that there was little use in his staying on. He took his leave of Tokushima and his men. He had a story to file.

The platoon rested as much as it could in Aomori and left the following day, the thirtieth of January, for Namioka. It was a simple march over a main road, but during their one day of rest the men had begun to feel how tired they really were. Also, their frostbite had become extremely painful: Tokushima had to ask two probationary officers to carry the rifles of two NCOs who suffered particularly badly. The platoon took unexpectedly long to reach Namioka.

The Tokushima Platoon left Namioka on the thirty-first of January, in light snowfall. On reaching Masudate, just outside the town, Tokushima assembled his men and explained to them the line he wished them to take concerning the two rifles.

"I had intended to tell Major Kinomiya, the commander of the rescue team, what we had seen at Narusawa and to hand the rifles to him, but I was so angry at the rude way he treated me that I told my first lie since I joined the army and said that we had not seen anything. Well, what's done is done. There's no use regretting it now. If there is any problem, I'll take full responsibility. But please have faith in me and pretend you never saw a thing."

It was a moving appeal. No one spoke a word.

The whole platoon was badly disposed toward Kinomiya, for the rumor that he had shouted at Tokushima had already circulated among the men. Also, they knew from their own experience how unfriendly their reception in Tamogino had been. That they were given shelter, food, and fire to warm themselves had not been thanks to the 5th, but to the people of Tamogino. The 5th had not even sent its medical team. That whole night Tokushima's men had sat fully dressed around the hearth, staring into the flames, waiting for the dawn. They all felt that if the 5th had given them food after their exhausted arrival or had inquired if they needed any medical assistance, Tokushima would have behaved differently.

Tokushima walked down the line, inspecting their faces, and each face clearly expressed the resolve to do as he had requested.

The entire 31st Regiment, from Colonel Kojima down, as well as a whole crowd of civilians had assembled at the northern suburb of Watoku to welcome the platoon back to Hirosaki. Amid loud cheers, Tokushima's men made their entry into the city. One-third of the men walked with a limp, but this only made it clearer how remarkable their achievement was.

On the parade ground of the barracks, Colonel Kojima gave an address in which he commended the platoon in the warmest terms, but Tokushima's reply was brief. After a few words of thanks, he declared the platoon dissolved.

After eleven days and a distance of over 130 miles, the Tokushima Platoon's struggle with the snow was over.

8

About the time Tokushima's men made their triumphal entry into Hirosaki, the 5th Regiment in Aomori also found something to rejoice in: news had come that Major Yamada and most of his men had been found and were in good shape.

Unfortunately, this report had been colored by wishful thinking. The truth of the matter was that Yamada and eight others had been found in the gorge of the Komagome River.

On the twenty-sixth, Yamada's group had separated from Kanda's and turned off toward the Komagome. They lost one straggler after another, and by the time they found themselves stuck in the vicinity of the Ōtaki Moor, only fourteen men were left.

They were unable to scale the steep cliffs that towered up on either side, they lacked the strength to retrace their steps through the deep snow, and they had used up all their rations. The only positive aspect of their situation was that, at the bottom of that huge crack in the earth, there was virtually no wind. All they could do now was wait for death.

Almost without exception, the fourteen survivors suffered from delusions. A man would say and do the strangest things, but if at such a time someone warned him that he was behaving strangely, he would come to his senses and stop immediately, often to find that the person who had warned him was now himself acting strangely.

In many cases the knowledge that the very river on whose banks they were stranded flowed straight toward their barracks in Aomori contributed to their madness. Yamada, for example, suggested that they build a raft and use it to go down the river—though he had been present when Kanda told a man who proposed a similar idea not to be ridiculous.

But their commander had spoken, so the lower ranks among the survivors immediately set to work. They took off their bayonets and with these began to hack away at the trees that stood buried in the snow. Only then did Yamada realize that the whole idea was absurd: the Komagome was riddled with cataracts and totally unsuitable for navigation. Immediately he told the men to stop.

Still, as long as they had something to do, however silly, it took their minds off their situation and made the time pass. In the long period of waiting that followed, they began to hear the inexorable footsteps of death coming ever closer.

On the afternoon of the twenty-seventh, Probationary Officer Imaizumi and an NCO presented themselves before Yamada:

"Probationary Officer Imaizumi requests permission to swim down the river to Headquarters!"

Yamada gave the feeblest of nods.

Imaizumi and the NCO walked about twenty steps downstream. Suddenly Imaizumi threw away his greatcoat and stripped his upper body to the skin. The NCO followed his example.

"Hey, stop! Stop! What do you think you're doing?" shouted Lieutenant Katō.

Before he could reach them, Imaizumi said, "Don't worry, Sir. I'm a good swimmer. I know what I'm doing."

And he dived in, immediately followed by the NCO. Their heads emerged once, then they were swept downstream. The Komagome is a swift-flowing river, so it was not frozen, but its water was so cold that anyone who entered it could not expect to survive for more than a few minutes.

The others had witnessed the scene uncomprehendingly. Most of them felt that this had been a clever idea of Imaizumi's. If you can't walk it, you've got to swim for it, they reasoned.

On the twenty-eighth, the weather was a little better. Captain Kurata and a few others made an attempt to scale the cliffs, but they could not climb even 7 feet. Exhausted, they returned to Yamada.

"I guess that by now Imaizumi has reported to Colonel Tsumura and is sitting at home, behind a bottle of saké," said one of them.

"Yes, that was quick thinking," others agreed.

At this point Warrant Officer Shindō, who had so far listened to their conversation in silence, jumped up and shouted, "I'll go and report to Headquarters too! Anyone who wants to come along, follow me!"

In a frenzy he tore off his clothes and dived into the river. An NCO and a soldier followed his example. But at that spot the Komagome was not as deep as where Imaizumi had jumped in. The three surfaced immediately and tried to stand up. One was swept off his feet and fell back into the water, one collapsed against a rock, and Shindō himself was caught in a sitting position between two boulders. In a few seconds he was covered by a film of ice and changed into a statue.

163

Right after Shindō jumped in, Yamada called Corporal Ōhara over and asked him to go and get some water. The realization that he had to carry out his major's orders momentarily cleared Ōhara's muddled head. On all fours he crept to the river and scooped up some water in a mess tin, but the sight of the stream flowing by set him woolgathering again. Imaizumi had certainly been onto something there, he thought. And Shindō and the two others would soon reach barracks too.

Ōhara had already lost the use of his feet, so with the mess tin in one hand and supporting himself with the other, he crawled back to Yamada, who was sitting on a boulder, his lower limbs frozen fast to the stone. After giving the major his water, Ōhara sat up in a straight, military posture, and said, "I can swim too, Sir. I'll swim down the river and get help from Headquarters."

But Yamada looked up wearily and pointed at the frozen, ice-covered body of Shindō.

"See him?" he asked Ōhara. "Anyone who goes in will end up like that."

These few words brought Ōhara back to his senses. He counted the number of survivors. There were only nine left.

On January 31 the weather was comparatively good, with higher temperatures than they had had so far. Yet no one moved and hardly anyone spoke, except for Kurata and Katō, who would occasionally get up and walk about.

Ōhara had a notion that the secret of Kurata's and Katō's unusual fitness was their rubber boots, a commodity so expensive that lower ranks could not afford them even in their dreams. Ōhara was not envious; he had merely hit on the idea during a moment of lucidity. The greatest cause of the disaster was inadequate footwear. Once the cold had begun to affect the men's feet, they died in rapid succession.

Those two are in such good shape because they're wearing magic boots, Ōhara mused. He noticed that Kurata and Katō wore their trousers over their boots and had tied the legs with strings, so that the snow would not come in.

"If they'd lend me their magic boots, I'd be able to go anywhere," he muttered to himself. "I'd hop and skip like a rabbit, even in this yellow snow. Oh, I bet I'd even be able to fly!"

He did not remember when it was the snow had begun to look yellow to him, but it did. He had wondered at times why the snow

164

was not white—as snow ought to be—but now that it was yellow it stood to reason that yellow was the color of snow.

"Those boots won't let themselves be licked by a little bit of yellow snow. No, Sir! With those boots on, I bet I could get to barracks in one leap."

As a rule no one paid attention to such ravings, but when Kurata saw Ōhara pointing and heard him going on about his boots, he asked:

"Well, what about my boots?"

"With those boots on, I could fly like a bird," said Ōhara, pointing at the sky. "I'll show you. I'll fly way up high and report to Headquarters."

His finger pointed straight to the top of the cliff.

"Look, you see that raven there? Watch me fly up to that raven."

"Raven?"

Kurata could not believe that these mountains harbored ravens in the middle of winter, for ravens usually went down to the villages before it got really cold. Couldn't possibly be a raven, he thought as he looked up to where Ōhara was pointing.

"Yes, you're right," he admitted. "It does look like a raven."

"Hey, raven! Raven! Come here, birdie! Come then!" Ōhara shouted and threw his cap up in the air.

The raven withdrew from the cliff, but after a little while he returned with two comrades.

"That's funny. Those ravens are waving their hands," Ōhara said.

He was lucid again. The thought occurred to him that these might not be ravens, but human beings.

All the survivors shouted in unison, but it seemed the distance was too great for their voices to carry, so they all threw their caps in the air. The three ravens vanished.

"Oh well, I guess they were ravens after all," sighed Ōhara.

"No, that was the rescue team," Kurata stated with conviction. "They'll come back and get us out of here."

Thirty minutes later they spotted ten ravens, and from then on their number never stopped growing. Out of this flock, one brave raven was finally seen climbing down some sort of rope. Then it became clear even to the survivors with their weakened eyesight that this was not a raven, but a man. And then they heard his voice, a human voice.

"Sir, the rescue team is here," Kurata said to Yamada.

"Ah, have they come?" Yamada answered, tears streaming down his cheeks.

When the rescue team learned that Yamada was among the survivors at the Ōtaki Moor, an all-out effort was launched. It turned out to be extremely difficult. Kurata and Katō somehow managed to clamber up the rescuers' telephone wire by themselves, but the others had to be wrapped in blankets and hoisted up. It was almost morning when the last man was safe.

9

When the rescue team returned to Tamogino with Major Yamada and the eight others, they were greeted with the news that that same day two more survivors had been found in a charcoal burner's hut near Narusawa. On the second of February, Warrant Officer Tanikawa and three others were found at Okuzuresawa, also in a charcoal burner's hut, and Corporal Murayama was discovered at one of the hot springs near Tashiro. All survivors were taken to the military hospital, where they joined Corporal Etō, who had been there since the day he was rescued. Their original number was seventeen, but five were so weak that they died in hospital. One committed suicide. The final number of survivors was eleven.

The one who committed suicide was Major Yamada.

At the time of his rescue, Yamada was so weak that he could hardly speak, but when he met Colonel Tsumura he apologized with tears in his eyes for having sent so many soldiers to their deaths. It was obvious he wanted to make a full report, but the doctor intervened and had him taken to a private room in the hospital. Here he spent a comparatively restful night, despite occasional complaints of pain. The following day, the first of February, he woke up late in the afternoon and requested to be taken to Regimental Headquarters, because he urgently needed to speak with Colonel Tsumura. This was clearly out of the question, but when the doctor passed his request on to Tsumura, the colonel went to the hospital himself.

"If it had not been my duty to render a full account to you, I would not have faced the ignominy of survival," were the words with which Yamada greeted his commander.

Bit by bit, with many interruptions, he told his story:

"The greatest cause of the disaster was my own absolute ignorance of conditions in the mountains in winter. The second cause was that I robbed Captain Kanda of the command I had entrusted him with. Everything that went wrong, went wrong because of this. The whole responsibility is mine."

He paused.

"Please look after the relatives of my dead men."

He closed his eyes, but the tears never ceased to flow from behind their lids.

Tsumura took these words very seriously. They suggested strongly that Yamada was resolved to commit suicide. Now that he had confessed his responsibility, he seemed ready to die.

"No, you're not the one who is responsible," Tsumura told him. "Responsible is the man who ordered this exercise in the first place—your regimental commander, myself. You must live, Yamada, to see to it that this tremendous sacrifice was not made for nothing. I am not the only one who thinks so. Tomorrow, Colonel Miyamoto, the emperor's aide-de-camp, will visit us to convey His Majesty's wishes for your complete recovery and speedy return to your military duties."

But Yamada gave no sign he had heard him.

Before returning to barracks, Tsumura warned the doctor that Yamada should be watched closely because there was reason to fear that he might attempt to kill himself. The doctor passed this warning on to the orderlies. However, after his interview with Tsumura, Yamada appeared to feel as if a huge burden had been lifted off his shoulders, for he fell into a deep, sound sleep. He did not seem like someone who would undertake anything desperate.

Late that same day Yamada's orderly, Private Takahashi, brought some food and clothing from Yamada's house. Takahashi would have accompanied the major on the exercise if he had not caught a nasty flu.

"I hear His Majesty's aide-de-camp will honor me with a visit tomorrow afternoon," Yamada told his orderly. "Sickness is no excuse for impoliteness. If I cannot greet him in uniform, the least I can do is have it by my bedside with all its accessories. A soldier must always show he is ready."

And he gave Takahashi a list of the things he wanted him to bring the following morning.

Waka, Yamada's wife, found it suspicious that one of the items on the list was the major's revolver. It immediately occurred to her that her husband might be contemplating suicide. He might very well be. Reports of the disaster on Mount Hakkōda had appeared in every newspaper. The public sympathized with the victims and was severely critical of the officers responsible for the deaths of so many enlisted men. Yamada, the survivor, was singled out as especially to blame, and the voices crying out against him seemed to be growing stronger every day. Waka had sensed this mood immediately and understood very well what her husband was thinking. She also understood very well why Captain Kanda had bitten his tongue.

For a long time she gazed at the word "revolver" on the list. At first she could not persuade herself to hand the weapon to Takahashi, but in the end she made it ready. As the wife of a soldier, she could not find it in herself to go against her husband's wishes. She consoled herself with the thought that if he did use the revolver to kill himself, she could always follow him later.

All preparations being finished, the hospital awaited the arrival of the emperor's representative.

During Colonel Miyamoto's visit, Yamada sat up in bed and listened in apparent composure while the emperor's representative inquired after his health and offered him words of encouragement.

After Miyamoto and his staff had left, the whole hospital breathed more freely. All doctors who were not on duty left for home as soon as the clock allowed them. The doctor and orderlies attending to Yamada had been so busy with the preparations for Miyamoto's reception that they had completely forgotten Colonel Tsumura's warning of the previous day. Besides, physically Yamada was doing as well as could be expected.

By eight in the evening, the whole hospital was silent. A bit bored, a medical orderly was sitting on a chair beside Yamada's bed.

At half past eight, Yamada muttered something to himself. The orderly thought he was talking in his sleep, but when he checked, he saw that Yamada's eyes were wide open.

About nine, Yamada asked the orderly in an unusually clear voice:

"Bring me as many recent newspapers as you can and read them to me, please."

Since the rules required that special permission be obtained whenever a patient requested something that fell outside the regular duty of the nursing staff, the orderly considered going to the doctor on duty. But Yamada forestalled him.

"The doctor has been busy since early morning because of today's visit. He must be exhausted. I don't think it's necessary to bother him for every little request."

The major had a point there, the orderly thought. He left the room, which was the last one in that particular ward and lay at the end of a long corridor. When he passed the doctors' room, it occurred to him that he might as well check if the doctor on duty was in and get his permission. He knocked.

At the same time a voice told him to come in, there was the sound of a report some distance away. The orderly rushed back to Yamada's room, the doctor on his heels.

It was all over. Yamada had shot himself straight through the heart. He had left no suicide note.

The doctor looked at the clock. The time was 9:09 PM.

Colonel Tsumura was notified immediately. He hurried over to the hospital, where he had a long conversation with its director.

The next day it was made known that Major Yamada had died after his condition had taken a sudden turn for the worse. Very few people knew that he had killed himself.

PART FIVE

JOURNEY'S END

THE SEARCH WAS OFF to a swift, if somewhat shaky start. Horrified by the news that the whole Hakkōda Company had perished, Regimental Headquarters in Aomori poured soldiers into Tamogino, but despite their overwhelming numbers these troops were not sufficiently equipped to go up Mount Hakkōda in winter. Any attempt to do so would have resulted in another tragedy.

Shocked by the magnitude of the disaster, the headquarters of the 8th Division issued standby orders to the 31st Regiment, which sent a company up to Aomori on the second of February. But because Tamogino was already overcrowded, these soldiers were billeted in Kōhata and told to wait for further instructions.

As the most suitable strategy for its search, the 5th opted for what mountaineers know as the polar method: a base camp was established at Tamogino, with advanced bases that gradually moved farther up the mountain. These bases were linked by telephone and known by their number, their location (for example, the Narusawa Base), or their commanding officer (the Takahashi and Shiosawa Bases).

After these bases, which were really no more than trenches in the snow, had been fixed up so that overnight stays were feasible, a ceaseless flow of soldiers was sent up the mountain. Day after day they combed its slopes, undaunted by the snowstorms. It was thanks to their frantic efforts and the unstinting use of materiel that two men were found in a charcoal burner's hut near Narusawa on the thirty-first of January, five days after Corporal Etō had been rescued. By any standard, the search proceeded quickly.

But this result was obtained only because so many people were used. The original number of participants in the search was 1,099: 40 officers, 12 medical corpsmen, 11 warrant and probationary officers, 776 NCOs and enlisted men, and 260 local civilians. These numbers gradually dwindled as the search progressed, but, until the middle of February, Mount Hakkōda regularly harbored several hundred men of the 5th and 31st, and even some from the 8th Artillery Regiment and the 8th Engineering Battalion. Later in February the 5th Regiment continued the search on its own. A group of Ainu—aborigines from Hokkaido—also helped look for the bodies, which could only be found by probing the snow with a bamboo or metal pole in the hope that it might chance upon a corpse. The work was extremely difficult.

The Japanese public was deeply shocked by the news that a winter exercise had cost the lives of a whole company of soldiers. The incident was covered by newspapers, by magazines, by every kind of publication. Some of these reported the facts comparatively faithfully; others were less conscientious. In this context, the 5th Regiment's official report said:

> The news of the disaster that had befallen the 5th Infantry grieved His Imperial Majesty and stunned 40 million Japanese. Without distinction of rank or estate, wherever people gathered, they discussed the tragedy and demanded to know the facts. In their eagerness to be the first to bring the story to the public, hundreds of newspapers quite sensationally printed the most insignificant details, irrespective of their authenticity, as long as they were related to the disaster. This is how all sorts of false rumors originated, such as the story that the soldiers of the Hakkōda Company burnt their backpacks or the stocks of their rifles.

But in its second chapter, "The March and the Circumstances Leading Up to the Disaster," this same report stated that when the major had lost consciousness on the third day, January 25, "the wooden frames of the backpacks were used to light a fire with which attempts were made to revive his spirits." The sophistry of the argument—that it was not the backpacks, but only their frames that were burnt—did not make the general impression on the public any better. However, because this report was published in June 1902, less than half a year after the incident, it may be assumed that the army had not yet regained its composure.

Not content simply to report the details of this tragic affair to the nation, some papers clearly blamed the Hakkōda Company's command. In an editorial entitled "Is the 5th Regiment Accountable?" the *Yorozu Chōhō* disclosed that the people of Tamogino had warned against proceeding without guides and that their advice had been dismissed angrily as being inspired by greed for money. The paper attributed the sad outcome of the exercise to the fact that the Hakkōda Company could do no better than blunder about in the snow, whereas the Tokushima Platoon never moved without guides and dug trenches when the weather turned bad. By and by, however, most papers seemed to change their tone. Only a few put all the blame on the incompetence of the Hakkōda Company's commanding officers; most inclined to the view that the freakish weather conditions had made the disaster inevitable. And it is a fact that both the blizzard and the cold spell that assaulted the Hakkōda Company remain among the worst on record.

The first signs of an abnormally severe cold front were observed on the afternoon of January 23, the day the Hakkōda Company left its Aomori barracks. A stubbornly stationary high-pressure area over Hokkaido extended its influence to the northern part of Honshu. Because of the accompanying radiative cooling, a temperature of $-42°$ was measured in Asahikawa, Hokkaido, on January 23. This was the lowest temperature ever measured in Japan, a record that has not yet been broken. The Hakkōda Company was overcome by a combination of snowstorms accompanying a passing nearby depression and the cold air mass that fell upon them later.

Ever conscious that hostilities between Japan and Russia might break out at any moment, the Ministry of War feared more than anything the emergence of an antimilitarist mood and seemed concerned that the people might lose confidence in the army because of the Hakkōda Incident. The army authorities therefore decided to publish a a collection of anecdotes based on the Hakkōda Exercise: stories of soldiers who died while nursing their sick officers, of officers who died while looking after their men, of soldiers sent out on separate reconnaissance missions, of the bugler whose mouth froze to his instrument but who insisted on blowing a signal and so tore the skin off his lips. . . . But if the army thought the public would fall for these uplifting tales, it was mistaken. The Japanese looked at the awful toll that had been paid—199 soldiers frozen to death—and they grieved, not so much for the dead career soldiers as for the dead conscripts.

Feelings ran particularly high in Iwate, which had suffered greater losses than other prefectures. In the northeast of Honshu, freezing to death has always been considered much more horrible than other, more usual ways of dying.

Angry parents would show up at the barracks of the 5th and tell the receiving officer to his face, "If our son had fallen at the front,

175

we could have borne it, but now they tell us he froze to death in the mountains! That's the hard part of it! First you draft him with a scrap of paper, and then you murder him this way! And you think we'll take this quietly?"

Almost all those—and they were many—who traveled up to Aomori after they received the telegram that their son or brother was missing shared this feeling.

To deal with the relatives of the dead, the 5th set up a special liaison committee. The Officers' Club was turned into a reception area, and military housing was made available for overnight stays. Even so, the regiment had to rent houses from people living near its barracks.

When a body was found, it was carried down to Tamogino, where it was viewed by relatives, who then decided whether to take the deceased back to his hometown for cremation. Because they lay buried in the snow, the bodies were not discovered easily. More than once desperate parents announced their intention to go search for themselves, much to the embarrassment of the liaison committee, which did not very well know how to appease them.

The 5th Regiment's attitude toward the kin of the dead was quite deferential. Strict orders had come from higher up that any further aggravation of the relatives must be avoided, whatever the provocation. This condition proved so frustrating that more than one liaison officer applied to the regimental commander for a transfer to the search team. The army sought assistance from the prefectural authorities, who at last managed to persuade the crowds of people who had come to Aomori to go home and wait until the bodies of their loved ones were found. In most cases they had to wait until spring, when the snow melted, although the search teams never let up in their efforts.

On May 28—when the last body was discovered, near the top of Three-Step Falls in the Komagome River—the search team returned to barracks. Only a dozen or so men stayed behind, to look for weapons and equipment that had not yet been recovered. They concentrated their search on two missing rifles.

2

The last of the bodies was found when almost all the snow had melted away. Soon now the mountainside would be covered with the green of spring. Most of the weapons and equipment had been recovered, with the exception of two rifles and a small number of bayonets. Of these, the rifles posed a problem. Because they were said to be their owners' souls, they were just as important to the army as the bodies themselves.

After the Tokushima Platoon's return to Hirosaki, Yūjirō Saikai had reported to his paper, *Tōō Nippō*, that he had seen the frozen bodies of two soldiers with their rifles at Narusawa. This caused some speculation in the 5th about the curious coincidence between the number of missing rifles and the number of dead sighted by Tokushima and his men. There were even voices that directly accused "those fellows" of the 31st of having taken the rifles home with them. Others suggested, only half-jokingly, that they ought to ask the journalist who had accompanied Tokushima, or even the guides.

It was inevitable that these rumors also reached Colonel Tsumura's ears, but Tsumura was not about to take action, for by inquiring if the rumors were true he would only cast suspicion on Tokushima. There was not one scrap of evidence that Tokushima had really taken the rifles, and if there was, it would only lead to the making of new victims. Tsumura felt he had better stay out of it.

He kept a dozen men or so in the mountains to continue the search, but in the end was forced to call them back. If any rifles or bayonets were still out there, they were now hidden by the sprouting vegetation. The search was officially called off on June 20.

Tsumura placed a direct telephone call to Colonel Kojima of the 31st Regiment to notify him of the decision. Such calls between the two regimental commanders were so rare that Kojima was a little apprehensive at first, but Tsumura merely thanked him for the assistance Kojima's regiment had rendered the 5th in the search and told him the search was over.

"We've given up on those rifles," he said, just before he hung up. "They're probably somewhere at the bottom of the Komagome Gorge. I'll report them as lost right away."

After Kojima put down the receiver, he sat lost in thought. Of course the search would be called off sometime; there had been no need for Tsumura to telephone merely to tell him that. No, the call must have had some other purpose.

Kojima pondered Tsumura's parting words. He sensed that 177 Tokushima had for some reason been avoiding the topic of the bodies and rifles he had seen en route. He had heard the rumor that Tokushima's platoon had taken the missing rifles to Hirosaki.

"If that's the case, we'll have to do something about it," he finally said to himself. He decided he could not afford to waste the chance Tsumura had given him.

He called for Major Monma.

"A few minutes ago, Colonel Tsumura telephoned to tell me that the search is now officially called off. He has given up on the missing rifles and will report them as lost."

Monma had listened silently, his face impassive.

"I think that's a wise decision, Sir. I don't believe two rifles warrant so much effort. The army has more important things to do," he answered, deftly dodging the issue.

"No need to be too fussy, I agree. And once those rifles have been reported as lost, it's as if they no longer exist. In fact, it would be awkward if they did exist, wouldn't you agree?"

He and Monma exchanged a look of understanding.

When Tokushima heard about this conversation from Monma, his response had nothing to do with the rifles:

"Our battalion has not had any night exercises recently, Sir. I feel we need one badly."

"As a battalion or in companies?"

"I was thinking of splitting up the battalion into two groups and having them exercise between midnight and dawn."

"Send the men out at night, eh?"

"Of course, Sir."

Monma could read Tokushima's mind.

"Good," he said, "I agree. We'll work out a plan as soon as possible and submit it to the colonel. When did you have in mind?"

"The sooner the better, Sir, I think."

Monma told his staff to draw up plans for a night exercise, but he did not involve Tokushima at this stage. Not until the outline of the exercise had taken shape did he show it to the captain.

"What about your company? Any special wishes?" he asked.

"I'd appreciate it if you could make us part of Group White, Sir."

When the plans were finished, Monma took them to Kojima and had them approved.

The exercise was to be held the first week of July. Tokushima asked Monma to tell Sergeant Sasaki that he would pick up the rifles at the armory on the day of the exercise.

On that day, Corporal Kichinosuke Saitō, whose dead brother Zenjirō had been the owner of one of the two rifles, and Private Fukumatsu Oyama, who had also participated in the Hakkōda

Exercise, were told by their platoon leaders to report to Toku-shima's office at 2:00 PM. This was a pretext to keep them out of sight until the beginning of the exercise.

Saitō and Oyama had understood that they were to do paper-work, so they carried only light equipment, but Tokushima sent them back.

"This job will take until dark, so go and get changed. I want you to be able to go straight to the exercise from here," he told them. A little while later they reported again, this time fully equipped. Tokushima's office was very small. A desk and a chair stood near the window, and against the wall there was a simple bed so he could lie down and take a nap when he was tired. In the center of the room stood a table with two chairs for visitors. There was not really enough space to do any work in.

"If you put your rifles against the wall they might get knocked over, so lay them down on the bed. And cover them with a blanket to be on the safe side," Tokushima told them.

Saitō and Oyama did as they were ordered. Tokushima did not put them to work right away, and after he did, he kept glancing at the clock. When it struck three, he got up and told them to come along, but without their rifles. They made straight for the armory, where Sergeant Sasaki eyed Saitō and Oyama with suspicion.

"I've come for the rifles Major Monma asked you to keep in storage," Tokushima announced.

From the depths of the armory, Sasaki produced two rifles.

"I've fixed them up a bit," he said.

Tokushima acknowledged this with a polite nod and gave the weapons to his two helpers.

"Thanks for looking after them all these months," he told Sasaki.

Nobody saw them leave the armory, and though on their way back to Tokushima's office they met a number of people, the sight of a corporal and a private carrying rifles raised no suspicions.

"Put these rifles on the bed too, and don't bother about the blanket. You don't want to mistake them for your own," Toku-shima warned.

By that time Saitō and Oyama had realized that these rifles were probably the same ones they had found on the mountain, but they had no idea what Tokushima was planning to do with them. However, as long as the captain was so completely relaxed about it, they felt there was no need for them to worry. They were given

179

something to do—measuring distances with compasses on a map and recording them on a chart—but it was nothing urgent. In the course of the afternoon, two or three officers dropped in, but Tokushima kept them standing, and the visitors, who saw how cramped the office was, did their best to finish their business as fast as possible.

For the night exercise, the battalion had been divided into two groups: Red and White. The exercise began at 8:00 PM, when Red left barracks to take up defensive positions at the target area. White was to leave at 10:00 AM and, with the help of reconnaissance troops, was to try and creep up as close to Red as possible. The main forces would clash at early dawn the following morning.

At 9:00 PM Tokushima stood up and told Saitō and Oyama to get themselves ready. This seemed a little early to them, because White would not assemble until 9:40, but they did as they were told. They checked their equipment and were about to take their rifles from the bed when Tokushima said in a serious tone of voice:

"Not your own rifles! Take the two you just brought in from the armory."

They did so. Tokushima marched them out to the parade ground, which lay completely deserted under a starlit sky. They cut diagonally across the ground, not in the direction of the gate, but bearing left, toward the drill field. When they had arrived more or less at the center of the row of cherry trees that lined the field, Tokushima ordered them to halt.

"Put the rifles over there," he added.

They noticed that they were standing near an old well.

"Thank you. Now go back to my office, take your own rifles, and rejoin your platoons. And don't speak a word about this, understand?"

They saluted and made a right turn.

"Be careful now!"

For a moment they halted. This warning could only mean that they should be careful to avoid questions. Both of them knew that Tokushima was going to throw the rifles into the well. Saitō felt a twinge of sadness at the thought of his brother Zenjirō's rifle lying at the bottom of that dark well until the end of time, but when he considered that the rifle was now dead, like his brother, instead of being used by someone else, he was able to accept the idea.

They listened sharply, but the splash of the rifles dropping into the well never reached their ears.

3

Immediately after the Hakkōda Incident, the Ministry of War appointed an investigative committee consisting of nine members: the director of its Personnel Affairs Bureau and his section chief for rewards and decorations, the section chief for army affairs of its Military Affairs Bureau, the section chief for daily affairs of the General Affairs Bureau and one of his staff members, the section chief for construction of the Bureau of Finance, the section chief for medical affairs of the Health and Medical Bureau, a military councilor, and an adjutant from 8th Division Headquarters.

This committee hurried to Aomori to inquire into the disaster, but never published an official report of its findings. It would seem therefore that the investigative committee was dissolved before it reached an official conclusion. The committee did submit a memo to the Minister of War, however, and in the memo the members expressed their opinion on a number of points.

The problem the committee considered the gravest was that of equipment. Its members stated it as their opinion that "during the Hakkōda Exercise the equipment of the soldiers was deficient in the extreme" and that "continued neglect of this problem could have the most serious consequences in an emergency."

Another point concerned the treatment of the dead, of their families, and of the survivors. The committee felt that "the Japanese people will not accept anything less than full compensation for the victims" and that "the manner in which the Army resolves this question will influence the morale of the nation in a time of crisis."

A third point was that "at a time when the life of every soldier, let alone every officer, must be held precious, the officers who may be considered responsible for the Hakkōda Incident are dead." The committee therefore recommended that "the question of responsibility not be pursued any further."

Emergency, crisis, a time when the life of soldiers must be held precious . . . unmistakable references to the looming war with Russia.

★

Once the search had been concluded on June 20, Colonel Tsumura sent Lieutenant General Tachikawa, the divisional commander, his formal resignation as commander of the 5th Regiment. He had already done so right after the disaster, but had been told to postpone resigning until all affairs resulting from the incident had been finalized. Now he was in Tachikawa's office at Division Headquarters, together with Major General Tomoda of the 4th Brigade and Colonel Nakabayashi, the division's chief of staff. Tachikawa tore up Tsumura's letter of resignation and threw it into a wastebasket.

"The whole responsibility rests with me, as commander of this division. The policy that sent the men of the 5th and the 31st out to Mount Hakkōda originated in this office. It was I who first conceived of the idea to have the two regiments compete in a winter exercise. You, as regimental commander, have nothing to reproach yourself for. In a few days' time I intend to present myself at the ministry to submit my own resignation."

After these words, Tachikawa called in Colonel Kojima, who had been waiting in the next room.

"I have just told Colonel Tsumura that I am taking the whole responsibility for this affair. I must be getting senile to have thought up something as wild as a competitive exercise on Mount Hakkōda in the coldest part of winter. It's a good thing the men of the 31st returned safely, or I would have to commit *seppuku*. And unfortunately, this is a problem that cannot be solved simply by cutting one's belly."

Tomoda and Nakabayashi both seemed about to protest that it was they who had suggested the whole idea in the first place, but they did not want to interrupt Tachikawa.

"It's hard, being a soldier, for you as well as for me. A soldier is forever fighting some hypothetical enemy, and to help him do his job it is necessary that regiments of the same division pretend they are at war. . . .

"Speaking of which, who in your opinion was the victor in this attack on Mount Hakkōda?"

Tachikawa had put the question to both regimental commanders. It came like a bolt from the blue.

"The loser was the 5th, sir, obviously," Tsumura answered.

"Wrong! The 5th was the victor! It won this battle by nobly sacrificing 199 of its men. Yesterday I had a visit from the director of the ministry's Bureau of Military Affairs, who told me that on the recommendation of the investigative committee it had been decided to upgrade all the army's winter equipment. I myself had been pestering the ministry about the same thing until I was blue in the face, but those bureaucrats in Tokyo, they have no idea how much cold and snow we get here in winter. They just sit there behind their desks on their lazy behinds, playing at being soldiers, without even making an effort to consider the requests of the people who are stationed here and know this area best.

"Oh, their mouths are full of slogans about military morale and military discipline, but this time they discovered that you can't fight a blizzard with morale and discipline alone. What do you think would have happened if this disaster had occurred during a war with Russia? Japan would have lost. But because it did happen now, the army decided it must seriously try to come to grips with the question of how it will protect its soldiers against the cold. That is a tremendous step forward! If I may exaggerate for a moment, it means that the tragedy of the 5th Regiment may have warded off the defeat of the Japanese Army. The souls of the dead soldiers of the 5th may rest in peace."

Tachikawa had spoken eloquently. Now he turned once more to Tsumura, who had listened with a face that showed how deeply the general's words moved him.

"But the Aomori 5th did not only win; its name is now known to the whole nation. At first public opinion may have been critical of its staff, but it now has come round to the view that the disaster was inevitable. Just consider the expressions of sympathy and the gifts of money that have reached us. They more than anything else tell us how deeply all the Japanese people feel the fate of the 5th. And the depth of their sympathy also tells us how strongly they have come to support their army. The name of the Aomori 5th Infantry has become immortal; it is more familiar to the people than the name of any other regiment. And do not think that it became known because of a shameful incident. Think rather that it earned its fame because of the heroism with which it fought the snow."

Now Tachikawa turned to Kojima.

"But that does not mean that the 31st lost. No, the 31st scored a magnificent victory! It will be a long time before others will dare attempt what the 31st accomplished so splendidly. For what is victory after all? . . . "

"But, Sir, is it possible for a war to have two victors?"

Nakabayashi's question stemmed the flow of the general's eloquence. If left to himself, Tachikawa looked as though he could go on for hours.

"Yes it is! In the sixteenth century, both of the opposing generals, Shingen Takeda and Kenshin Uesugi, claimed victory after each one of the battles of Kawanaka Island. In any major conflict it is difficult to distinguish between the victors and the vanquished. You've won if you think you've won, and you've lost if you think you've lost."

When they left Tachikawa's office, Tsumura and Kojima waited in front of Division Headquarters for their horses.

"Well, it's as the general said. We lost," said Kojima.

"No, no, it's we who lost. The 31st was magnificent," protested Tsumura. "You didn't lose a single man!"

Both men were silent. There was nothing else to say. Whatever needed to be said, had been said by Tachikawa.

"I have a feeling there'll be real gunfire at our next contest."

"Yes, next year, or rather, the year after, I suppose."

They were both thinking of the war against Russia.

Their horses arrived. They saluted each other and went their ways.

PART SIX

AUTHOR'S COMMENTS:
THE AFTERMATH

THE GOVERNMENT AND THE ARMY were quite sensitive to the mood of the people. The whole nation paid such close attention to the manner in which the Hakkōda Incident was settled that it seemed very likely the course of action taken by the authorities would decide whether the people and the military would drift farther apart or grow closer.

To placate the public, the Ministry of War used the prestige of the imperial family. Not only did aides to the emperor and the crown prince frequently travel to Aomori to comfort the bereaved relatives and visit the survivors at their bedsides, but they even inspected the progress of the search on the site of the tragedy. The ministry had resorted to this stratagem to neutralize the general condemnation of the levity with which so many young soldiers had been sent out to die in the snow. On April 25, the empress donated artificial limbs to those survivors who had suffered amputations. The emperor and empress also contributed toward the funeral expenses of all the dead, from officers to privates. Such acts signified that the emperor himself was greatly distressed at what had happened but at the same time approved of the exercise itself. Day after day, such favors were reported in the daily papers, for the emperor's interest, the ministry hoped, would be oil on troubled waters. How could the people continue to grumble after their emperor had made his pleasure known?

The anger of the relatives of the victims gradually subsided. But the amount of the emperor's contribution toward funeral expenses was determined by the rank of the deceased, which meant that the family of a major received 75 yen, and that of a private a mere 5 yen. This difference was too great. Some relatives grumbled that they did not see why the dead should not all be treated equally, irrespective of the ranks they had held while still alive. Was not death the same to all? They supposed that the difference in funeral contributions had been the idea of the emperor's advisers and did not reflect the wishes of their master. Because these sentiments could not be expressed openly, the indignation of the relatives turned inward and, the public mood being what it was, stirred up new feelings of distrust toward the highest military authorities.

With the permission of the government, the Ministry of War submitted, and the Diet approved, a supplementary budget bill providing for the costs of the search, for the construction of a common cemetery, and for a one-time compensation for the dead.

As the following table shows, the difference between the amount received by the family of a major and the amount received by the family of a private was 15 to 1 when the funeral money was awarded, but with the payment of compensation the difference diminished to 6 to 1.

	Funeral Money	Compensation
Major	¥75	¥1,500
Captain	¥50	¥1,000
1st Lieutenant	¥35	¥750
2nd Lieutenant	¥25	¥600
Warrant Officer	¥10	¥500
NCO	¥10	¥350
Private	¥5	¥250

This settlement appeared acceptable to the families of the dead. When it was announced that the victims were considered battle casualties and would therefore be enshrined at Yasukuni Shrine in Tokyo, the bereaved relatives as well as the Japanese people felt satisfied. By then, half a year had passed. On June 23 a magnificent funeral service was held at Tamogino, with the commander of the 8th Division officiating.

Since the incident many individuals and groups had, as an expression of sympathy, sent money to the kin of the dead and to the survivors. All the newspapers joined in a funds drive. When, toward the end of June, the money thus collected was counted, the total surpassed 210,000 yen. Contributions varied in nature. There were donations for specific individuals, for the bereaved families as a group, for dead privates only, or exclusively for the dead from Iwate Prefecture; yet other donations came with the request to allocate the money among the survivors in proportion to the degree of their injuries. The total of all this money was distributed according to the wishes of the donors, but the surviving officers and warrant officer declined their shares.

Many persons sent donations in kind, especially while the search was still in progress. Under the entry "Gifts of Confectionary," one of the records lists 5,000 "pine-wind cakes," 6 boxes of "shapes," 6 boxes of wafers, 1,000 bags of "celestial beans," and 15 boxes of "garden dew"—sweets whose appearances and tastes are lost to history.

Of the eleven who survived, the two officers and one warrant officer had suffered only light injuries; they were able to resume their duties on February 18. But the remaining eight NCOs and privates had lost both hands and both feet, or both feet.

A breakdown of the survivors' ranks presents an interesting picture:

	Number	Survived	Survival Rate
Officers and warrant officers	16	3	1:5
NCOS	38	3	1:13
Privates	156	5	1:31
TOTAL	210	11	1:19

Not only was the survival rate much, much higher for officers than for privates, there was also a remarkable difference in the degree of their injuries. This fact, one of the distinctive features of the Hakkōda Incident, was among the reasons why public criticism of the officer corps was so fierce.

The three lightly injured officers fought at the front during the Russo-Japanese War, which broke out two years later, in 1904. In one of the war's bloodiest battles—that of Heikautai in 1905—Captain Hajime Kuraishi ("Kurata" in the novel) was killed, and Lieutenant Kakumei Itō ("Katō") and Warrant Officer Teizō Hasegawa ("Tanikawa") were severely wounded. Captain Taizō Fukushima ("Tokushima") died in the same battle, and half the members of the Tokushima Platoon were either killed or wounded.

The other eight survivors of the Hakkōda Company underwent operations in the military hospital in Aomori and were sent to a sanatorium in Asamushi to recuperate. Thanks to the care they received, all eight recovered satisfactorily. When they left the hospital, it was early summer, the season of fresh green leaves. Their artificial limbs covered by new uniforms, they posed for a group photograph before returning home with their attendants.

189

After the incident, these eight became nationally famous as the heroic—some said, miraculous—survivors. They received piles of letters from all over the country. Especially in their hometowns they were regarded as heroes, sources of pride for the regions that had produced such brave men.

Typically, when a survivor's train pulled in at the station, it was met by crowds of people waving flags. A rickshaw stood ready to wheel the local hero triumphantly through the streets of his town to the door of his parents' house. If his hometown did not lie on the railroad, he was afforded similar welcomes in all the communities that lay on his route, with mayors and local politicians following him like shadows. When he arrived in his own village, the reception reached a peak of frenzy. Tears streamed down people's cheeks, and their throats were hoarse with cheering. Then, almost before he had had time to sit down, the donations and compensation money would arrive—about 1,000 yen per person.

What the surviving eight invalids had in common was that they were all farmers' sons who, at one time or another, had done some charcoal burning, which meant that they had to spend autumn and part of the winter in the mountains. They were therefore accustomed to the snow, and they survived because their experience had taught them how to protect themselves against the cold. Most of them came from poor families.

At the time, 1,000 yen was a lot of money, the equivalent of almost an acre of farmland or 74 acres of forest. Some of the eight invested their money in land; others put it in the bank so they could live off the interest. As it turned out, those who used the money to buy land or commodities chose wisely, whereas those who deposited their money soon used it up.

All eight were single, and they were overwhelmed with offers from young women who wanted to marry them. One of the survivors was a quadruple amputee—he had lost both hands and feet and could write only with the brush clenched between his teeth—but for him too there were marriage candidates. Such a husband's disability spoke volumes for his courage; it was a visible proof of his valor, something for a wife to be proud of.

All eight married happily. Some of them served for many years as village assemblymen or as village clerks, but for one the acquisition of a hero's reputation and an undreamt-of sum of money became his undoing. This man had lost only one leg, a minor handicap compared to what the other seven had suffered.

190

Because he was good-looking, many girls were interested in marrying him, and the bride he chose from among them made him a good wife. But, because he was a good storyteller, he was often invited to other towns and villages to talk about the brave feats of the Hakkōda Company, and after concluding his tale he was invariably treated to a few cups of saké. This happened time and again, and in the end he became quite fond of the bottle. After the Russo-Japanese War broke out, however, heroes were a dime a dozen in Japan, and people wanted to hear about bullets whistling overhead—not about hardship in the snow. A few years after the war this Hakkōda hero was completely forgotten. To cope with his resentment, he turned to drink. Ten more years, and he had become an alcoholic whose wife had left him in despair.

Three years after his wife's departure this man sat, drunk, in one of the bars in his town.

"I'm one of the heroes who survived Mount Hakkōda," he said to a young man who was also drinking there.

"Mount Hakkōda? Never heard of it."

The young man did not know what had happened twenty years before. He probably had not even been born then.

For one second the old soldier looked up and glared at the youngster; then his head dropped on the table. The hero was dead.

But one of the eight survived to tell the tale in his own humble way until he died in 1970, at the venerable age of 91. This was Corporal Chūzaburō Obara ("Ōhara"). Thanks to him the truth about the fate of the Hakkōda Company reached the world.

The brilliant achievement of the 31st was completely overshadowed by the tragedy of the 5th. The success of the 31st was occasionally referred to when someone wished to criticize the 5th, but that was all. Few Japanese ever even heard of Fukushima ("Tokushima") or his platoon.

For many years the seven guides from Kumanosawa preserved the silence to which Fukushima had sworn them, but in 1930 Yoshishige Tomabechi first published the facts. In his book, *The Untold Story of the Hakkōda Exercise*, he recorded a number of oral statements by one of the guides, who assumed that by then it was safe to speak out. Frostbite had given almost all the guides crooked fingers or toes and made them unfit for work on their farms or in the mountains. They had led Fukushima and his men to success, but their own lives had been spoiled.

Irrespective of success or failure, the ultimate destiny of the Fukushima Platoon and the Hakkōda Exercise was generally sad, for almost all those directly involved met with a tragic end.

> Oh, the snow lies deep and heavy
> on the heights of Mount Hakkōda
> and the bugle's call hangs frozen
> in the bitter winter wind.

This army song—"The Snowstorms of the Northeast"—has kept the memory of the Hakkōda Company alive from the beginning of the century to the present day. But the question of why this disaster occurred at all has been seriously investigated by very few.

It is a question that defies explanation unless one keeps in mind that the Hakkōda Incident took place just before the Russo-Japanese War. Insufficient equipment, confusion in the chain of command, unprecedentedly bad weather—none of these factors gets to the heart of the matter, which is that on the eve of war with Russia the military authorities decided to conduct an experiment to see how well soldiers could cope with the cold. This was the greatest cause of the disaster.

None of those involved in the incident, from the commander of the 8th Division down, was ever called to account. Without one transfer, without making any command changes at all, the army marched against Russia.

★

When I visited Aomori Prefecture during my research for this book I was struck by the difference between then and now.

The old grounds of the barracks of the 31st Regiment in Hirosaki are now a residential area, and a high school stands on the site of the 5th Regiment's barracks in Aomori.

The vicinity of Tamogino does not seem to have changed much from the way it looks in old photographs. There are still houses there with thatched roofs, but the road the Hakkōda Company took has disappeared without a trace. It has been replaced by a fine paved road that roughly follows the course of its predecessor.

Near Sainokawara there is a stand of pine trees said to have been planted the year after the disaster. Despite the years that have passed, they are only 16 feet high and 12 inches thick at the trunk. Apart from some stunted alders and birches, nothing else grows here that deserves the name of tree.

On top of the Umatateba stands a bronze statue of Corporal Fusanosuke Gotō ("Corporal Etō" in this book). He has a magnificent view from there.

Good Fortune Rock, which served as a landmark for the Fukushima ("Tokushima") Platoon, still lies on the Tashiro Moor, but the route the platoon followed around Lake Towada has become a paved road, too, as has the route from Utarube to Herai.

The cemetery for those who lost their lives during the exercise is in Kōhata. Surrounded on four sides by an earth wall, lined with cherries and red pines, and with a lawn at its center, it bears some resemblance to a Western graveyard. The stone that marks the grave of Major Shin Yamaguchi ("Major Yamada") rises up across the lawn from the entrance. It is one step higher than the tombstones of the other officers, which are on either side. Among them is the stone of Captain Bunkichi Kannari ("Captain Kanda"). One level lower, at the northern and southern sides of the cemetery and separated by a path for visitors, are the markers for the NCOs and enlisted men. Even in death, the differences in rank between them have been strictly preserved. There is something forbidding about the place.

Afterword by the Translator

WHEN A JAPANESE AUTHOR has trouble meeting a deadline, it is common practice for his publisher to put him into a "cannery"—a hotel which he is not allowed to leave until he finishes his manuscript. This happened to Jirō Nitta when he was writing *Death March on Mount Hakkōda*. So difficult did Nitta find it to come to grips with the material of the story that at one point he escaped from his cannery for a change of scene at home. After his return to the hotel, things at first did not get much better, and as he was pacing up and down the corridor, searching for inspiration, he bumped into a famous historian, his arms loaded with reference works. "I wish I were a novelist," said the historian, "so I could forget about my sources and write only from my imagination." "I wish I were a historian," retorted Nitta, "so I could forget about my imagination and write only from my sources."

In the end, Nitta used both. "The historian establishes facts," he was fond of saying, "and the novelist spins the thread that connects them." That is exactly what Nitta did in *Death March on Mount Hakkōda*. Meticulously researched, with each of its many quotations and references verifiable, the book appears to be a typical example of the documentary novel—and to the extent that it is a novel based on documents there is nothing wrong with this characterization. But the term "documentary novel" raises false expectations. It leads the reader to assume that the authenticity of the documents extends to the entire novel, whereas a novel by definition is a work of the imagination. The result is that the fictional re-creation of a historical event may become "truer" in the popular imagination than the event itself.

Death March is a case in point. Although it was fairly common knowledge that almost two hundred soldiers froze to death in 1902, after the true scope of the disaster became known the authorities went to great lengths to suppress the details, and as a result the historical circumstances of the Mount Hakkōda disaster were virtually forgotten until 1971, when Nitta published his novel. Civilians were forbidden to own books about the event, and even the 5th Regiment's own report of July 23, 1902 (from which Nitta quotes), was soon withdrawn from circulation because of the criticisms it leveled at the way the exercise had been prepared and conducted. The Japanese government, fearing the consequences of a public backlash against the army just when it was gearing up for a possible war with Russia, did all in its power to sell the idea that the Hakkōda Company had become the victim of freakish winter weather and that all its members deserved to be enshrined as martyrs for the national cause. It would have been awkward to make a martyr out of someone who was demonstrably to blame for the disaster.

For the same reason, the 31st Regiment's successful completion of a much longer and much more rigorous march over identical terrain and in possibly even worse circumstances was given no publicity whatsoever, and Captain Fukushima ("Tokushima" in the novel), who had done such a brilliant job in its preparation and execution, was quickly promoted out of sight. The comparison with the 5th would have raised too many awkward questions.

It was against this background that Nitta started his research for this novel. His widow relates how he struggled to get access to the historical materials and how some of the information he was looking for did not turn up until after the novel had appeared. He had very little to go by: a few reports from 1902 or 1903, many of them based on hearsay; an army report of questionable reliability; a few pamphlets and privately published books by amateur historians; a survivor's memories, blurred by the passage of over half a century. Also, Nitta was not a trained historian; nor was he an expert on military matters. Under the circumstances it is surprising he managed to reconstruct the historical course of events as well as he did.

But although Nitta aimed at historical accuracy, his main purpose was to write a novel about human suffering and human endurance, and for that reason he did not always stick to the facts. The impact of the novel, and later of the film that was based on it, was so great, however, that many people still believe the Hakkōda disaster took place just as Nitta described it. An ironic consequence of Nitta's success is that the new research it prompted into the causes of the incident clearly shows how *Death March* is in some points wide off the mark, but a careful study of what Nitta added or changed may tell us why he wrote the novel in the first place.

To begin with, there was not one unified Hakkōda Exercise, but two independent exercises, entirely different in scope, planning, and execution. The exercise by the 31st Regiment of Hirosaki had been in planning for three years. For most of 1901, its Captain Taizō Fukushima had prepared intensively for an eleven-day march past Lake Towada and across Mount Hakkōda. He had made a practice march over the proposed route in July and had arranged not only for shelter, but also for guides. This means that the seven guides from Kumanosawa who have such a terrible experience in the novel were not recruited on the spot, but hired well in advance. That Fukushima was able to complete his exercise on schedule, under the awful circumstances Nitta describes in the novel, is an incredible feat of courage and stamina and a testimony to the accuracy of his preparations. As it turned out, the data collected by his observation teams proved to be invaluable in the war with Russia, which makes it seem all the more unfair that Fukushima's success was hushed up to save the reputation of the Aomori 5th.

The 5th Regiment's plan was much more limited. The decision to carry out a winter exercise on Mount Hakkōda had only been taken in late 1901. Captain Bunkichi Kannari ("Kanda"), recently promoted and still fairly inexperienced, had not been entrusted with the preparations until January 5, 1902, and Major Shin Yamaguchi ("Yamada") waited until January 20 before he decided the destination and time schedule: a one-day march to the hot springs at Tashiro, and back again the next day. Under normal circumstances this would not have been difficult, and the practice march Captain Kannari organized on January 18 suggested no different. But as we know, everything went horribly wrong. The blizzard that hit the 5th Regiment on January 23, 1902, still breaks all the records of the Japanese Meteorological Agency for cold and intensity. Preparations, equipment, and leadership proved woefully inadequate, and 199 soldiers froze to death.

Several differences with Nitta's novel here are immediately obvious. Since the Hakkōda Exercise was not a joint exercise, the competition between the 5th and 31st Regiments is entirely fictional. Captain Fukushima's personal records contain no trace of a correspondence with Captain Kannari, but even if they had exchanged letters it is doubtful that they discussed the possibility of

197

meeting on Mount Hakkōda, for Kannari's company was scheduled to return to barracks on January 24, when Fukushima was still supposed to be in the village of Herai. Before accusing Nitta of falsifying history, however, one should know that at least one of the books he may have read for *Death March* states unequivocally that the 5th Regiment's ultimate goal was Sanpongi. Also, when Yamaguchi and Kannari failed to return to barracks on the appointed date, their own colleagues assumed they had pushed on for Sanpongi and called the police there, much as Nitta describes.

It is unclear whether Nitta was misled by his sources or decided, for reasons of his own, to elevate a contingency plan to a main plan, but in his description of the relationship between the characters Tokushima and Kanda he obviously used a novelist's license to capture his readers' interest through added human drama. And although that relationship is a fiction, it works. It appears not only as something that could have been, but almost as something that ought to have been true--and to the extent that two fellow officers went through much the same experience with such different results, on a symbolic level it was true.

Nitta appears to have had the same purpose in mind with the story of the two brothers Zenjirō and Kichinosuke and their sad reunion in the snow. Here again he may have wished to symbolize the brotherhood between the two groups of soldiers, but most readers will have sensed that this was too coincidental to be true, and they are right. It is a typical example of the kind of melodrama so beloved by the Japanese, although it may strike Western readers as contrived.

Less obvious from the historical outline above is the fact that Nitta misunderstood the line of command in the Hakkōda Company. For this he may perhaps be excused, as it really is a little fuzzy. Captain Kannari was in practical command of the company, but he was outranked by Major Yamaguchi, who therefore technically was the officer in charge. Even when Yamaguchi was incapacitated, the command devolved not to Kannari but to another officer on the battalion staff. This takes nothing away from the fact that Yamaguchi should have interfered less. The disastrous decision at Ōtōge to continue toward Tashiro instead of turning back to barracks was Yamaguchi's, for instance, and other examples may be given. The point remains that Yamaguchi was within his rights to issue orders and that his subordinates, including Kannari, recognized this.

But problems in the line of command were not the main reason the 5th Regiment perished, nor was it simply a result of incredibly bad weather, as the military authorities later claimed. The soldiers of the 5th died because of the incompetence of their commanding officers, including the energetic but overconfident Kannari. There were problems with the soldiers' equipment, such as the lack of adequate footwear and clothing. Considering the size of the company, there was not nearly enough medical staff on hand: one doctor and five orderlies for 210 men, against two doctors and one orderly for Fukushima's platoon of 38. Some of the decisions that were taken simply did not make much sense. The company could still have returned to Aomori after abandoning the luggage train or have bivouacked beside it, instead of using soldiers as carriers. Later, many lives were lost because of the order not to abandon the heavy cauldrons used for cooking. Also, notes found on the dead officers demonstrate plainly that the steadily worsening weather was largely disregarded. It is not a pretty tale. Considering the strong feelings against military conscription that existed at the time, one can understand why the authorities decided that this was one story that needed to be killed.

Most of this information was at Nitta's disposal, and he used it effectively. The one deliberate change he made, however, is crucial to our understanding of his purpose in writing this novel.

By shifting the blame for the disaster from Kanda to Yamada (as I shall call them here, to avoid confusion with their historical models) and thus creating the impression that the problem lay in the line of command, Nitta was really attacking the vertical structure of Japanese society. Whatever goes wrong in the novel, goes wrong because of problems inherent in Japanese society and Japanese behavior: Yamada looks down on Kanda because he did not go to the right school; Kanda does not dare exceed Yamada's orders on his practice march to Kotōge; enlisted men are not allowed to warm themselves at their officers' campfire; soldiers sacrifice their lives to save their blundering commander; rank and seniority override merit and common sense. The built-in unfairness of the system even reaches beyond the grave: monetary compensations are higher for officers than for enlisted men; the height of a gravestone depends on the rank of the person buried underneath; an army rifle is more important than a soldier's life.

When *Death March* first appeared, one Japanese reviewer remarked that Japanese society and Japanese politics had hardly

199

changed in the previous seventy years. He managed to see the point and miss it at the same time: Nitta's true topic was not Japan in 1902, but Japan in 1971. That much was recognized by the company that ordered fifty copies of the novel so its executives could study the dangers of bad communications with their staff. In Nitta's vision, the 5th Regiment's doomed Hakkōda Company becomes the symbol of a society which blunders on in blind obedience to a divided and incompetent leadership bound by rigid hierarchical ties. It is a society that produces well-meaning but weak-kneed people like Kanda, and where there are Kandas, there will be Yamadas to exploit them.

Not all Japanese are as incompetent as Yamada or as ineffective as Kanda, however. There is another brand of Japanese, exemplified by Tokushima. The fact is hardly reassuring. Tokushima succeeds, not because he is necessarily a better planner than Kanda, but because he refuses to be intimidated by his superiors. At first he makes an excellent impression. Tokushima seems the hero of the book. But then he curtly dismisses the woman Sawa, who guided his platoon across Inubō Pass. That was insensitive, to say the least, and this insensitivity expands to monstrous proportions when Tokushima browbeats the seven guides from Kumanosawa into years of fearful silence. When push comes to shove, the army cares only for its own and disdains its duty toward civilians—a point underlined by the way even Tokushima's men ignore the guides as soon as they reach safety. For all his admirable qualities, Tokushima is not necessarily an admirable person. He is the Japanese soldier the world learned to fear during the Second World War: courageous, efficient, tough, and arrogant.

All this is terribly unfair to the real-life Captain Taizō Fukushima, who seems to have treated his guides quite conscientiously, even the seven from Kumanosawa. For the fate of these guides, Nitta relied entirely on a report published by the local historian Tomabechi about thirty years after the event. But from an exchange of letters between Fukushima and the mayor of the village where the seven guides lived it becomes clear that after the march Fukushima was in fact quite concerned about his guides' physical condition—convincing evidence that their experience was not the closely guarded secret Nitta presents it as.

Because these letters were found in military archives, it is doubtful that Nitta knew of their existence. Yet one wonders why he was so ready to believe the accusations of the guides in

Tomabechi's book, the more so as his credulity spoiled his estimation of Fukushima, who does not at all appear to have been the sort of officer who would underpay his guides and then dump them in the snow.

The answer probably lies in Nitta's family background. Nitta was born into a samurai family of the lowest class. His ancestors had to take orders from just about anyone and lived lives of stoic poverty, "hiding their hunger behind their toothpicks" as the saying goes. Patient endurance was built into their behavioral code, and while Nitta was quite willing to endure much, he was not by nature a very patient person. His frustrations vented themselves in an almost visceral dislike of people in positions of authority, whether in the military or in the civilian world, while at the same time his samurai upbringing forced him to champion the cause of the weak and the powerless. He would snub his publishers when he met them in the street, but he would also pay the medical expenses of one of his subordinates in the Meteorological Agency out of his own salary.

Such a personality would naturally bias Nitta in favor of the seven guides and would also explain why he again opted for the least flattering interpretation of the matter of the two missing rifles. It is a fact that two rifles belonging to the 5th Regiment were never recovered; it is also a fact that on January 29, 1902, the journalist Yūsaburō Tōkai ("Saikai") published a report in an extra of his newspaper *Tōō Nippō* that he personally had carried two rifles down the mountain. Possibly, Tōkai wrote the truth, but it is peculiar that he always refused to discuss what happened and soon afterward resigned from the newspaper. The likeliest explanation is that he or his editor added this passage to his report to liven it up a bit and that the real rifles are still rusting away somewhere on the mountain. Nitta chose to believe Tōkai's report, however, and spends a disproportionate amount of time—in the Japanese original even more than in this translation—trying to explain why the discovery of these rifles was never reported and what might have happened to them, while in passing taking a swipe at the army's disregard for its own principles.

Finally something needs to be said about Yamada's and Kanda's suicides. The records published by the army only mention that Major Yamaguchi died in hospital. His family maintains, however, that he really killed himself to assume the responsibility for the Hakkōda disaster, and that this was hushed up to prevent the other

201

surviving officers from assuming their share of the responsibility in the same way. As such behavior is not implausible in Japan (and also because it is dramatically more satisfying, perhaps?), Nitta took the family's word over that of the army. Although there have never been rumors that Captain Kannari committed suicide, it must have seemed less than just to Nitta if he allowed Yamada, the villain of the novel, to do the honorable thing without offering Kanda the same option. Within the cultural context of the novel, it is an extremely effective scene. Even Western readers will find something undeniably pathetic in Kanda, the innocent victim of arrogance and stupidity, bleeding slowly to death in the snow.

If there remain any doubts that Nitta intended his retelling of the Hakkōda disaster as an indictment of Japanese society, they will be quickly dispelled by a look at the last section of the book, when all the survivors have been rescued and the authorities are faced with the problem of spin control, as it would be called nowadays. Unfortunately, this is the least satisfying part of the novel, for it is necessarily anticlimactic and the historical facts are too clear-cut to allow for deviation. Here for once Nitta was forced to rely on his sources rather than on his imagination.

Nitta changes his novelist's hat for that of the investigative reporter and ends the book with a long string of scathing comments on the vanity of human wishes. But for all the genuineness of Nitta's indignation, his ending does not convince.

One can not fault Nitta for trying, yet it could hardly have been otherwise, for he was attempting to find a meaning for something that was, like all tragedies, ultimately meaningless. Not even the greatest tragedians, from Aeschylus on, have managed to find a satisfactory answer to the question why human beings suffer. But the reason a modern audience still responds to the old Greek plays transcends the boundaries of time and culture. It is, quite simply, pity—pity magnified by the recognition that there, but for the grace of God, or Fate, go we.

Pity undeniably plays an important part in Nitta's novel—such an important part that one wishes he had refrained from distilling any other messages from the Hakkōda disaster. For in the last resort, *Death March on Mount Hakkōda* is not about the success of Tokushima's platoon or about the darker aspects of Japan's vertical society, but about the dying soldiers of the 5th Regiment. Captain Kanda makes such an unforgettable impression precisely because he is weak and fallible, and we identify with him, whereas we do not identify with Tokushima. In an age when no event is real unless it has been reported in the mass media, it may not hurt to point out that Kanda's desperate exclamation, "Heaven has abandoned us!" is not the stuff of fiction. These are the real words of a real person, recorded by one of the survivors who stood close to Captain Kannari at Narusawa, and the hopelessness they express is as real as the gruesome suffering that provoked them. Under its fictional cover, *Death March on Mount Hakkōda* contains a hard layer of truth. If the truth moves us to pity, so much the better. Heaven knows we live in an age that could use some.

★

Hiroto Fujiwara, better known under his pen name, Jirō Nitta, was born as the second son of an old samurai family on June 6, 1912, in Suwado, Nagano Prefecture, the most mountainous region in Japan. After graduating from the Wireless Training Institute, he was employed by the Central Meteorological Institute, which transferred him to Manchuria in 1943.

In 1945, at the end of the war, he was interned in a detention camp near the northern Korean border, while his wife (the well-known essayist Tei Fujiwara) and children, the youngest a baby of only seven months, had to walk back from Manchuria to the southern tip of the Korean Peninsula before they could be repatriated. The hardships they endured on the way nearly killed the children, who survived only by their mother's refusal to give up. On their return to Japan, Nitta's wife became dangerously ill, and when Nitta finally joined his family in 1946 he had to nurse her back from the brink of death.

In 1949, Nitta's wife recounted her experiences of that terrible journey in her first book, *Nagareru hoshi wa ikite iru* (*There Is Life in Falling Stars*), which immediately became a best seller and is still widely read. Her success stimulated Nitta to try his own hand at writing, and in 1951 his very first novella won the Sunday Mainichi Prize. In 1956 he was awarded the 34th Naoki Prize for Popular Fiction for a collection of stories that included "Mount Hakkōda," the seed which grew into *Death March on Mount Hakkōda*. This novel, which was published in 1971, quickly sold close to one million copies and was made into a highly successful film in 1977. In the meanwhile, Nitta had become one of the most popular writers in Japan.

203

In *Death March on Mount Hakkōda*, the various elements in Nitta's background combined to make it his best book. Nitta had worked and lived in the mountains most of his life and was an enthusiastic mountaineer, and while he loved the mountains, he also knew how dangerous they can be. His training as a meteorologist enabled him to write so vividly about the snow and the weather, two of the most important characters in the novel. Nitta's working methods, too, contributed to the realism of his descriptions. Before he started a novel, he would read up on the subject and the region in which the story was set, and then go there—several times, if necessary—and spend as much time on location as possible. But perhaps most crucial to the composition of *Death March* was Nitta's lifelong championship of the social underdog, which determines the tone and the message of the novel.

Nitta wrote many books, including historical and detective novels, but he remained best known for his mountain stories. He died unexpectedly of a heart attack in his house near Tokyo on February 15, 1980.